THE DUKE AND THE SIREN

JESSIE CLEVER

SOMEDAY LADY PUBLISHING, LLC.

THE DUKE AND THE SIREN

Published by Someday Lady Publishing, LLC

Copyright © 2021 by Jessica McQuaid

ISBN-13: 978-1-7362903-2-3

Cover Design by The Killion Group

Edited by Judy Roth

For JQ
We met for the first time in a public restroom because that is how
the best stories go.
Thank you for everything.

CHAPTER 1

*D*uchesses did not open doors.

Propriety dictated a servant do so. But when the knocking was as frantic as this was, and she was in such close proximity to the door on which the knocking occurred, it seemed only prudent that she answer it.

Viv pulled open the front door of Ashbourne Manor and in tumbled a thoroughly sodden young man.

The day was cold and sleeting as was expected at the seashore in December, but it was all the more unfriendly for what the day marked.

It was Viv's twenty-eighth birthday.

She had been careful not to think of it.

As her birthday was only three days after Christmas, she was still in residence with the rest of her family at Ashbourne Manor as it had become custom to gather in Glenhaven, the home of her brother-in-law's country seat.

She did not explicitly request to be alone on said birthday, but she need only make mention to her sister Eliza and the rest would be taken care of. Eliza was just the type of person to understand a suggestion like that.

Because every time Viv looked at Eliza's son, George, a pain so terrible she was afraid it would rob her of her breath erupted in her chest.

She was eight and twenty, and she should have had a son of her own by now.

But that's not how things had transpired.

Instead she was a wife without a husband, a wife without children, a woman stuck in limbo because of her husband's adultery.

So she'd spent the morning rambling through the halls of Ashbourne Manor wondering how she could possibly be the only married spinster in all of creation while the rest of the family had taken young George to see the dairy cow who herself was carrying a babe she would have come spring.

Even dairy cows were having babies instead of her.

"Dear heavens, are you all right?" Viv said now to the puddle of young man on the vestibule carpet.

"Quite all right, miss," the young man stammered as he sloshed to his feet.

The first she caught of his face, it was turning red as the man finally registered to whom he was speaking.

"Your Grace!" he nearly shouted as he surged to his feet, his arms rigid at his sides as if he thought he were reporting to a military commander. "I do beg your pardon. I didn't know it was you." He eyed the door warily. "Did you just answer the door, ma'am?"

Viv studied the young man. "Geoffrey?"

The young man pulled his soaked cap from his head, droplets of icy rainwater springing from his red curls.

"Yes, Your Grace." He gave a respectful bow. "I'm very sorry, ma'am. But there's been an accident."

Geoffrey was the son of the stable manager at Margate Hall. Her *husband's* country seat.

While she registered his words, they made little sense.

"An accident? Well, that's terrible, but I'm sure it mustn't be so bad as to—"

"His Grace is dying, ma'am. You must come at once." Geoffrey's words flew from his lips so quickly, she stood mesmerized by his features. The way his eyes went wide with pronouncement and yet instantly narrowed with concern. The way his chin wobbled with pain.

Was it for Ryder or was it for her?

Horribly, it made her want to laugh because in just that moment she experienced a flutter of relief at the possibility— well, to put it rather cruelly—that she might be freed from the prison of her marriage should her husband die.

The young man's lips wobbled as if reluctant to say more, but she already knew the rest.

"The phaeton," she said.

Geoffrey's face flushed, and her mind wandered, picturing Ryder the day he'd procured his beloved high-flyer. He'd acquired it from Weatherby's, the most renowned phaeton manufacturer in London. The day had been crisp with the subtlest hint of warmth the first days of spring have to offer.

She recalled the almost boyish enthusiasm evident in Ryder's smile when Weatherby himself presented Ryder with his phaeton. Her husband had swung himself up into the vehicle without hesitation and snapped the reins for the horses to carry him off.

He'd left her standing on the pavement.

A flash of anger surged through her. He'd loved that phaeton more than he loved her. Morbid thought that it was, she found it somehow fitting that it might now be the cause of her husband's demise.

"Your Grace, you must leave at once," Geoffrey said, and

she had a feeling it was not the first time he'd spoken the words, so lost had she been in her own memories.

For the first time, she realized Geoffrey's teeth chattered, and without further thought, she took his arm and pulled him into the drawing room off the vestibule to plant him squarely in front of the fire.

The carpet beneath his feet was soaked within moments, and he gratefully tugged his gloves from his hands, holding his likely frozen fingers up to the flames.

She witnessed this, and yet she didn't. She was suddenly lost in her own mind, her thoughts sloshing back and forth between the cruelty of death and the tantalizing wisps of happiness that awaited her should she become a widow. It was as though her thoughts were tangible and her mind an empty cavern. The thoughts tumbled and bounced and seemed to echo in the emptiness of her suspended existence.

She could remarry. She could have children. She could have...

This.

Her eyes wandered the room, taking in the evidence of a happy family gathering. George's wooden block tower, scattered across the floor from when he'd knocked it over in his first clumsy attempts at running. The ottoman Sebastian had used to prop up Louisa's feet. She was due to have their first child in three months' time and how her feet swelled. The red and green tapers burned down to nubs on the piano where they spent the evenings singing Christmas carols.

She could have a Christmas of her own with her own babes and a loving husband. She could be happy if only...

If only Ryder Maxen, the Duke of Margate, would simply die.

No, you wouldn't.

The thought skittered through her mind silencing all the

rest of them, and she closed her eyes against it. She wouldn't be free of Ryder when he died because she still loved him.

"Your Grace, I must insist you come at once. You see…" Geoffrey's voice stumbled, and she opened her eyes to watch him. He swallowed. "His Grace is in a bad way, ma'am. The doctor gave him laudanum straightaway, but—" Geoffrey licked his lips nervously. "Well, the duke is not making sense, you see. But one thing we understood, ma'am."

"What is it?" Somehow she knew she didn't *want* to know what it was.

"Well, ma'am, he's asking for you."

Later, when she had time to reflect, she would identify this as the moment her very person split in two. Half of her wanted nothing to do with the matter. Half of her wanted to wrap her arms around her hurt and hide until Ryder's death was nothing but another event in the timeline of her sorry marriage. She *craved* that thought. The idea of just slipping away, disappearing until it was all no more, and she could start anew.

But the pleasure she derived from such thoughts faded as quickly as it came. Because at heart, she was Lady Vivianna Darby.

And Lady Vivianna Darby never shirked her duty.

She went to the corner of the room and tugged the bell pull.

When Mrs. Donnelly, the housekeeper, arrived, Viv gave instructions to fetch food and drink for Geoffrey and to see if any of the footmen had suitable dry clothing for him. If they were to leave immediately, it would simply be torture for Geoffrey to continue in the same sodden clothes.

She sent a footman to find her sisters as she made her way to her rooms. Her lady's maid was already filling trunks when Viv finally arrived.

"Pack everything, Samuels. We shan't know what is to

happen, and it would be best if we're prepared for anything. We'll sort it out when we get to Margate."

"Very good, ma'am." The woman gave a sharp nod as she disappeared into the dressing room.

Viv called after her. "Do pack a single bag for me to carry on horseback. Just the things I'll need for this evening."

"Yes, ma'am," Samuels called from the other room without question.

Viv shed her morning gown just as her door flung open, bouncing against the wall behind it.

"Viv, what's happened?" Eliza strode into the room first, Johanna helping poor Louisa to shuffle in behind.

Her dear middle sister was clearly out of breath from the walk from the barns, and Viv pulled out the dressing table chair, pushing Louisa into it.

"Did you make her run?" She asked the accusing question of Johanna, the youngest of the sisters and the most likely to goad her sister on.

"Make her run?" Johanna's eyebrows went up. "I was holding her back. A woman in her condition shouldn't be moving with such zest." She spoke the last word as it were some kind of tropical disease.

Louisa opened her mouth as if to retort, but sensible Eliza interrupted.

"Viv, what's happened, darling?" she said again, although more softly this time.

Viv didn't realize she was still holding the back of the dressing table chair until the wood bit into the softness of her palms. She released her grip and gathered her courage before meeting Eliza's gaze.

"It appears Margate has finally pushed his luck too far. He crashed his phaeton. They say he's dying, and I must come at once."

She didn't know why she kept the fact that he'd asked for

her to herself, but for some strange reason, she wanted to keep it her secret.

An odd look came over Louisa's face, and Viv thought she might have mistaken it for something else like curiosity, but then Louisa said, "Oh, Viv, I'm so sorry." It sounded like she meant to say more, so Viv waited. Finally, Louisa licked her lips and said, "Well, I'm just surprised to find you're going to him. After everything. But I suppose…well, it's none of my concern."

Louisa was right.

Why should Viv run to his bedside when his carelessness had finally caught up with him?

Because you love him still.

No. She shoved the thought away as soon as it came.

No, it wasn't that. It was because she was a Darby at heart. And a Darby never let anyone down.

As she stood there in her bedchamber, her three sisters before her, she knew with greater certainty that was the heart of the matter.

Four years ago she'd returned home to ensure her sisters would never suffer the same fate she had, and now here they were. Eliza happily wed and a mother to precious George. Louisa newly wed and her first babe on the way.

And Johanna.

Viv's heart squeezed whenever she saw Johanna.

For reasons only known to her, Johanna had been reluctant to enter the marriage mart, and so nearly four years later, she was still unwed.

Viv could not forget that. She would do her duty by her husband, and she would return to London in time for the season. She would see Johanna wed in the coming year. She would be certain of it.

"Oh, Viv, that's terrible," Eliza whispered, her brow creased with concern. "I'll have the carriage fetched—"

"No." Viv hadn't meant the word to be so sharp. It was just the urgency that gnawed at her now that the decision was made.

But had she really made a decision?

Of course, she would go to Ryder. How pathetic to think it. But this wasn't about unrequited love. This was simply a matter of duty.

She softened her voice. "I must go on horseback. A carriage will take too long."

"You're going to ride to Margate on horseback?"

The note of incredulity in Johanna's voice was alarming. Of all the sisters, it was most like Johanna to take on such a feat as a midwinter ride through the English countryside from one end of Sussex to the opposite end of Kent. For the first time, Viv felt a niggle of trepidation for what she was about to endure.

But hadn't Geoffrey just traversed the same course and in the middle of an ink-black night no less?

She tugged on the trousers she would wear beneath her split skirts.

"I must go as quickly as possible. Horseback is the only option."

Samuels emerged from the dressing room then with the shirt and jacket that completed the outfit. Viv fingered the fine fabric with a sinking heart. She'd need her cloak with the fur trim and yards and yards of scarves.

Perhaps Mrs. Donnelly would see to some warming stones for her pockets.

"You can't make that ride by yourself," Eliza said, not with a note of criticism but rather with marked practicality. "You'll need protection if you plan to ride on the open road. If only Andrew hadn't left yesterday," she said, referring to their brother, the Duke of Ravenwood.

Andrew had returned to London yesterday to attend to

business matters, but she knew he really just wanted some quiet time to himself. With a house full of sisters, these few days before they returned after the holidays was the only chance he got for some peace.

She did up the last of the buttons on the jacket as Samuels pulled at the pins in her hair, releasing the red-gold locks in a cascade down her back.

"I'll have Geoffrey, the stable master's son. He's the one who came with the news."

"That little boy we saw in the front drawing room?" Louisa's voice nearly squeaked with concern. "You'd get more protection from Henry."

Henry was Eliza's collie, and honestly, Louisa was not wrong in this regard.

Samuels's deft fingers finished plaiting her hair, and she tucked the long braid into the back of Viv's jacket. It was bad enough she would be forced to wear split skirts. She didn't want to attract attention with her brilliant hair.

"Be that as it may, it's my only choice." She answered Louisa, but her gaze was on Eliza.

Her sister placed a hand at Johanna's elbow. "Let's let her finish getting ready. We'll send your things along behind you in the carriage."

Viv could only nod her thanks as Samuels tightened the last of the jacket's ties.

The room seemed suddenly empty when her sisters had departed, but in her mind, there existed nothing but clear resolution. She would make the torturous ride to Margate. She would fulfill her duty. There was nothing else to be done.

It was only minutes later when she reached the vestibule, her riding boots ringing in the sudden quiet. The past few days had been filled with her family's usual boisterousness, the laughter and the good cheer. It was gone now, and only the sound of a winter rain, weak and half-hearted, beat at the windows.

Her sisters and their husbands were lined up at the front door. Mrs. Donnelly was the first to step forward, though, two towels held between her hands.

"Warming stones, ma'am," she said, and Viv couldn't help a smile.

Mrs. Donnelly would have known, of course. Viv took them with a nod and slipped the warm towels into the pockets of her jacket beneath the heavy cloak she'd donned.

She gave each of her sisters a hug and kiss, their goodbyes brief. It wasn't as if she were never to see them again. They were all being terribly maudlin about the whole thing. She was only riding across the countryside.

Just then a gust of sea wind blasted against the manor house, and the panes of glass shook in the windows flanking the door. The party in the vestibule stilled, their eyes traveling ominously to the manor's exterior walls.

Viv gave Eliza a quick hug before moving to the door. She must be brisk about this or she would change her mind. After all, what did she owe Ryder?

But that was just it. She owed him nothing. He, however, owed her everything. And she would start with an explanation. If he stayed alive long enough.

Dax, Eliza's husband, stopped her at the door.

"I understand you know how to use one of these." He handed her a black velvet pouch, the weight and shape of it leaving no question as to its contents.

"Yes, I used to shoot with my father." She took the pouch, slipping it into the pocket of her skirt. She was no fool. She would welcome any means of safety including a pistol.

"I wish I could ride with you." His face was stern with gravity.

"You know I would never allow you to leave Eliza and George."

"I would expect as much from you." He pressed a kiss to her cheek, and not bothering with propriety, opened the door himself.

It seemed everyone was capable of opening doors that day.

The icy sea wind struck her full in the face, needling her tender skin until she could raise her scarf so only her eyes were bared to the onslaught.

Geoffrey stood there with two fresh horses, harnessed and biting at the bit. She felt a pang of remorse that Geoffrey would be forced to endure yet another icy ride, but she had little choice. She needed his protection as a male on this journey, and she would not ask another to fulfill such a role. Not for Ryder. He didn't deserve it.

They would need to swap horses several times over the journey, and she only hoped they would find such fine horse-flesh along the route. Without another word, she strode forward and lifted herself into the saddle of the closest horse. With Ashbourne Manor at her back, she struck off onto the icy drive that would lead them to the road, ready to face her fate.

SHE NEVER EXPECTED to spend her twenty-eighth birthday with her dying husband.

Although she wasn't entirely certain it was still her birthday. Darkness had fallen swiftly some hours ago, and they'd been forced to pick their way over the road by what little light pierced the thick, menacing clouds. The journey had taken much longer than she had anticipated because of it and now she could not be certain of the time.

She could be certain of one thing, however.

She had not been prepared to see her husband.

She studied what little of his face she could see as he lay at death's door, covered in bandages and plasters and ointments. The room was rife with the odor of oil of earthworm, and she felt the urge to hold her breath against it.

Somehow she couldn't quite believe it was him.

But it was. Those were his chiseled cheekbones, his jet-black hair, his full mouth.

Could she even recall what it was like to kiss him?

She swallowed against the thought.

He had always seemed invincible. The Rogue Duke who captured hearts and dashed dreams. The handsome duke every marrying mama coveted; for herself or her daughter was open to debate.

To say nothing of his legend as a phaeton driver.

If Ryder was not seducing a widow, he was raking in coin by obliterating his competition in death-defying phaeton races across England.

But perhaps he'd pushed his legend too far this time.

Icy water dripped from her split skirts and riding trousers, off the brim of her hat in cold, numbing rivulets onto her shoulders, slipping off the cuffs of her jacket to squirm their way through her sodden gloves.

The ride from Glenhaven had been treacherous, worse than she had anticipated, and frankly ill advised. But they'd made it far sooner than a carriage would have seen to it, and now she could only hope not to catch a fever.

She would need her strength to nurse her husband back to health if that were even possible.

Now that she stood beside him, saw the extent of the damage, she willed herself to feel something, even if only the clawing fingers of the icy rainwater that soaked through her traveling clothes and chilled her skin to gooseflesh.

But she couldn't feel anything because this was not how it was supposed to end.

Ryder was supposed to come after her.

In her daydreams that was what happened. Ryder would finally realize the gravity of what he'd done, realize the atrocities he had committed, and come running back to her, begging her for forgiveness.

Instead, he'd gotten himself killed. Or almost anyway.

She could feel nothing as the doctor told her what to expect. Dr. Malcolm, he had said when she'd tramped into the room moments earlier, heedless of Mrs. Olds's cry that she get out of her wet clothes.

Ryder had broken his right leg. He may have broken several ribs or, at the very least, bruised them. Several lacerations had required stitches, and should he live, he would have a nasty scar down the right side of his face.

Should he live.

Those were the doctor's actual words, and she roused herself enough to question him.

"Should he live?" She worked to keep her voice even. "Aren't you a doctor? Aren't you supposed to *ensure* that he lives?"

The doctor was a tall, overly thin man of middling years with little hair on top of his head, which he made up for in dense muttonchops that cradled his cheeks. When he swallowed, his Adam's apple bobbed, and he pushed his spectacles back up his nose, his lips working without sound emerging.

Guilt swamped her. She had no reason to take any of this out on the poor country doctor. It wasn't his fault Ryder had never come after her. It wasn't his fault Ryder had never come to his senses.

It was her fault for still loving the husband who had betrayed her.

She closed her eyes, pushing the painful thought aside.

"I'm sorry, Dr. Malcolm. I've had a terrible day, and I'm suffering from strain and fatigue. Do accept my apologies."

The doctor swallowed again, but it no longer looked like it hurt. He gave a nod as he said, "I can't be sure what internal damage His Grace may have suffered. Unfortunately, he was moved from the wreckage of his phaeton before I could get there. I cannot tell you what further damage may have been done from his mishandling."

She considered the doctor before returning her gaze to Ryder's prone body. "Mishandling? Surely they couldn't have harmed him much. The main road is only a few kilometers from here."

The doctor blinked several times before saying, "Has no one told you? His Grace suffered the crash on the other side of Canterbury."

Her gaze flew to the doctor's face, a sense of dread curling in her stomach. "Canterbury? That can't be."

Canterbury was more than twenty-five kilometers from there. Surely they wouldn't have tried to move a man in Ryder's condition such distance and in midwinter no less.

"I'm afraid it is, Your Grace." The doctor wiped his hands on a rag before turning to the table beside the bed where his kit lay open. The soft light of oil lamps that had been lit glinted off the rows of glass bottles nestled inside it. "If His Grace does not die from whatever internal injuries he may suffer, he will very likely succumb to infection."

He paused in putting away his tools to turn his gaze on her. He seemed to consider her for several moments, and she realized he was weighing how much to tell her.

She squared her shoulders, and despite the water that dripped from her chin, she spoke with assurance. "Please tell me everything, Doctor. I must know it all if I am to care for him properly."

14

The doctor replaced a shiny implement in his bag, a torturous-looking device she knew not the purpose of, before emitting a soft sigh. "Your Grace, the bone of the right leg perforated the skin upon breaking. It was not bandaged when I got to him, and considering the length of his journey to get here, I cannot say what filth and possible disease he encountered in his travels. The infection will likely get him before any loss of blood."

He'd spoken the words matter-of-factly, and while she registered their meaning, they did little more than settle into the numb hollowness she already suffered.

The bone had broken through the skin. Likelihood of infection was high. Very high. That was why they'd come for her. Ryder really was going to die.

"I'm sorry, Your Grace. But I feel in these circumstances it's best to be practical."

The reality of it hadn't hit her until just then, and involuntarily, she reached out a hand, placing only her fingertips on the edge of Ryder's forearm. It was wrapped in bandages, and she pulled her hand away almost immediately, not wanting to ruin the clean wrappings with the sodden gloves she hadn't bothered to remove when she'd arrived.

She'd tossed her reins to a footman as soon as they'd made the front door of Margate Hall. She'd strode inside and up the stairs to the ducal chambers, ignoring the protests of the housekeeper and her scurrying maids bent on relieving her of her soaked outer garments.

Viv had had no time for such frivolity. She couldn't have stopped in her progression until she'd seen Ryder. Now that she had, the hollowness plagued her.

What had she been expecting? Geoffrey had said he was dying. Had she really thought she'd get an explanation from her husband? An explanation for why he had ruined her entire life the moment she'd found him between the thighs of that opera singer?

It had been nearly four years since she'd discovered him in bed with the soprano from the Theatre Royal, and in that time, she'd not heard from him once.

Not once.

She'd never gotten the chance to ask him what she wanted to know most.

Why hadn't he come after her?

She knew why, but instead, she foolishly held out hope. Hope that it wasn't what she feared. That he never really loved her.

Four years was a long time to feel all of the emotions she thought would undo her. Bitterness and humiliation. Loneliness and despair. It was the pitiful looks from matrons and the worried gazes of debutantes who feared they'd fall victim to the same fate as she that gnawed at her but couldn't touch the part of her that hurt the most.

The part of her that believed he had really loved her.

Clearly, she'd been wrong.

If the existence of the opera singer were not enough to convince her, four years of utter silence were.

"Is there anything else that can be done?" She felt the futility of the question. If there was anything to be done, the doctor likely had already done it.

"I washed his wounds with liquor. It's an old trick my grandmother used and swore by. Based on the extent of his injuries, I thought it warranted to exhaust all avenues of healing."

He snapped his bag closed and moved to where a coat had been discarded. Viv only noticed it now as he picked it up, and she wondered just how long the doctor had been there. How long had it taken to set Ryder's broken leg, stitch the wound, and set it in plaster? The lacerations—

how long had this poor man spent stitching and bandaging?

"Will you take some food, Doctor? I'm sure Mrs. Olds can bring some tea and sandwiches…" She let the sentence drift off as her eyes searched for the windows, again wondering as to the time.

The doctor's smile was soft. "My wife shall be waiting for me, but I thank you for the hospitality, Your Grace." He buttoned his coat, pulled the collar tight to his neck as the sound of rain was a constant staccato against the windows and roof of Margate Hall. "You must watch for signs of fever. The next few days are critical. Should he suffer any change at all, you must send for me immediately."

She couldn't stop her eyes from traveling to the laudanum bottle sitting on the table by the bed, a used spoon lying innocently next to it. Geoffrey's words whispered through her mind. *Ryder had asked for her.*

But why?

She closed her eyes against the pain that rocketed through her at the possibilities of just why her husband should want her now, at the seeming end of his life.

The doctor seemed to sense her thoughts as he said, "I gave him some for the pain, but I'd hesitate to give him more. The stuff is powerfully alluring. We want him to have his senses about him to accurately monitor his condition."

"Thank you, Doctor," she said, even as she kept her eyes closed.

The doctor said his goodbyes, and she only opened her eyes when the sound of the door clicking shut echoed through the room.

She was suddenly alone with her husband. She studied him, so quiet and harmless in sleep.

Anger bubbled up first. She swallowed, trying just as she had for four years to keep her civility when she explored what had happened and how it had led to where she was now.

Now that the urgency and need to get to Margate Hall had passed, she was left with nothing but to stare into the chasm between them, the void that had filled with recriminations and doubts, accusations and hurt.

She was afraid they would consume her whole.

The sound of the door opening startled her, and Mrs. Olds swept in, a stack of towels in her hands. Maids followed with a full teacart and pitchers of warm water.

"Your Grace," Mrs. Olds said only and nothing more as she set down the towels and reached for Viv's sodden jacket.

Viv let her.

Mrs. Olds had been the housekeeper at Margate Hall for many years before Viv came along, and she was more of a mother to the place than servant. Viv allowed the woman to strip her of her sodden outer garments, ply her with towels and warm tea.

The maids scooped up the used towels and her garments, leaving behind no trace of what Viv had endured to get there. Just as suddenly as they had come, they left.

Viv stood in her riding trousers, shirt, and bare feet, her hair undone and flowing down her back to dry.

Somehow a cup of hot tea had made its way between her hands, and her fingers tingled with sudden warmth. She turned back to the bed, but Ryder hadn't moved. His breathing was shallow, his brow tense.

There was nothing else to be done. What had seemed insurmountable that morning was now finished. There was nothing more to do now.

She pulled a chair over to the bed and sat down to wait for her husband to die.

CHAPTER 2

*H*e opened his eyes only to immediately shut them again.

God, he swore this would never happen again.

He swore he would never wake up in a strange place, swore to never again *not* remember where he was or what had happened, or worst of all, whom he was with.

His eyes pulsed at the backs of his eyelids, and his head throbbed against the pillows. At least he'd made it to a bed this time. Waking on the bench of the Earl of Langford's piano was not the most enjoyable thing he'd ever endured.

Why couldn't he simply stop?

In his younger years, it had been fun. It had been… distracting. The thrill of the race followed by a good debauchery at an equally commendable bloke's house, and Ryder could squirrel away an entire fortnight avoiding responsibility and duty.

God, *duty*.

What a terrible word.

The throbbing behind his closed eyelids did not subside.

He should've gone for Viv the way he had planned. If anyone were to stop him from this madness, it would be she.

He'd tried once. That night of the Kittridge ball the previous season. He'd been in London to procure a new set of wheels for his high-flyer, and he wasn't sure what had overcome him.

A sense of nostalgia?

No, nothing so maudlin.

It was worse than that.

It was as if he could feel his own fate pressing down on him. It was as though he could sense what was about to happen. He was slipping further and deeper into the hedonism he had once found refuge in. But it no longer felt like that. Now it felt like a prison.

Why he thought Viv could save him he wasn't sure. He was drawn to her, though, like a monk to a relic, seeking salvation and perhaps worse: forgiveness.

But the moment he'd set eyes on her that night, fear had tightened his throat, rendered his feet useless. She stood with her brother and the Duke of Ashbourne, a man well known for his polished reputation in Parliament, and if he'd heard correctly, Eliza's new husband. Ryder had never felt inadequate in all his life, but just in that moment, he felt like nothing more than a discarded gossip rag.

He'd left the Kittridge ball without speaking to her.

That was when the incident with the piano bench had occurred.

It was just so much easier than to face the weight of history carried by the title Margate.

This morning, however, he was rethinking that. The pain was rather unbearable even for him, one so used to such ill-advised use of one's body. There was nothing to do about it except get up, he supposed. He would see if Mrs. Olds had some of that tonic that seemed to help on the worst mornings.

Except…

Well…

That didn't seem to be right.

Ryder couldn't move.

His right leg was pinned to the bed, weighed down by something heavy and immovable. The realization swept through him in pieces; one by one each bit came into his muddied mind. His hands reached out compulsively, but they caught in nothing but bedclothes, his fingers twisting through the sheets uselessly.

But having attempted to move his arms an entirely new pain shot through him so crisply it rendered him breathless. He stilled immediately, his mind absorbing and cataloging the kaleidoscope of pain that cascaded through him. But even as he moved through the hot tightness in his chest, the way his arms seemed to weigh as much as a quarterhorse, he couldn't seem to keep his mind from attempting to his lift his leg.

But it wouldn't move.

Panic gripped him. He hated panic, hated the weakness it showed. He kept his eyes shut and forced his mind to carefully review the situation.

He remembered waking up at the Earl of Rutherford's estate. Was it yesterday? Was it two days hence? He couldn't be quite sure. Rutherford's estate was just two estates over from his own in Kent. The man was legend for his holiday parties, and Ryder never missed one. But something had been different this year. Perhaps the drinking was more to excess than it had been once, the women looser, or was that unhappiness he saw bringing them to his rooms at night? Whatever it was, the entire thing had had a pall to it, one that had never been felt before. It left him with a sourness in his stomach and a hollowness to his chest.

He'd realized on the seventh day of the party why.

He didn't want to be there.

It was the first time in the twelve years since his majority that he'd had such a thought, and it had perplexed him, yes, but more so, it had worried him. If he did not wish to be at a house party, then where else did he wish to be?

If he were honest with himself, he would admit the parties had been growing lackluster for some time, the drinking repetitive, the sport unchallenging. So why should it come to a head at Rutherford's party?

Because it was Christmas.

Such nostalgia for the time of year was utter nonsense. Only…it wasn't. Not that year. That year he'd found the holiday trappings sad and not quite complete without an adoring family to accompany them.

The restlessness that had driven him away from duty and responsibility since his majority seemed to have suddenly turned inward. He now found himself running away from… well, himself.

Instead of doing the sensible thing and leaving, he'd thrown himself into the festivities, participating in every challenge that involved drink, hunting, and women.

Until he'd awoken in Rutherford's fountain.

He was lucky he hadn't frozen to death, and he was even luckier that Rutherford had shut off the water to prevent freezing damage in winter. Otherwise, Ryder might have died that night in the bloody earl's fountain.

That had been the last straw. He'd packed what little he'd brought and headed back to Margate to collect his horses and phaeton. Suddenly the restlessness inside of him had been pointing in a single direction.

London, and more specifically, Viv.

The thought should have repelled him, but whatever had been brewing in him for some time had finally come to a head. Viv was the only clear thought in his mind. If he could only get to Viv, she could...

What?

Save him?

But what did he require being saved from?

His thoughts had rampaged the way his insides did, and he'd hitched up his phaeton without bothering to pack.

And then—

He couldn't remember.

He'd left Margate. He was sure of it. He headed west toward London not two days after Christmas, he was certain. So where was he? Whose bed was this? Why couldn't he move?

The questions hurtled out of the void at him one after another until he couldn't bear it. His eyes flew open, and he attacked the bedclothes that pinned him. He hadn't accounted for his weakness, though, hadn't known to expect it. But his arms were as futile as cooked noodles, striking the bedclothes with little more power than a pony against the bit.

He must have made enough of a stir, however, as sound erupted somewhere to his right.

"Ryder! You must stop."

Viv.

A new pain, so exquisite and pure, rushed through him at the sound of her voice. He must have made it. He must have made it to her, to London, to everything that would keep the restlessness at bay.

Except...why couldn't he move?

It seemed an eternity before she appeared above him. The light in the room was soft, and it cradled her face until she appeared cherubic, angelic. She *was* angelic. She was the thing that would save him.

He licked his lips, realizing for the first time how dry and cracked they were. What had happened to him?

"Viv." The word barely came out.

His throat scratched, the dry muscles pulling against one another until he was coughing—great heaving coughs that had him struggling to sit up, gasping for air.

Viv's arms were around him, helping him to settle against the pillows at his back. Something cold pressed to his lips, and he realized she was attempting to give him drink. Cold tea swept into his mouth like a welcome tidal wave, the cool essence passing so quickly over the desert of his mouth, he lapped at the cup she held to his lips for more.

It was gone all too quickly, and he collapsed against the pillows, unable to even hold himself up. Viv's arms were gone all too quickly as well, and it left the hollowness raging in his chest.

He followed her with his eyes, unable to move his head.

"Viv." This time the word emerged more easily, but it was gravelly and broken. "Viv, what's happened?"

He watched her turn to a teacart set at the bedside and refill the cup she had pressed to his lips. Slowly, the other parts of the room began to filter through his foggy senses.

He was in his bed at Margate. He recognized the bedclothes and the window dressings. He couldn't be sure if it were night or if the drapes had been drawn so tightly as to shut out what light there was in midwinter at the coast. Candles dotted every surface, and it was as though he and Viv were alone in existence, the rest of the world held at bay in the rim of shadows that surrounded them.

The thought shot a thrill through him that he couldn't quite understand, once more only knowing that Viv was the answer to his gnawing restlessness now. Viv was everything.

"You've had an accident, I'm afraid." Her tone was crisp, jarring, and it took him a moment to adjust to the reality of the situation instead of the reunion he had dreamed of.

He was the husband who had betrayed her while he hoped she was his savior. He swallowed against the self-recriminations that sprang to his lips.

"Accident?"

She returned to the bedside and held out the refilled teacup.

"You crashed your phaeton." She pursed her lips, her eyes narrow and unfeeling.

"I…" The words swept over him, their truth and what it would mean taking time to settle. He accepted the teacup without saying more, but his arms were too weak, and he set the teacup down in the bedclothes.

Viv snatched it from him before he could spill a single drop, but her face pinched as if in frustration or disappointment or—

He surged forward and grabbed her arm, his sudden ability and strength surprising her, true, but surprising him as well.

"Vili and Ve—are they all right? Were they hurt?"

A line appeared between her brows as she studied his face. "Vili and Ve?"

"My horses. Please tell me I didn't hurt them."

Her expression blanked, her lips parting but no sound emerged as her eyes swept over his face. He tightened his grip on her arm, using what little strength he had left.

"Viv, please. My horses. Please tell me they're all right."

She nodded furiously, the candlelight flickering off her red-gold hair. "They found their way back to the stables yesterday."

He collapsed at her words, the pillows engulfing him as

his heart raced with the release of adrenaline battling with the fatigue the outburst had caused.

"One of them was dragging the pole from your phaeton. They must have snapped the traces when the phaeton overturned."

He closed his eyes, unable to keep them open any longer, relief at knowing he hadn't hurt Vili and Ve making him realize just how tired he was.

He opened his eyes one last time, his gaze sweeping over her face, still so mottled in a confusion he didn't understand.

"I'm dying, aren't I?" The thought shouldn't have brought him the relief that it did. How morbid. How expected. How welcomed would it be to just die. Maybe then the restlessness would stop haunting him.

"You're not dying." She spoke the words automatically, and he couldn't help the smirk that came to his lips.

"Yes, I am." His words were gravelly again, and he wondered how long he'd gone without drink, but he didn't think on it long. The blackness was calling to him again. He'd need only shut his eyes, and it would all go away.

"How can you say that?" Her words were whispered.

"Because they wouldn't have sent for you if I wasn't," he said just as the darkness took him.

* * *

SHE WASN'T sure how long she sat there, the sudden silence buzzing in her ears. It was certainly too long to have remained perched on the side of her husband's sickbed like that, and embarrassment flooded her cheeks with heat as she slid from the bed and into the chair she hadn't left for longer than necessities entailed in the three days since she'd arrived.

The fever had been the worst of it.

It had started not long after she'd arrived. The burning

heat of his skin had sent a new wave of nausea through her at the very real evidence that death was not only possible but likely. The thrashing had begun soon after, and she was far too consumed with trying to hold him still so as not to upset the plaster about his leg or whatever other internal injuries they could not see.

Mrs. Olds had brought endless teacarts and a stream of clean towels. While Viv could not recall eating much, she'd plied tea against Ryder's cracked lips with a spoon, urging some between his lips but not enough that he might choke. She'd rung for cool water almost constantly, wishing for only the coldest water freshly pumped from the well to soak the flannels she was using to bath Ryder's fiery skin.

She first saw the streaks of sweat along his temples when she'd been applying her own mixture of honey, tallow, and peppermint to the skin that had become chafed from the raw edges of the bandages around his face. She'd pulled down the only sheet she'd left him to find his shirt soaked through with sweat.

She still couldn't admit to the elation that had coursed through her at the sight.

The fever had broken, and he was still alive.

He'd beaten it.

She'd stared uncomprehending at his soaked linen shirt, her emotions swirling with such ferocity she couldn't make a single decision on how to act.

Because deep down, very deep down where she never wanted anyone to see, she knew she felt relief and worse, hope.

If Ryder lived, she might yet get her answers.

So she'd pulled the sheet from him, along with the other bedclothes, and summoned the strongest footmen to lift Ryder while she pulled his sodden shirt from him. The trousers he'd been wearing the day of the accident had been cut for the doctor to mend the broken leg, but their tattered remains still clung with human filth to Ryder's lower body.

She'd recoiled at the sight, not realizing he'd lain like that for nearly four days. How uncomfortable it must have been, but as she had witnessed firsthand, he hadn't been conscious for any of it. But when her eyes caught sight of the telltale splotches of darker color, she felt her stomach heave. She ordered them off, which was easier accomplished by finishing the hack job Dr. Malcolm had begun.

By rolling Ryder from side to side, they were able to change the sheet beneath him, along with the linens covering the pillows. It took four footmen, the butler, Geoffrey, and Geoffrey's father to complete the task, but when they finally settled Ryder back on the bedclothes, dressed in a clean nightshirt, she felt a sense of rightness about it.

He may have ruined her life, but that did not require she abandon her sense of duty.

When everyone had finally left, she'd given herself permission to sit and catch her breath. It hadn't lasted long. Without giving her hands something to do, her mind was left to wander, and soon four years of emotions threatened to suffocate her.

She'd pushed to her feet and paced to the windows, her muscles protesting at the further exercise, but she didn't care. Back and forth she went, her eyes darting surreptitiously in Ryder's direction as one thought tumbled over the next.

The thought that scared her the most was the realization that the physical attraction was still there. She couldn't blame herself for it. Ryder was a handsome man. Too handsome. That's what had started the whole mess. But while she couldn't blame herself for still feeling the magnetic tug that seemed to keep her attention constantly pulled in his direction, it could still frighten her.

Would she be strong enough to resist it?

If she demanded answers—no, *when* she demanded them —she would need all her strength to defy the sexual tension she felt brewing at seeing him again. Even if he were covered in bandages and plaster. Even if his leg were swallowed by the stark white of a plaster cast.

Because she knew what he looked like despite all of that. Memories of his smile haunted her. The way he'd studied her face like it was the most exquisite thing he'd ever beheld. The way he'd cup her cheek before pressing perfectly sculpted lips to hers in the briefest of kisses meant to entice her.

Those same lips had been pressed to the soprano's left breast the last time she'd seen him.

She rubbed a furious hand at the back of her neck, tension clawing at her muscles. It wasn't fair that he should have this kind of control over her, that he should be able to render this seesaw of emotions in her.

And she couldn't even be certain yet if he would live.

Would the fever come back? Would infection set in where the bone had punctured the skin?

There was still too much unknown, and until then, she would not allow her thoughts to rampage over her direction of duty. Ryder was still not better. Danger lurked in every corner until he was once more on his feet, his leg healed and the effects of the accident long behind him.

Until then she would stay the course. Her emotions mattered little.

But what did she do now?

Now that he'd woken up?

For the first time in three days, she became aware of herself. She wore the same clothes, having only taken time to bathe herself from the bowl and pitcher Mrs. Olds brought her every day.

A messenger had arrived the previous day with a note from Samuels saying the carriage had become stuck in the muddy roads, and they were delayed a day. Viv still hadn't anything clean to put on. Mrs. Olds had tried to launder the shirt Viv suspected had become sealed to her body, but Viv refused the offer. It needn't matter if she were to still attend the sickroom of her husband.

Except now he was awake.

He would see the way her hair fell greasy and lank in a braid across her shoulder. How many times had she pushed her hair off her forehead with a hand sweaty from exertion or caked in cream? The cuffs of her shirtwaist were gray, and she only wore her riding trousers, Mrs. Olds having deemed the riding skirt beyond saving.

Would this be how Ryder saw her when he first came to his senses for longer than a single exchange?

He'd asked about his horses.

The thought struck an uncomfortable note in her chest. Uncomfortable because it was easier to hate Ryder, hate *all* of him, than to believe he wasn't entirely bad. But asking if the horses were all right first, before he thought to ask of himself, well, that was just terribly typical of him.

She rubbed at her chest, trying to dispel the pain.

Why couldn't it be easier to hate this man?

He looked so peaceful in sleep. The fevered fits of earlier were gone, and now he lay perfectly still, not even a worried crease to his brow.

Duty had gotten her this far. There was no reason it shouldn't guide her further.

She stood and went to the bell pull in the corner. When the footman arrived, she instructed him to fetch Dr. Malcolm and to have sent up two pitchers of fresh water, one warm, and a large enough basin in which she could wash her hair. She also requested Mrs. Olds to be fetched. The footman gave a nod and slipped out the door.

She pulled the tie from the end of her braid before he'd

even gone through the door. She scraped at the matted strands until she could free her hairbrush from the bag Samuels had packed for her to carry on horseback.

Mrs. Olds arrived moments later, one of the pitchers in hand, the other along with a basin carried by an accompanying maid.

"You do not wish for a tub to be brought up, Your Grace?" Mrs. Olds said by way of greeting.

Viv shook her head. "There isn't time. Margate awoke briefly, and I've sent for the doctor. I should like to at least remove the detritus that has found its way to my hair before the doctor arrives. I shouldn't like him to think we do not keep a clean sickroom."

Mrs. Olds's eyes flew to the bed at the mention of Ryder waking up, but her lips firmed as she turned back to Viv.

"Are you certain, ma'am? A tub would be no trouble."

There was a weight to the housekeeper's words that Viv considered. Was she suggesting that Viv should wish to enhance her appearance now that Ryder was showing improvement? Such an insinuation would suggest Viv cared what Ryder thought of her.

And she did.

The thought whispered through her mind like a thief, robbing her of her confidence, and she pushed it away. She did not, in fact, care what Ryder thought of her. He had given up that right four years ago.

"No, thank you." She kept her voice crisp and indicated the pitcher. "I shall be quick."

Mrs. Olds's eyes traveled to the bed again, but she was smart enough not to say another word.

When she was gone, Viv used the pitcher of cold water to dampen her hair. She perched over the table where the maid had placed the basin. The water was icy, and Viv's skin prickled against the cold. She didn't pause, however. She wasn't sure how long it would take to fetch the doctor, and she wanted to be somewhat more presentable when he returned. It wouldn't do for a duchess to appear so unkempt in front of a man of medicine.

She lathered quickly. The soap Mrs. Olds had brought smelled of lavender and basil, and with it came a sharp memory of her first summer spent here in Margate. The scullery maids made the soap from local herbs, and the scent was entirely unique, striking in Viv a memory from before.

From before Ryder had betrayed her.

From before her life had been sent off course.

From before she had begun to think she might not be worthy of a man's attentions.

She had always suspected. While she may have been attractive enough, she had heard the other rumors, the ones about her attitude. *Brash* was one word she'd heard used. A marchioness had once called Viv mannish in her boldness while an earl had said she was headstrong. He'd said it with a wicked glint in his eye that suggested more than Viv was willing to imagine.

She rinsed her hair with the second pitcher, the warm water welcome against her chilled scalp. She scrubbed and rinsed and scrubbed and rinsed, and still she felt unclean. Perhaps that was to be expected. She was, after all, nurse to the unfaithful husband she had expected to die.

She turned back to the bed thinking she'd heard a noise, but Ryder still lay in slumber.

Was he out of the woods now? Would he recover? Or did death still lurk at every turn?

Her hair had dampened spots along her shoulders and the front of her shirtwaist, and she picked up a towel to blotch away the wet spots. As carefully and quietly as possible, she pulled her chair closer to the fire so she could dry her hair in its warmth.

Meticulously, she separated the sections, concentrating on drying each carefully with the towel. Such intricate work was highly unnecessary. At home in London she had always allowed her hair to simply dry whilst she tended to the rest of her toilette. But right then, she welcomed the distraction, anything to keep her from remembering where she was and what it meant.

It worked until a gravelly, low voice came from the bed. She swung her head about and resisted the urge to hide her face when Ryder's gaze met hers.

"You're still beautiful," he said as she willed her body not to thrill at his words.

CHAPTER 3

*H*ow had he not remembered how beautiful she was?

It wasn't as though he were unaware, but like memories often did, his recollection of her beauty had taken on a sort of pearled existence. He knew she was beautiful, but perhaps not quite *how* beautiful.

Her expression closed at his words, however, and he felt a spike of pain at knowing his voice could do that to her.

She stood, setting aside the towel she had been using to dry her hair by the fire. The room was still dark, and he couldn't make out many details, but her hair—he would know that anywhere.

It was an ethereal red gold, and he could remember with perfect detail what it had felt like to run his fingers through it, to see it spread across his pillow, to push it from her face so he could kiss her.

Remorse crashed into him, sudden and breathtaking. He scrambled mentally to keep himself composed, and in his earnestness, he realized the restlessness was absent.

For good? Or was it only temporary? Perhaps the sight of

his estranged wife was enough to quiet the noise inside of him, at least for a little while.

He swallowed uncomfortably and struggled to sit up, feeling suddenly vulnerable.

She quickened her pace back to the bed.

"You really mustn't move. I've sent for the doctor. If you could only hold still for a little while longer, he may assess you and see how you fare."

Her words were clinical, almost cold, and he collapsed back against the pillows.

"The doctor? I will not have some outlandish fiend take my blood—"

"Dr. Malcolm is a reserved man of scientific study. I saw no evidence of leeches on his person. I think you're quite safe."

He eyed her. "You would enjoy that, wouldn't you? Watching a subterrestrial creature suck my blood?"

Her smirk was self-satisfied. "If you could only imagine." She stopped several feet away at the teacart. "Are you feeling up to eating something more than broth? I can send for a fresh tray."

Her words were stifled, so unlike the woman he remembered, and her manner was brusque and cold.

For the first time, he understood his miscalculation.

He'd believed Viv his savior, but she only saw him as her ruin.

Why had he not understood as much before now? If he were to consider things from her perspective, he was an adulterous husband, a rogue and a cad. A cold hollowness descended on him with the realization.

What had he been expecting? That she would welcome him with open arms?

Well, yes, frankly.

No woman had ever refused him.

He adjusted against the pillows, but the motion sent a tight pain through his chest. He sucked in a breath.

Viv turned in an instant at his outburst. "Are you all right? You must hold still until the doctor comes."

"And just what, pray tell, is the good doctor going to tell me?"

If he hadn't been watching her face so closely, he would have missed the way her eyes slid to his legs. He followed her gaze, but the bedclothes hid anything from view.

A sudden trepidation fell over him.

"Viv, what's happened? Am I—"

He was grateful when she spoke, preventing him from saying what he feared.

"You've broken your leg." She licked her lips, her eyes traveling down the bed where his legs were as if she were deciding just how much to say. "It was a difficult break according to the doctor. I really think he should be the one to explain it."

He knew he hadn't the strength to lift even the bedclothes to see for himself, and yet somehow his hand shot out and captured hers. She stood near enough the bed now that he easily grasped her hand, but he hadn't anticipated the spark that coursed through him at the sudden contact.

He didn't let go, even when she reflexively tugged her hand away.

"Viv." He poured all he had into her name, keeping his gaze locked on hers. She pulled at her hand again, but he only tightened his grip. "Viv, please. I know things are not right between us, but I need you now. I need you to tell me how bad it is. Please."

Even in the dim light of the candles, he saw the way her eyes changed, darkening, flickering with apprehension, and yet he somehow thought he'd startled her.

She watched him, her eyes searching, even as she said,

"The bone broke through the skin. Dr. Malcolm is most concerned for infection. They—" Again, she licked her lips. "They moved you from where you crashed outside of Canterbury. They should have waited until the doctor saw you."

Canterbury?

So he'd made it that far then.

He broke away from her troubling gaze long enough to look down at his legs. Foolishly, he attempted to lift his right leg even though he already knew he wouldn't be able to complete the feat.

"What else?" he asked even as he willed his muscles to move. The pieces came together suddenly. The immovable weight, the uncomfortable all-encompassing itch that seemed to burn its way up his thigh.

His leg was in a cast. The thought sent another wave of hollowness through him. He knew what came of a man who was reduced to wearing plaster. Immobility. The wasting of muscles. Sometimes men didn't recover from it. He'd seen it himself. They were doomed to the Bath chair for the rest of their days. He had to get up. He had to move. He had to—

Pain hissed through him again, hot and searing, and he realized in his jumbled thoughts that he'd attempted to sit up again.

Viv was next to him now, her hip pressed to his as she sat on the bed, pushing his shoulders back against the pillows.

"Ryder, please."

The sound of her voice stopped him, and his gaze flew to hers, all of his thoughts surrendered.

She was pleading with him. Her voice was moist with tears, but her eyes—her eyes were aflame, begging him to heed her warning. His body stilled completely, falling victim to her spell.

She was so close as she leaned over him, her hands on each of his shoulders.

How could he have forgotten the gold flecks in her irises? Or the way her eyebrows were so perfectly arched? The way her upper lip was just the slightest bit heavier than the bottom one? The way she studied him as if she could see deep inside him, so deep she could know his truth?

The thought sent a bolt of fear through him, and before he knew what he was doing, he lifted his head just enough, closing the distance between them until finally, achingly his lips met hers.

He'd expected her to recoil, pull away in dignified horror. But she didn't.

She *sighed*.

It was like coming home and finding everything just as he'd left it. She was everything he remembered. No, that wasn't right. She was *more*. She was what he'd been searching for this whole time. He wasn't sure how he knew that, but he could feel it. This. This was his salvation, just as he'd expected all along.

But even as the thought settled in his mind, he knew it for the brief reprieve it was. Because while Viv could calm him, she couldn't erase the ugly thing that gnawed at him.

For now, he just wanted to kiss her, to lose himself in the taste and feel of her. If he was surprised when she didn't pull away, he was stunned when she kissed him back, meeting him for every thrust, every nibble, every caress.

He wasn't sure when the kiss turned from something innocent and pleasurable to something passionate and consuming, but he didn't hide from it. He plunged, he devoured. He drank from her lips like a man dying of thirst.

His fingers had somehow made their way into her hair, spearing the red-gold locks in passionate fits. Her hands kneaded his shoulders as if she needed him to hold her up.

This was what he'd given up in one stupid, careless act. He wanted to curse his younger self, damn him for the purgatory he'd been living in for the past four years. But he hadn't known. He hadn't known what ecstasy awaited him as the husband of Lady Vivianna Darby.

He'd gotten a taste of it, a glimmer of what could have been, but he'd been naive, ignorant, foolish. He'd thrown it all away for one night of base carnal pleasure with some woman, the name or face of whom he could not recall now.

He groaned, both for the regret of his past and for the current pleasure that rippled through him. It was as if he were finally alive again after so long spent feeling nothing. Taking drink he did not taste, touching women who brought him no pleasure.

He was tortured with the sudden return of all his senses, and he plundered. Her hands streaked their way down his chest, exploring, and he deepened the kiss, sensing his body tightening in response to her.

Gone was the sickroom with its acrid smells and riddled air. Here there was light and sound and magic, just in the kiss from his wife.

The sound of the knock at the door had the effect of a pistol's hammer. His wife shot off the bed and out of his arms, throwing herself to the other side of the teacart before the door opened.

Mrs. Olds came in followed by a nondescript sort of man carrying a black case. The doctor he presumed.

It was several breaths before he realized he was sitting up, freed of his pillows prison, and yet he felt none of the pain that had held him down. His eyes drifted to Viv even as she ran a hand quickly over her face before greeting the doctor.

"Dr. Malcolm, I'm so glad you were able to make it so quickly. You see His Grace has awoken."

Dr. Malcolm's gaze had already traveled to the bed, and

oddly, Ryder wondered if the man could tell he'd just been thoroughly enjoying his wife's pleasures.

Ryder plastered on the smile that wooed many a widow. "Hello, Doctor. I understand I have you to thank for my life."

The doctor's expression was unchanged. If anything, he glowered in Ryder's direction.

"You shouldn't be sitting up. We can't know what trauma you've suffered. Are you having any difficulties with your breathing?"

Ryder glanced at Viv before replying. "Not now. In fact, I feel splendid."

The doctor's grimace deepened as if he didn't care for Ryder's flippancy.

"You've broken the small bone of your lower right leg. The bone punctured the skin, and I would warn that infection is still a worry."

The man set down his intimidating black case, unlatching it with efficient clicks. He withdrew a small wooden tube and motioned for Ryder to lie back. As he'd just managed to sit up, Ryder was not keen on obeying the doctor, but he caught a flash of Viv's concerned expression out of the corner of his eye, so he reclined without further comment.

The doctor placed one end of the wooden tube to Ryder's chest and placed his ear against the other. Ryder couldn't help but catch Viv's gaze, and he sent her a lopsided smile that had her turning away and fumbling with the tea things.

"Your lungs sound good," the doctor said after some time as he moved the wooden tube lower on Ryder's torso. "When was the last time you voided, Your Grace?"

"I beg your pardon."

The doctor moved the tube like he was arranging pieces on a chessboard. "Defecated. When was the last time you did so?"

"I hardly see how that's relevant."

The doctor straightened, holding the wooden tube between both of his hands, his expression bland. "Inability to defecate would indicate an obstruction or other malady of the digestive organs, which, if left untreated, could lead to infection and eventual death. Now then, Your Grace, when did you last defecate?"

"I can't remember," Ryder said quickly, reality settling hard on his chest.

"He hasn't had much to eat in the last three days," Viv said from the opposite side of the bed as the doctor.

Dr. Malcolm gave a nod. "We'll need to monitor your bodily functions closely. We want you eating, drinking, and expelling as usual, Your Grace." He replaced the wooden tube in the black case. "Now then, we should discuss the next part of your recovery."

"He broke the fever sometime in the night, Dr. Malcolm. I should think in a few more days he should be well on his way to mending."

Viv spoke as if she were assuring herself of his speedy recovery. But why? He eyed her, understanding wedging uncomfortably in his chest.

She wanted to leave, as quickly as possible. Run away from him for a second time. The thought made his teeth grind.

Dr. Malcolm crossed his arms over his chest. "The fever and possible infection were only the beginning hurdles to recovery, I'm afraid."

This caught Ryder's attention. "You mean I'm still in some kind of danger?"

Dr. Malcolm shrugged. "You're in a great deal of further danger, Your Grace."

Ryder kept one eye on Viv, saw the moment she registered what the doctor was saying as her eyes narrowed and her mouth slackened with inevitability.

The doctor continued. "Without proper care in the coming months, you may never walk again."

* * *

PROPER CARE.

He meant her.

Dr. Malcolm meant she would need to see to her husband's recovery as his leg healed. There would likely be exercises, of course. Some kind of work to rebuild the muscle and allow him to regain his feet.

She stepped forward, clasping her hands efficiently in front of her. "I'll begin the search for the best nurse immediately."

Even as the words left her mouth, a sourness settled in her stomach. Ryder's expression suggested he knew the futility of her statement as he raised a single eyebrow in her direction.

She couldn't let a nurse care for him.

But she'd already kissed him.

The need to flee was strong, but her sense of duty kept clawing at her.

She wouldn't let a nurse care for Ryder, just as she hadn't thought twice about riding through the frozen English countryside to get to him when she thought he was dying. It was her place to care for him, her duty as his wife.

"I can make recommendations." The doctor's voice was not as strong as it had been, and the last word tapered off almost incomplete.

"I don't think that will be necessary, Doctor." Ryder kept his gaze locked on her even as he answered the doctor. He stared at her, his eyes boring into her, uncovering the deepest of her weaknesses.

That kiss, God. It had been a mistake, and yet she would

hold the memory of it close to her forever. His lips were supple, his skill unmatched, but it wasn't about the physical aspects of it. It was the way he made her feel cherished with just a simple caress of his lips.

She felt like a woman in Ryder's arms. She wasn't the brazen Vivianna Darby everyone whispered about. She was sensual and alluring. She was desired.

And it would be her downfall.

He would be her downfall.

"I believe my wife more than capable of handling my rehabilitation," Ryder said after a noticeable beat.

How had he won without her speaking a word in defense?

Dr. Malcolm glanced at her as he rummaged in his bag. "Are you certain, Your Grace? Your recovery will not be easy. It will take great fortitude and exquisite knowledge on the part of your caretaker."

"I am quite certain." Did anyone else notice the subtle growl in Ryder's voice or was it only her? "Her Grace excels at seeing things done. Properly." The word oozed sensuality, and her cheeks flamed.

How dare he stroke her pride like that?

She raised her chin. "But I think a nurse would have far more knowledge in the medical arts. Wouldn't you agree, Doctor?"

Dr. Malcolm snapped his bag shut. "A nurse would be trained in certain aspects that may be unfamiliar to you, Your Grace."

He spoke with careful respect and gave a nod in her direction as if he feared offending her. How little did he know she thrilled at his mention of her unfamiliarity with the sickbed.

She was fortunate not to have cause for such familiarity in her life. While her mother had wasted away for days with influenza, Viv had only been a child and could remember very little. Her father had passed after a very short illness in his extreme old age. Perhaps Ryder would reconsider. Perhaps she would feel at ease recognizing her shortcomings and seeking an alternative—a better alternative at that—for Ryder's care.

Yes, surely that would silence that nagging voice that beckoned her to do her part. She would do it. She absolutely would. By hiring the best nurse money could buy. After all, the Duke of Margate had enough of it to spend.

But the intensity of Ryder's gaze on her never lessened.

"While I can see your point, Doctor, I should think I would be more at ease should I be cared for by someone with whom I have an established relationship." Finally, he broke away his gaze from hers to look at the doctor. "Isn't there something to be said for being cared for by a loved one?"

The doctor seemed to consider this. "There is anecdotal proof that the support of loved ones does aid in one's recovery, but there is no medical fact to suggest the truth of such a thing."

Ryder's smile was swift. "Anecdotal is enough for me." He shifted against the pillows and, had she not known him so well, she would have missed the tightening of his jaw.

Something had hurt when he moved, and she took a step toward him without realizing it. He stopped her with a look, his eyes falling pointedly to her feet.

She stepped back and squared her shoulders.

He raised an eyebrow.

Damn that eyebrow.

Perhaps she could shave it off in his sleep.

"Now that that is settled, what should be the next phase of recovery?" Ryder's smile was innocent enough, but she didn't miss how his gaze lingered on her.

The doctor hesitated as he studied Ryder. "I'm rather perplexed that you're alive, Your Grace."

This had Ryder's attention, and finally, she felt relief from his consideration.

"The crash of which you were a victim must have been rather terrible judging by the state of your injuries." He pointed to Ryder's broken leg. "You broke the fibula in your lower right leg. That is the small bone at the back of the leg. In order to break this bone in such a way as to cause it to puncture the skin, it would require an incredible force to strike the leg. I was not privy to the accident scene, so I can only imagine what happened to your body."

She saw Ryder swallow uncomfortably at this.

"What do you think might have occurred?"

"The phaeton flipped and crushed you." The way the doctor spoke the words would suggest he was telling Ryder how he took his tea. "You were lucky your vital organs were not crushed as well. From the sound of your lungs and digestive organs, you should consider yourself lucky. No. More than that, some higher power was looking out for you that day. If you believe in that sort of thing."

Dr. Malcolm picked up his case and held it between both hands, but Viv didn't miss Ryder's glance.

At her.

She swallowed, her thoughts scattering at the look's meaning.

"You still have a broken leg, Your Grace, and that is in addition to the many lacerations along your arms and face. Those will need to be kept clean to avoid infection. The plaster is to remain on your leg for at least eight weeks, at which time I shall remove it and examine the condition of the bone. If it has healed enough for my liking, I'll allow you to walk with the assistance of a cane. Do not pretend you should be walking again on your own before summer, Your

Grace." Here the doctor turned his clinical gaze on her. "Unless your wife is particularly good at nursing you back to health."

She hated the way her face heated at his innocent words. It was only luck he hadn't seen how she'd been nursing Ryder before he'd entered the room.

He gave a nod and turned to the door, but he stopped and looked back at Ryder in the bed. "You've only surmounted the first obstacle, Your Grace, in the fact that you're still alive. Your life is in no way guaranteed from this point. Your body has much healing to do." He turned his gaze to her. "Send for me should anything develop. Otherwise, I shall plan to return to remove the plaster in eight weeks' time."

Eight weeks.

She quickly did the math in her head as the door shut on the doctor. It would bring them to the end of February, first of March at the latest. She could still return to London in time for Johanna's season. She swallowed and pushed her palms against her thighs. Gathering her resolve, she returned her attention to her husband.

"I shall remain as your nurse, but I intend to leave before the season begins in London. I have other duties to see to then. If you cannot agree to those terms, I shall leave immediately and hire a nurse to care for you."

She felt the emptiness of her threat, but she hoped he didn't. However, he had already intimated that he knew perfectly well the power duty held over her.

"Ah, yes, the great quest to see your sisters wed. I believe congratulations are in order. Eliza and Louisa are happily settled then?"

There was something about the way he watched her that left her weary.

"Yes, they are quite happy."

"It's funny that you should spend so much on seeing to

46

their matches when you were so quick to flee from your own."

Anger bubbled up inside of her.

"How dare you." It was nothing more than a whisper as she tried to maintain her composure. "I did what was necessary to preserve what was left of my dignity."

She prepared herself for his retort but none came. Instead, he seemed to deflate, almost as if he regretted the outburst. She held still, unsure of what she was seeing. He reached up as if to rub his forehead, but his fingers struck the bandages still wrapped about his face. He pulled his hand away and inspected his fingers as if they were foreign.

"You have a laceration on your cheek. The bandage is keeping it covered."

His inspection continued down his arms as he touched the bandages wrapped around him.

"Lacerations." He spoke the word as if repeating what Dr. Malcolm had told him.

Finally, he settled his arms on top of the bedclothes on his lap, his shoulders slumped. For the first time since he'd awoken, Viv felt a slip of assurance, that maybe, perhaps just maybe, he wasn't going to be all right. That maybe…he might give up.

She stepped toward the bed without thought.

"You need to drink something. And eat if you're up for it." She poured a fresh cup of cool tea and brought it over to him, but instead of taking the cup, he merely peered up at her.

"It is truly bad, isn't it?"

The cup threatened to wobble in her grip, and she cupped the palm of her other hand under it to steady herself.

"It is." She tried to keep emotion from her voice. He didn't need a show of hysterics right now. Not that she'd ever proven herself prone to such things before, but never before had she been tried like this.

If she had thought him capable, she might have thought his expression was pleading as he looked up at her.

"Please, Viv. Please. I know I don't deserve to ask this of you, but I can't bear to think of being at the mercy of a hired nurse." He reached up a hand, and at first she thought he wanted the tea in her hand, but no. He was reaching for her.

Her heart pounded in her chest, and she set down the teacup quickly, afraid of spilling it. She pressed her hands together and ignored his hand.

She drew a breath so deep it reached back the entirety of the four lonely, heartbreaking years of estrangement from this man.

"You hurt me," she said.

The words shocked her. Not because she meant them but because she'd said them. She'd imagined saying them so many times, pictured every way of wording her meaning so as to cause the most damage, but in the end, it only mattered that he heard them.

He dropped his hand, but she wasn't done.

"I trusted you, and you destroyed that trust. We are no longer husband and wife in my eyes. We are no longer even friends. I want that to be perfectly clear. I shall stay here until the plaster is removed, but I will be in London for the start of the season. I will not bend on that."

She studied him, studied his eyes, his lips, his brow. What was he thinking? What had he been expecting?

That kiss had been so much, *too* much, but what had it meant? Did he truly wish to kiss her or was it just a reflex of his roguish ways?

Whatever it was, there would be no more of it until he explained himself. She wasn't naive enough to expect an apology. All she wished for was recognition of the pain he'd caused her. That was all. That would need to be enough.

Before he could answer there was a sharp knock at the door, and Mrs. Olds entered.

"Your carriage has arrived, Your Grace," Mrs. Olds said with a small nod in Viv's direction. "I've shown your maid to your suite of rooms. I trust you should like to finally change out of those clothes." The housekeeper pointed to the connecting door that led to the duchess's rooms and gave a knowing smile. "I shall stay with His Grace until you return."

"Thank you, Mrs. Olds," Viv said, and with only a brief glance in Ryder's direction, she headed for the door, leaving everything unsaid between them.

CHAPTER 4

*H*e'd thought having his wife as his nursemaid would have meant he'd see more of her. But he, in fact, had not.

He'd enjoyed a rousing tete-a-tete with his housekeeper in which Mrs. Olds frowned at him a great deal. And now, three days later he was still wrestling with the emotions stirred up by what Mrs. Olds relayed to him in order to catch him up on what had been happening while he was asleep.

The first order of which was Mrs. Olds's detailed recounting of how Viv had come to Margate.

He wasn't sure if he wished to throttle her for careless stupidity in riding horseback across from Sussex to Kent, in the middle of winter no less, or if he should consider her daring a glimmer of hope.

Did he have a chance of regaining her trust?

You hurt me.

The words echoed in his head and haunted his nightmares. Some part of him knew he'd hurt her. There was her obvious reaction of running away, but if he were honest, at the time, her reaction had confused him. Didn't all husbands take lovers? Shouldn't Viv have expected the same behavior from him?

He knew now that not all husbands did, in fact, take lovers, and that he was a right ass for thinking Viv should not have been upset.

He ran a hand over his face, only to collide with the bandage that still covered the right side. God, his *skin* hurt. Every bit itched as if crawling with earthly critters, and he had entire conversations with himself about how he could not rip the plaster from his leg no matter how much he believed it was filled with ants.

He grabbed the bell by the bed and shook it violently. Viv had brought the bell on the second day after he woke and invited him to use it should he have any need whatsoever.

He knew she was attempting to get herself settled at Margate now that the carriage and her lady's maid had arrived. He had been gentleman enough not to point out the fact that she'd had a home at Margate since they were wed five years ago.

He knew she was avoiding him, but was it because of the kiss or what she had said?

He thought himself a fool now for thinking she would welcome him with open arms. But then, he really hadn't been thinking. The restlessness had threatened to overpower him and he—

Well, he'd fled. Just like she had.

His injuries and the recovery he faced held back the restlessness, but he knew that was only a matter of time. Soon he would need to deal with it. Soon he would need to find answers for the gnawing sense of time fleeting away from him. His accident would only be a distraction, and he was no longer certain Viv was the answer to it all.

Or was she?

He had loved her once, but it was as a young man loves

anything pretty. He felt a thrill at being her husband, at *owning* her. The thought made his stomach turn now. How could anyone own a person, let alone a someone like Viv? It would be like trying to hold a flame in one's hand. Beautiful and powerful but in the end, you would get burned.

His wandering thoughts were interrupted by the door opening, and the wife in question entered. The room was still dim as the drapes were left drawn, but he could make out her red-gold hair in the candlelight. It was up now in a simple chignon and her gown was of a soft green. The perfectly respectable madam of Margate Hall.

He would remember her as she'd been when he'd awoken though. Her fiery hair hanging like a curtain about her face, the outline of her legs prominent through the trousers she wore with the firelight behind them.

He cleared his throat. "I'm going mad. Something must be done."

Her frown was swift. "The doctor said you're not to attempt moving for at least another week, and then it will only be advisable to have you move with the assistance of a Bath chair. If the footmen are able to lift you into it."

The idea of having other able-bodied men do anything to him had his teeth grinding.

"We will discuss that when the time comes. For now, I should settle for a bath of sorts. My skin has grown to hate me, I should think."

Her expression softened, her lips parting ever so slightly as she considered this. He knew she would detest the intimacy of the act, but her sense of rightness would have her fulfilling his request.

She gave a nod. "I believe you are right. A little freshening would do you good perhaps."

She went to the bell pull in the corner and gave it a tug. She kept her gaze averted though and busied herself with the teacart a maid had brought earlier and left within his reach by the bedside.

"You're not eating."

"Send me something edible, and I shall."

There was the frown again. "You've suffered a shock. We can't know how your stomach will take to heavier foods."

"I can tell you how it will take. With celebration and jubilee. Would you like to see?"

Finally, she considered him. "I'll speak with Cook about sending up some soup. I believe she's made a batch of split pea."

"With the chunks of ham?" His mouth began to water at the mere mention of it.

Viv placed fisted hands at her hips. "Yes, but I will only allow them to send you up some if you promise to stop should you feel unwell."

He gave her a lopsided smile that always worked to woo many reluctant widows. "I promise."

"Don't use your smirk on me. Its powers are wasted on my stony heart." Her tone was sardonic, but he couldn't help but feel the sting of the truth behind her words.

Mrs. Olds arrived, and the bath was accommodated. Pitchers of warm water were brought along with a basin, towels, and soap. Viv requested the tray of soup stuff as promised to be delivered in an hour's time.

"Do you think the drapes could be opened? I've rather grown tired of sitting in the dark."

Viv glanced at him from where she was sorting through the flannels they'd brought with the pitchers of warm water.

"The doctor said—"

"Hang the doctor. He's not the one stuck in this bed."

"That same doctor saved your life or have you forgotten?"

She seemed to find a suitable flannel and moved over to the bed with one of the pitchers and the basin. She placed both on the table by the bed and surveyed him like a butcher would a choice round of lamb.

He swallowed. "I have not forgotten. But don't they say sunshine is the best healer of all ills?"

"They don't say that."

"Are you going to be this obstinate the whole time?"

"You asked me to be your nurse. You didn't ask me to play nice." She gestured toward his body. "Where does it hurt? I should hate to cause you further pain." Her smile was tight as if she meant the exact opposite.

"It hurts everywhere including in my teeth."

"If you wish for me to feel sorrow for your condition, I should tell you it's not possible. You were the one being careless with the phaeton."

Because I was coming after you.

"My reckless ways catching up with me?" He tried for a sarcastic tone, but his badgering thoughts had the question coming out weak and rattled.

"Something like that." She eyed him curiously.

She picked up his hand, but while he wanted to say it sent a spark through him, her touch was far too cold and removed. It only served to draw his attention to the wedge between them.

She examined the bandages along his arms. "Do you think we should take a peek under here? I can imagine the wrappings are none too comfortable."

"They are not."

She peeked beneath the first wrapping and, seemingly satisfied, peeled back the fabric to reveal a hash of small lacerations gone pink and soft with healing. There were two cuts in the upper part of his shoulder that had required stitching, but they were small and already pink.

"I should say you're healing rather nicely if this is any indication."

She unwrapped the rest of his arm and turned it over so it lay palm up on the bed. She came around the bed to begin work on the other arm and soon he could move both of his arms without the chafing confines of the bandages.

She studied his face next. "The laceration on your face required stitching, and while I think it might be best to keep it covered, I can also understand how it might be bothering you. Let's take it off and give your face a thorough scrubbing. We'll just be careful of the stitches. I'll see if Mrs. Olds has something we can use as a fresh covering."

She moved to walk back around the bed, but he grabbed her hand in his own before she could leave. He didn't know why, but he was suddenly overcome, words pushing at his lips.

"Viv, I want you to know I'm sorry. I'm sorry I was unfaithful. I'm sorry I broke your trust in me." Her eyes were wary, and he tightened his grip on her hand. "I know that means nothing to you, and I know an apology is worthless without the actions with which to support it, and I've given you no cause to believe the sincerity of my regret. But I want you to know that I believe what I did was stupid, foolish, and selfish. It was the actions of a careless young man heady with his first taste of the world. You were the victim of my selfishness, and I wish every day it hadn't been you that I hurt. Because—" He licked his lips, his chest suddenly growing tight. "Because you're the least deserving of such treatment, and it has meant I've spent the last four years without you."

It was one of those times in his life when he hadn't known what he felt until he spoke the words, and it left him just as rattled as she likely was. He let go of her hand, knowing he had not earned the right to touch her.

She stood there for several breaths, and he watched her, recalling how happy he'd been on their wedding day. How genuinely happy. He hadn't been happy in a very long time.

"Thank you for telling me." Her voice had lost its sarcastic edge, and he sensed the soft underbelly he'd exposed with his admission, and he felt a flicker of hope that maybe she was not lost to him. "But I would ask that you remember I am here as your nurse and not your wife."

He gave a quick nod, even as disappointment flooded through him. "I understand."

She moved away from him then and started in on bathing him. Again he wanted nothing more than to say the act was the stuff of his dreams, and his wife's touch like the first sip of water after a long drought. But it wasn't. Her movements were efficient, her touch cool. She went about scrubbing and rinsing as if it were everyday she bathed dukes in their beds.

She helped him off with his nightshirt to scrub his back and torso. It was the most erotic thing a woman had ever done to him, but the stony expression on Viv's face extinguished any ardor he might have felt. Soon he was in a fresh nightshirt, a fresh strip of linen applied to the neat row of stitches on his face and shoulder, and Viv was setting aside the last of the towels for the maids to take away.

She brushed off her hands as if signaling the end of her ministrations, but then she rummaged on the bedside table, selecting a small pot of what looked like a yellowish cream.

"This should help with the irritation from the bandages." She pulled a chair over to the bedside and sat, the small pot nestled on her lap as she tugged his hand into hers. She applied the salve with the same careful and efficient strokes she'd used on the rest of him. But this was different.

The salve was *divine*. Its buttery texture cooled his irritated skin almost instantly, and he let his head drop back on the pillows with utter satisfaction. She didn't speak, and neither did he. He simply let her slather him with the mystery concoction. But like the rest of it, she was done too soon, and she once more brushed her hands together.

"The soup should be here soon, and then you should get some rest. I'll be in later to check on you. If you need anything before then, there's always the bell." He couldn't be certain, but he might have said her lips weren't as tight when she looked at him.

"Thank you." His voice was more gravelly than he'd meant it to be, and he didn't trust himself to say anything else.

She gave a nod as if to leave and turned in the direction of the connecting door. But instead of leaving, she slipped over to the bank of windows opposite and pulled back a single drape, allowing a modicum of sunshine to spill into the room. He watched her disappear through the door, a decision forming in his mind before he consciously realized it.

She was no longer only the savior he sought. She was also the wife he wanted.

And he would win her back.

He just had to get out of that damn bed.

SHE WASN'T sure how long she sat perched over the unwritten letter, her eyes lost on the rolling hills that disappeared down to the channel below that lay somewhere beyond the horizon outside her window.

The duchess's rooms faced north just for that reason. While the light was appalling, the view more than made up for it.

If only Viv could see it.

But instead she replayed what had happened in Ryder's room the day before, heard his words over and over again in her head.

I'm sorry I was unfaithful.

She had thought she wanted to hear those words, yearned

to hear them. But when they were actually spoken, she felt... nothing. Ryder was right. The words did very little good because while he had finally said them, they did not undo the past. They could not erase the memory of seeing him with that woman, the way his hands caressed her body, his skin so dark against the creamy white of the soprano's breast.

Viv coughed, sputtering erratically until she could pick up her teacup only to find it had grown cold. She sipped at it anyway, trying to clear her throat and her mind.

So Ryder had finally said he was sorry. So what? Was that what she truly wanted him to say?

No.

An apology from him was the last thing on her mind. It seemed so useless after the deed was done. What she wanted was an explanation. *Why* had he done it?

What had she done to cause him to find pleasure in the arms of another woman?

She tried to remember that first year of their marriage. She'd never refused him her bed, and while she wasn't schooled on the topic, she thought he had found pleasure there. She'd done everything he asked, made all the appropriate noises, and smiled and showered him with compliments when it seemed appropriate.

How could he have wanted someone else?

The thought felt selfish and arrogant. Who was she to say what he wanted? How was she to know she wasn't enough for him?

She could have sat there ruminating in her maudlin thoughts all day, but the letter to Eliza letting them know how Ryder was faring remained unwritten. She picked up her pen just as the knock came at her door.

Samuels entered with a bow, and Viv noticed a bundle in her arms.

"I'm very sorry, ma'am. It seems the post was a victim of

the recent weather. Mrs. Olds did not wish to disturb His Grace with this, so she sent it up with me."

Viv eyed the bundle and for the first time noticed just quite how soggy it was.

"Good heavens." Viv stood and pointed to the stone tiles on the floor in front of the hearth. "Set it down there."

The maid did as instructed and carefully brushed her hands along the sleeve stockings of her uniform. "It seems there's a great deal of post for His Grace, but it is rather all ruined, I'm afraid. Mrs. Olds wondered if you should still like to see if some might be saved, ma'am." Samuels gave a tilt of her head as she eyed the bundle. "I should think it wouldn't harm them to let them dry for a bit, would it? Perhaps I could bring up tins from the kitchen in which we could collect the water."

Samuels was a young woman Viv had promoted from upstairs maid after Viv's first lady's maid married a footman and opened a haberdashery on Bond Street. It meant that Viv was still new to her relationship with Samuels and was often surprised by the woman's industrious aptitude. Had Viv's previous lady's maid been given a pile of soggy post, she would have quivered in tears should her uniform be ruined.

Viv knelt carefully next to the hearth and bent over the post. She could make out Ryder's address without difficulty on several pieces, but as soggy as they were, she feared attempting to open them would cause their utter destruction.

"I think allowing them to dry for a bit wouldn't do any harm. Please fetch the tins from the kitchen, Samuels."

Samuels gave a nod. "Very good, ma'am."

Using only the tip of her index finger, Viv prodded at the soggy lump with a heavy sigh. She only hoped there was nothing of import in there. She hadn't received a note from Glenhaven in several days, but then she hadn't sent her sisters any news.

Without Viv in residence to shoo them back to London, she wondered if Johanna would linger into the new year. Sebastian was likely inclined to stay because he knew it would make his wife happy, but Viv knew he would make some kind of excuse of having Parliament business to discuss with Dax.

An ache, heavy and solid, formed in her chest as she yearned for her sisters. She could have used their guidance right now, or at the very least, a shoulder on which to cry.

But Viv didn't feel like crying. She felt like weeping.

She saw no way out of the exile she'd lived in for the past four years, especially now that she had Ryder's apology, and it had done nothing to ease her turmoil. Because it wasn't enough. She had spoken the truth. The trust between them had been shattered, and she didn't know if it could be rebuilt. She felt that it could not. So where did that leave her?

In love with a man she could never be with.

By virtue of his apology, she wanted to believe he had changed, but the fact of his phaeton accident proved otherwise. He was still the same careless, reckless rogue to whom she should never have entrusted her heart.

She kept prodding at the pile of letters, hoping to catch a glimpse of her sisters' handwriting. It was strange how something so innocent could lead to something so terrible. But when the words *manly cock* jumped out at her, it had the effect of arresting one's attention.

She stared at the phrase, the dark ink muddled with damp. She tried to read more but there was another letter clumped to the top of it blocking the writing. She picked up the whole bit and began the arduous task of separating the letters.

What on earth was she doing?

Didn't the saying suggest such care would kill a cat? She should put the letters down and allow Samuels to tend to them. No, she should just toss them into the fire and pretend she'd never seen them.

But she couldn't help it.

What was this nonsense about a manly cock? And was it Ryder's cock to which the writer referred?

Viv had never had cause to use such a word in truth or in writing in all her years, and while she knew she should stop, she wanted to know what kind of person would use it.

The top letter peeled away from the one she wanted with a sick, slopping sound, and she worried the paper would tear with it. But luck was with her, and the bottom letter held. Carefully, so painfully carefully, she pulled back the top layer and then the bottom, unfolding a neat square of paper on which a short letter was written.

She spent several minutes studying it, her eyes slipping over muddled words as she tried to make sense of them. Even when she could ascertain the word, the sentence often left her confused, forcing her to reread the whole thing. Finally, the entirety of its meaning sank in like a knife spatchcocking a bird, and she dropped the letter on the hearth, sitting back on her heels as if it might dirty her.

* * *

My dearest lover,

* * *

News of your accident has just reached me, and my heart has been rendered useless by the fact. I wept when you departed Willie's with such haste, even though I had begged you to stay, and now I can only fault myself with what's happened to you. I should have convinced you. I shall never forgive myself. I only hope the knowledge that my wet loins ache for your manly cock will help in your recovery. Please do say I may come nurse you back to health. You know what wonders my mouth can do.

* * *

THE SIGNATURE WAS BEYOND COMPREHENSION, but it needn't matter. Viv had read enough, more than enough really. She sat there on the carpet, her heart racing as her brain scrambled to make sense of it all.

Absurdly, her first thought was that the writer lacked in common vocabulary.

Her loins were wet? No one used such silly theatrical nonsense, which could only mean the woman was of low class. Could the writer be the soprano herself?

Viv shook her head as if answering her own question. She'd heard somewhere the soprano had gone off to America after that. But she could have come back. Couldn't she?

She plunged forward on her knees, picking up the letter once more, her eyes scanning it for anything she might have missed. In the end, it was still the same letter.

Still the same betrayal.

But was it?

She already knew Ryder was not faithful to her. He had apologized for hurting her, but he never claimed he had stopped his wandering ways. So why should the letter both be a surprise and feel like another betrayal all at once?

Because she had wanted to believe his apology was the start of something more.

How foolish she'd been. Of course, he wasn't about to change now. Not for her anyway.

She set to work on the other letters, attempting to separate those that would come apart easily, resolutely ignoring the letter from wet loins. None of it mattered. She might be trapped in exile, but she was far better than many women in the ton. Her husband did not drink to excess nor did he harm her in any physical way. She had her freedom as well. Not once in four years had Ryder demanded anything of her.

Damn him.

By the time Samuels returned with the tins, Viv had most of the letters separated on the stone tiles. Carefully they placed each onto a rack inside the tin so the water could drip down while leaving the papers to dry.

"There. I think that should do it," Viv said when they'd placed the last letter into a tin. "Now I only hope there was something worth saving in here," Viv muttered under breath.

"I beg your pardon, ma'am." Samuels turned her head from where she added coal to the fire, sending the flames up in a noisy burst.

"Nothing at all. Just woolgathering, I suppose." She straightened and pushed at the wrinkles that had formed in her skirts from her labor. "Thank you, Samuels, for your quick thinking with the tins. We may just save the lot of it."

Samuels gave a quick nod as she dusted off her hands from the coal. "I should only hope it doesn't happen again. I'm not familiar with such workings in country homes. Is the post often subject to such happenstance?"

Viv paused, considering her answer. She wasn't often at Margate, perhaps two or three times in the past four years. It left an uncomfortable hollow reminder in her chest.

She smiled. "I should hope not, or we would all be rather a mess, wouldn't we?"

Samuels's smile was soft as she curtsied. "Yes, ma'am. If there's nothing else for me—"

"Go along. I'm sure you've much to do to get us settled."

She gave another small bow and left, leaving Viv to her thoughts and the cursed letter on the hearth.

What if she were to just throw the damn thing in the fire? That would serve him.

But would it really?

It would only work to cause him harm if her actions meant anything to him, which she was sure they did not.

That was that then, wasn't it? She had her answer.

She meant nothing to him, so he would mean nothing to her. No matter what skillful seduction he attempted on her, she would shield her heart from him. No matter the cost.

CHAPTER 5

*H*e was fairly certain if he remained in bed for much longer his buttocks would never resume their normal shape.

Seven weeks.

He still had seven weeks until the horrid plaster came off.

Seven weeks for his bum to become as flat as a drunkard singing at the docks.

He'd tried lifting the leg a few times to see just how heavy the thing was. Now that he had a bit more strength, it didn't feel quite so impossible.

Not quite.

It was still absurdly heavy, and he knew whatever plan he formulated for getting out of bed, it would need to accommodate the weight of the plaster. He was not stupid enough to think he could carry it. Not if he wanted the bone to heal and not rip off the entirety of the leg should he take a misstep on the stair.

The plaster came to just above his knee, which was the most excruciating part as he longed to bend the joint there. But he remained thankful the cast stopped where it did. At least he could swing the leg about with careful determination. Like, say, over the side of a bed should he choose to leave said place.

Maids brought his trays regularly, and he ate with a vigor he hadn't known recently. He needed his strength if the bone were to heal in just eight weeks, and time was running out to woo his wife.

Said wife he saw very little of. Some nurse she was turning out to be. He couldn't blame her, though. It was almost as if he held her prisoner there, prisoner to her own sense of duty.

He should have let her go. He should have agreed to hiring a nursemaid. But he simply couldn't.

Not after that kiss.

He still didn't know for certain where any of this would lead, but something clawed at him, gnawing at him to make this right, to win his wife back no matter what it might take.

And then what?

He didn't know.

He couldn't look that far ahead. He couldn't think of the restlessness that waited there just beyond his vision. For now, he would focus on Viv. Only Viv. She was all that mattered.

He scratched at the irritated skin along his jaw where the last of the bandages remained. Viv continued to worry he'd rip out the stitches in his cheek whilst asleep. Judging by how taut the cheek went when he tried to eat, he felt fairly confident the stitches were not going anywhere.

There was a sharp knock as Mrs. Olds entered.

"Your Grace, Mr. Stoker to see you." She gave a small bow and moved aside to allow the man to enter. "Will there be anything else?" she asked, her hand on the doorknob.

"No, thank you, Mrs. Olds." He cast a wide smile in her direction.

It affected her not in the least.

"Very good, Your Grace." She gave another nod and left, closing the door behind her.

"Mr. Stoker?" He couldn't stop the eyebrow that raised sardonically.

The man in question's mouth twisted into a smirk. "Your Grace?" he quipped with as much sarcasm.

"Did we not realize how awkward it would be one day when I inherited the title and you—" Ryder paused in his perusal of his friend. "Good God, Daniel, are you the blacksmith?"

Now that a week had passed since everyone believed him to be at death's door, Ryder had convinced Viv to leave most of the drapes open so he could have sunlight in his bedchamber. It was only because of the bright winter sun that he saw his childhood friend's cheeks warm with embarrassment.

Daniel held a felt hat between his hands that he tossed back and forth nervously now. "It would appear that I am."

"But what about the hops?"

As soon as the words left his lips, Ryder regretted them. It was apparent he'd already made his friend uncomfortable, and now he'd only made it worse.

"The hops aren't what they used to be, Your Grace."

"If you call me Your Grace once more, I'll be forced to throttle you, which the lady of the house will not like in the least, and then you'll be forced to endure her wrath. Now what is this about the hops?"

Hops had always been a valuable crop on Margate lands, so much so, that Ryder's father had hired a man to see to their harvesting alone. That man had been Daniel's father. Ryder always assumed when the time came, Daniel would take his father's place.

Apparently, that hadn't been so.

Daniel gave a shrug, his brow wrinkled as if in confusion. "You mean you really don't know?"

Ryder hated how vulnerable he felt being stuck in the damn bed, and this was not the kind of conversation he wished to have in such a position.

Daniel scratched at his neck. "That act the Parliament passed—God, nearly ten years ago now—it allowed everyone to brew their own beer and ale. Now everyone's fancying himself a brewer. They don't want the good hops my father used to produce. They want the cheapest you can turn up. That's the only way they've managed to keep the fields turning a profit since then. My father wouldn't have any of it. He lives in the cottage down by the church now. All but given up. Blacksmithing under old Tobias Minter was the only thing I had left to me."

Nearly ten years ago Ryder would have been on his Grand Tour. It was when he'd raced his first phaeton.

He pried his back teeth apart. "I didn't know any of this, Daniel."

He gave another shrug. "I suppose I can see how you wouldn't. The fields are still bringing in coin. There would be no reason for your steward to alert you to it. Everything is the same except nothing is. The hops workers' barracks have gone to ruin, and Margate is no longer the desired job it once was."

Hops had been a staple of his childhood. He couldn't remember a summer without the mention of the hops harvest. He and Daniel would race Mr. Stoker to the fields in the spring to see how the soil had fared over the winter. To think it was so much less than what it used to be gave him a tightness in his chest.

"Your father used to check every field before it was planted to ensure it was the proper kind of soil for the hops. He was so…"

"Stubborn," Daniel said with a soft laugh.

"I suppose he might have been that," Ryder said, his own voice full of humor. "But he was a damn fine farmer, too."

Daniel nodded. "He was at that." He gestured around them. "I was told you had need of a blacksmith."

Ryder cleared his throat and cast his gaze down to his leg. "I've gone and done something foolish, I'm afraid."

"I heard it was a phaeton accident." Daniel followed Ryder's gaze. "I happen to have come into possession of one by trade recently. I'm not sure I would wish to race such a vehicle."

"I have admitted it was rather foolish."

"The chaps at the pub said it was downright reckless." Ryder did not miss the smirk on Daniel's face.

"It might have been, but I had good reason."

Daniel laughed. "It was a woman, wasn't it?"

Ryder could only frown. "Something like that." He patted his broken leg. "I broke my leg, though, and the plaster weighs more than a keg. I can't get up on my own, and I feel—"

"Helpless as a child?" Daniel's voice was thankfully neutral.

"Exactly. You've got to get me out of this bed, Daniel."

Daniel tucked his hat under his arm and pulled a small notebook from his pocket.

"I can make a Bath chair, if that's what you're looking for. I had to make one for Mrs. Feathers just last month."

"Mrs. Feathers is still alive?"

Mrs. Feathers played the organ for church services in the village. Mrs. Stoker, Daniel's mother, had always insisted on bringing Ryder to services along with Daniel when they were boys. The sermon would run about as long as an age, and halfway through, Daniel and Ryder would start making faces at one another to pass the time.

Mrs. Feathers would glare at them from her organ, and after services, she'd remind them what hell was reserved for little boys who misbehaved in church.

Daniel looked up with a surprised smile on his face. "Aye, she is. The woman must be a hundred if she's a day. Twisted her ankle coming out of services, though, and now she's afraid of walking on it."

"She must have someone to push the chair for her, doesn't she?"

Daniel pulled a stub of pencil from between the pages of the notebook. "Her daughter has the duty of it. Why? What did you have in mind?"

Ryder crossed his arms over his chest. "Well, that's just the thing. I don't want anyone's help. I want to do it myself."

"Spoken like a true petulant child."

"Did you just call a duke petulant?"

Daniel's smirk was quick. "When the word fits…"

Ryder couldn't stop the laugh. He stilled suddenly, trying to recall when last he'd had such an engaging conversation with someone who truly made him feel…well, he didn't know what. He'd spent so much time ignoring the hollowness in his chest he'd forgotten what it was to feel joy, happiness, like he belonged.

He swallowed, rubbing absently at his breastbone. "Be that as it may, I should like to be independent in this. I don't wish to seek out another's help should I wish to leave this bed."

Daniel made more notes in his notebook. "So you'd like to propel it using your own person?"

Ryder gave a nod. "Yes, exactly." He patted his broken leg. "But you'll need to consider the weight of this thing. I wouldn't want the chair to tip over and tumble me out because of the heaviness of the plaster. With my luck, I'd break my other leg."

Daniel looked up, tapping his pencil against the note-book. "Your body weight should be enough to counter the weight of the plaster, but you'll need to be careful when getting in and out of the chair. You'll want sturdy arms for the chair to help leverage you into it. Have you attempted getting out of bed?"

Ryder blinked. "I haven't," he said slowly, realizing this entire feat may be more complicated than he'd anticipated. "I have been practicing trying to raise my leg with the plaster on, and I've gotten it several inches off the mattress."

"Perhaps you wouldn't need to lift it. I could fashion a prop for the broken leg that would sit at the same level as the mattress. You'd need only slide your leg over to it."

Ryder eyed the height of the bed. "Wouldn't that be laugh-ably high?"

Daniel shook his head, placing the pencil back into the notebook and snapping it shut. "No, the chair will already put you higher because of the necessary circumference of the wheels." He tucked the notebook in one pocket as he with-drew a circular leather case from the other. "Do you mind if I take some measurements?"

"You're like some sort of strange tailor," Ryder said, eyeing the leather case.

Daniel raised an eyebrow. "I've never been afforded such comparison. Thank you, Your Grace."

Ryder laughed as he indicated for Daniel to continue.

His friend pulled a flat piece of metal from the leather case that was marked with measurements along one side. He measured the distance from the floor to the bed, and then seeming to find this satisfactory, he measured from a space above the floor to the bed.

"Bath chairs require a certain amount of wheel to keep them upright with the occupant, but if you would like to manage the chair yourself, it's going to change the dynamics."

He straightened, holding the flat metal strip up like a lance. "I must measure your leg, good sir."

They'd played at catching frogs when they were young, but they were no longer boys.

Ryder frowned. "This is entirely awkward."

"I would agree. You're the one who put us in this position, though, I'm afraid."

Ryder flinched. "I suppose you're right."

He shifted and pulled back the bedclothes to reveal the plaster. Daniel was efficient as expected and had his measurements within seconds. Ryder flipped the bedclothes back.

"Do you know about how long it will take you to fashion such an apparatus?"

"You're lucky you broke your leg in the middle of winter. Any further into spring, and you wouldn't have gotten a chair at all. As it is, I'll have time to make this a priority."

Ryder felt some relief that he would soon have some version of freedom from this bed, even if it didn't involve his own legs. He thanked Daniel with a firm handshake.

"You're really the blacksmith?" Ryder asked of his child-hood friend.

"You're really the duke?" Daniel's smile was full of the mischief they'd terrorized the servants with as boys.

It was really his friend, and being there with him had Ryder's head filling with questions.

Daniel was almost to the door when he turned back. "I just have one question."

"What is it?"

"Was she worth it?" he asked, one side of his smile tipping into a smirk.

Ryder didn't hesitate. "Absolutely."

* * *

"I've never played backgammon."

"And you feel like starting now?" She gestured around them as she stood next to his sickbed.

She'd been sorting linens with Mrs. Olds when the maid had come with Ryder's request to see his wife. Viv had figured while she was in residence she should attend to some of the matters the duchess would normally see to and figured the linens were a good place to start. She'd hardly gotten into her task when the maid had arrived, and curiosity more than duty had compelled her to answer the request.

Ryder shrugged. "What else am I going to do?"

She eyed the pile of discarded newspapers on the side table as well as the two untouched novels.

"Anything else?" she offered.

"Shouldn't I wish to spend time with my wife?" he replied.

"You haven't wished to spend time with me in the past four years. Why start now?"

He closed his eyes briefly as if her words had actually made a mark.

When he opened them he said, "Be that as it may, I should very much like to spend time with you now."

She tugged at the sleeve covers Mrs. Olds had given her to keep her gown clean while they tended to the linens. "I should think your sudden desire for my presence is only caused by your current incapacitated state."

"Couldn't it be possible that I desire your presence simply because I desire it?"

She didn't like how smooth his voice was, but more, she didn't like the flare of heat it caused deep in her stomach.

"No." The word was flat and left no room for argument.

They studied each other in silence for several seconds then, and she wondered why she wished he would say more.

Was it his words that teased her or his tone?

Neither should have. She recalled the letters drying in her rooms, and it would do her well to remember their contents.

She straightened her shoulders. "Should you wish to learn backgammon, I should be happy to teach you."

She went to the corner and pulled the bell pull. When the maid arrived, she requested the backgammon board and a bed tray on which they could play.

She turned back to the bed when the maid had left and eyed Ryder's position with trepidation. In order for them to play properly, she would need to sit on the edge of the bed. It wasn't as if he could get up and occupy one of the chairs in the sitting arrangement by the windows.

Even though logic would suggest otherwise, her eyes drifted to that sitting arrangement as if it were a final hope. Perhaps she could lift him...

No, she was being utterly foolish. She could no more lift him than to turn her hair purple with the twitch of her nose.

"Perhaps you would be more comfortable playing with one of the staff. Mrs. Olds, I'm sure, is—"

"Are you afraid to be alone with me?"

If he had said anything else...

She only just stopped herself from gritting her teeth. "Not at all. I am only concerned for your happiness." Her smile was feral.

"Well, if my happiness is your aim, might I suggest we pass the time with other...activities?"

She didn't know why her bravado fled at the mere mention of the expected relations between husband and wife, but when faced with the truth of their circumstances, her stomach turned at the thought.

She didn't trust him. She didn't know how she could after everything, and didn't trust serve as the basis of any kind of worthy relationship? What did that mean for them?

There was no *them*. The letters she had uncovered were proof of that.

She recovered her feral smile. "I'm terribly sorry, but I reserve my participation in such activities for gentlemen of a more deserving nature."

If she hadn't been looking directly at him, she would have missed the way his jaw loosened, and his eyes widened just the smallest degrees as if what she'd said surprised him. No, not surprised. Startled.

Why should her personal business be any concern to him? He'd made the terms of their marriage clear four years ago, and it didn't involve intimacy.

Sex, sure. But not intimacy.

Her chest squeezed, and the reality of the past four years descended on her like a mourning veil. She picked up her skirts and made her way to his bed.

"I'm surprised you haven't played…backgammon before with a lady friend. I'm sure you've had several."

The muscle over his right eye twitched.

"You are suggesting I make a habit of collecting…lady friends."

"Do you not?" She nestled one hip on the side of the bed, careful not to let the mattress consume her.

"You may be surprised to learn that I do not."

She laughed. "I do find that surprising."

And untruthful.

So he would continue to lie to her. Had she expected anything else?

He crossed his arms. "I don't make it a custom. I enjoy sport and drink. The women have always been auxiliary to my interests." His playful tone was gone, and for a moment, she wondered if he were actually telling her the truth. The idea so shocked her, her mouth opened without sound emerging.

They sat like that for several moments. He with his arms crossed, his expression plain and open. She with her lips slightly parted and her brow wrinkled in question.

"Your reputation proves otherwise," she finally said.

"If you're referring to that ridiculous name the *ton* has assigned me, I regret to inform you there's no basis for such application."

She was prevented from requesting further explanation when the door opened and a footman carried in the bed tray with the backgammon board atop it. He bowed and settled the tray over Ryder's legs.

"Will that be all?" the young man asked.

"Yes, quite. Thank you," Viv finally managed.

The footman gave one more bow and departed.

She busied herself with setting up the board and tried to ignore the heat of Ryder's steady gaze. She carefully placed the dark checkers in the spaces in front of her, counting each one with unnecessary care to ensure the set was complete.

"Backgammon is a game of chance and skill. You'll roll the dice to see how many spaces you can move your checkers and the objective of the game is to remove all your pieces from the board." She held up an ivory-colored checker. "You move the light pieces."

She arranged the ivory-colored checkers on the board in a mirror image of her own.

"Your pieces will move clockwise whereas mine will move counter-clockwise." She removed the dice from their leather pouch and gave them a small shake. "I'll go first to show you how to count the spaces."

She kept her focus on the game, but she couldn't help noticing his expression didn't change for the whole of her explanation. He watched her carefully. Not the board or the way she gestured the game play with her hands. *Her*. He watched her.

Had he been telling the truth?

Ryder was incredibly handsome, yes, but it was more than that. With his jet-black hair and piercing green eyes, Ryder was…alluring. She wouldn't blame a woman for falling for his charms. Viv had, after all. But didn't the blame still lie at Ryder's feet for not resisting the women who propositioned him?

And what of that letter?

The letter suggested such familiarity and longstanding acquaintance. It wasn't as if she thought someone would write the words *wet loins* to a near stranger. If Ryder didn't seek out the relationships, he certainly didn't stop them.

She rolled the dice and picked up a brown checker.

"I shall move this one four spaces for this die." She tapped the die in question and moved the checker four spaces counter-clockwise across the board. She selected another brown piece and tapped the other die. "I'll move this one three for this die." She settled the checker three spaces away and placed her hands in her lap. "Now then. You roll the dice."

"How many other men have you been with?"

Her eyes flashed to his, the question ringing in her ears. "I beg your pardon."

He leaned forward and for the first time, she saw a sharpness to his gaze. "How many?"

Her brain swam with the accusation underlying his question, and for a moment, she was paralyzed. She returned his hard gaze with one of her own, summoning the strength she carefully controlled.

"How dare you," she whispered for the second time since conversing with him again. "You would suggest I would break my vows made in a church before God. You would suggest I would take my commitments with such a cavalier attitude as to smear the name of my husband. You would think me so crude?" She spat the last word, feeling its vileness on her tongue.

He blinked and licked his lips, his attention turning inward as if considering his own question. "Viv, I didn't mean to suggest that you're—"

"That I'm what? A whore?" The word came far too easily, and she hated its depravity.

"No." He spoke the word swiftly and firmly, but it needn't matter. Why would he ask the question if he didn't believe she'd taken a lover?

No, *lovers*.

How many other men?

How many?

God, why did she continue to love this man when he continued to rip her heart to shreds? She had been right to guard her heart from him, and she should have listened to her own wisdom.

But what of her explanation? Why hadn't he come after her? Why had he strayed in the first place? Did he believe as the rest of society did? That she was too bold, too loud, too…much?

Were the answers worth too much if the cost was her heart?

"I never said such a word." He leaned forward now across the bed tray.

"You needn't have bothered. You made your meaning perfectly clear when you asked such a thing of me." She realized she was gripping the bed tray as if it prevented her hands from closing around his neck. "How many men, you ask? Do you really wish to know?"

A muscle moved in his cheek, and she realized he was grinding his teeth.

"Do you really want to know how many men have pleasured me when you couldn't?" The words flew from her mouth before she could stop them. There was utterly no truth to them, and yet power surged through her to throw them in his face.

There. His eyes went blank, and his lips parted on the softest exhale.

She'd hurt him. *Finally*. But it meant nothing. The words were a lie, and even if they had been the truth, she felt no triumph in her win.

She felt dirty. She felt despicable. How could she keep letting him have this power over her?

She closed her eyes, willing the blood in her veins to stop pounding so hard through her body, willing her mind to quiet and allow her to regain control of her senses.

When she finally opened her eyes, she found Ryder studying her, his eyes quiet yet alert.

"How many?" His voice was gravelly now as if he wrestled with his own emotions.

She wouldn't do this. She *couldn't* do this. She had wanted her answers but not if it meant playing the game at his level. She was better than that.

She scratched her arms, feeling the filth as if it were real. Slowly, she placed her feet on the ground, one at a time, and stood, smoothing her hands down her skirts. She lifted her chin and squared her shoulders.

"I think that's enough for today. Should you wish to play in future, I request that you ask Mrs. Olds to partner you. I seem to have lost my taste for the game."

She was nearly to the door when his voice stopped her.

"Viv."

There was something in his tone, something she hadn't heard before. She wanted to say it was remorse, regret, apology, something... But Ryder was never sorry for anything. So she didn't stop until she had closed the door between them.

CHAPTER 6

When he thought he might go mad, he had the footmen help him move to the settee by the window. It was a herculean effort, one he would never mention to anyone based on how much it unmanned him, and he could only hope his servants were loyal in their silence. One man was entirely dedicated to carrying his leg and the heavy plaster while another was responsible for keeping his nightshirt in place. At least he could try to maintain some kind of dignity.

In the end, it had been worth it. If he had had to remain abed a single day more, he didn't know what would happen.

Especially as his mind swam with images of his wife with other men. Her long legs wrapped around some man's torso as he—

He tossed back the last of his tea, wishing it were something stronger. He peered around him at the carts Mrs. Olds had left with tea fixings and breakfast. He'd touch hardly any of it. The low table beside him was strewn with discarded newspapers and empty teacups. Sitting atop it all was his bowl of butterscotch candies, and he reached for one now.

Tucking the sweet morsel in his cheek, he turned his attention back to the window to properly brood.

It was one of those winter days when the sky was so blue and empty, he could feel the cold of the air even from where he sat indoors, ensconced in blankets and bathed in the heat of the fire. His rooms overlooked the gardens at the back of the estate, and in the middle of winter, it was all rather dreadful. Where there should have been color, there was drab and brown and emptiness.

If he were the maudlin sort, he would say it was a reflection of his soul. He wasn't, and yet, staring at the brown tangle of the barren rose bushes below, he could understand how they felt.

He'd never thought Viv would take a lover.

Now that it had occurred to him, he figured himself daft for not thinking it earlier. Of course, Viv would take a lover. She was beautiful and vibrant. Any gentleman would seek her attentions. How could he have been so stupid?

He scratched at his cheek where the bandage continued to irritate. The doctor wanted the stitches left in for a few more days, but Ryder could feel them tug every time he tried moving his jaw. While he was sure everyone was quite concerned for the possibility of fever, he considered this ongoing irritation hellish. The fever had been hardly a foe at all. Now the real recovery began.

Once the stitches were removed, he would feel marginally better. Although his arms itched where the skin was still healing, and he could only move his shoulder as far as the stitches there would allow. He'd bribed Mrs. Olds into getting him a jar of that magical salve Viv concocted.

It was more than a week after his accident, and he still had difficulty raising his arms. As soon as he attempted it, tightness spread through his chest and pain had his breath hissing between his teeth.

Broken rib? Perhaps. But the dear Dr. Malcolm thought it more likely the muscle strain from the accident. According to the men who had found him, it appeared Ryder had been thrown over the top of the phaeton and landed directly on the hard earth before the seat of the phaeton had crushed his leg. The body absorbing such a shock was enough to leave him sore and frustratingly weak.

He remembered none of it, which was even more of a frustration.

He picked up his teacup again only to remember it was empty. He set it back down and ran his hand through his hair. God, he needed a bath. Viv had done her best while he was fevered to keep him clean, but he wanted nothing more than to dump a bucket of delicious warm water over his head. He eyed his plaster.

How was he to go about such a thing and not get the damn thing wet?

Viv would have his head if he ruined the plaster. The doctor would need to be called to reset it. No, it just wouldn't do.

He reached for another butterscotch.

The knock at the door was sharp and startling. He knew only one person who knocked as such, and she'd been avoiding him all day.

She was wearing a blue gown he vaguely remembered from the early days of their marriage. It had a way of warming her, setting her hair alight and making her eyes sparkle. It was faded now, though, and he could see where she'd turned the cuffs up.

He puzzled at that, but she spoke before he could ask her of it.

"Mrs. Olds said you're not eating. Are you feeling ill?"

He gave her a tight smile. "The servants are tattling on

me, are they? I shall have to remember that when it comes time to evaluate their wages."

She folded her hands in front of her and tilted her head with the slightest degree of arrogance. "I know you already had Reynolds allocate their Christmas stipends, so you will not convince me of your miserly ways. You were rather more generous than usual this year. Feeling guilty about something?"

He felt a responding sense of kinship at the sarcasm in her voice, but he didn't like the direction her words had taken. If she only knew of the legions of guilt he carried with him.

"You're rather fetching today, Your Grace. Are we to be receiving callers?"

"Hardly." She glanced out the window as if gathering herself. "If I am to be in residence for the foreseeable future, I think it a wise use of my time to inventory the household goods. Mrs. Olds and I are working on the silver services today."

"There's more than one silver service?"

"We're currently at seven, but we haven't gone through the east wing drawing rooms as of yet."

"The Duchesses Margate did enjoy a good silver service, did they not?"

She seemed to consider him before her eyes slid slowly shut as if in pain or frustration. When she opened them again, he didn't like the tiredness he saw there.

"Ryder, would it be too hard for you to be serious for once? I really must know if you are not feeling well."

He hated seeing the weariness on her face, and more, he worried he was the cause of most of it.

"I am quite well. I'm just not feeling particularly hungry is all." He scratched at his beard. "I wouldn't mind a bath, however, if you're offering."

The smirk came to his lips before he could stop it, but when he saw the tight expression on her face, he felt instant regret.

"Ah, I see what you mean." He picked at the blankets covering his legs. "Perhaps I've spent too much time in frivolous company. I appear unable to converse in a serious fashion."

It wasn't that, though. He knew only too well how quickly the restlessness returned if he should assume any manner of seriousness. If he never spoke a single word of import, he could pretend the blackness wasn't licking at his heels.

Only he didn't like the tightness that came to his chest when he saw Viv's disappointed expression.

"I would, indeed, enjoy a bath. Do you think one might be arranged?"

Her eyes were watchful as if she waited for him to slip into humor once more. He wasn't surprised to find it was easier with her to have a serious conversation. The need to be flippant and humorous wasn't quite so strong.

He felt the pull of her, the calming, the easiness, the peace. He had been right to seek her out. He didn't know how he had known it, but he had. Viv could banish the restlessness for good. He knew she could.

"I think we can devise something that should work. You must be careful of the plaster. I don't think Dr. Malcolm will be keen on redoing it."

He gave her an honest smile now. "I promise I shall do my best."

She considered him once more with that wary eye, and he didn't like it. Again, he felt the fool for thinking she had been waiting for him, pining for him. Lady Vivianna Darby waited for no one and pined for nothing. He should have realized that.

Did that mean all was lost?

No, he simply couldn't accept that.

But perhaps his usual roguish ways wouldn't be enough. If she wanted sincere, he could be sincere.

"I'll speak with Mrs. Olds, and we'll see what can be done." She hesitated. "This would be a great deal easier if only you employed a valet."

He pursed his lips. "He would only slow down the phaeton."

She did not bid him good day when she left, and he hoped that meant he would be seeing her again at some point. His plan had seemed much more inclined to be met with success when he had the function of both of his legs. It wouldn't do for him to continuously watch her leave him, stranded on whatever surface he currently found himself. He hoped Daniel was making progress with the Bath chair.

Mrs. Olds soon arrived with a flourish of footmen, a copper tub, a trove of towels and flannels, and a veritable train of maids carrying steaming pitchers of water.

"You're not to get your plaster wet, Your Grace," Mrs. Olds said from where she conducted the troop of servants.

"Yes, ma'am. I have been told as much."

Mrs. Olds's look was swift. "Then you should know how much your behavior will affect a certain person's perception of you."

Mrs. Olds had been housekeeper at Margate Hall since he had been in the nursery, and it was not unusual for her to give him cloaked guidance, no matter the topic. Including the relations between him and his estranged wife.

"I had an inkling of such."

She folded her hands in front of her as the maids filled the copper tub that had been set on the floor beside him. Once all the pitchers had been emptied, the level of water was easily within reach, and he yearned for a wet flannel to run along his neck.

He eyed Mrs. Olds. "This will do nicely. Thank you."

The footmen and maids filtered out, but Mrs. Olds remained.

"Is there something else you would desire for luncheon, Your Grace? You seem uninterested in the cart that was brought to break your fast."

He was ready to dismiss her with a halfhearted reply when he recalled the reason for Viv's visit earlier. If he were to stay in her good graces, he would need to make a small effort at least. Even if that included consuming his meals.

"I should be interested in some stew if Cook has it. This cold weather has me in mind of something warm."

Mrs. Olds gave a bow. "Of course. I shall see to it immediately."

As she made her way to the door, he picked up his cup again only to find it empty like it had been the first three times he'd tried it.

"Mrs. Olds," he called before she could close the door behind her.

She peered back at him around the edge of the door. "Yes, Your Grace?"

He was prepared to ask for a fresh pot of tea when something stopped him, a niggling sensation of a recent conversation poking at his memory.

"Mrs. Olds, do the footmen still brew a batch of beer from the leftover hops?"

Mrs. Olds stepped back inside, her hands falling away from the door.

"Yes, it is a custom the footmen still maintain."

"Might they have any left from a recent batch?"

Mrs. Olds's expression remained unchanged. "Yes, I believe they might."

"I should like a tankard brought up with my luncheon."

"You should like a tankard of the house ale brought up

with your luncheon?" While her expression remained stoic, she was not so good at keeping the incredulity from her voice.

The house ale was traditionally only consumed by the servants as it was deemed to be of lesser quality.

"Yes, I should very much like that."

She gave a nod. "Very good," she said and shut the door behind her.

He shucked his banyan and nightshirt as soon as he was alone, wincing only a little at the sore muscles in his arms and the pull of his stitches. The first touch of the warm water against his fingertips was heaven, and he couldn't help but wonder if he might coax more kisses from his wife if he didn't smell like soured cabbage.

* * *

Viv tried to concentrate on the pile of pillowcases she held in her hands, but when she counted them for the third time and still could not remember the correct count, she gave up.

"Mrs. Olds, do you think the number of pillowcases is adequate for the number of guest rooms currently in order?"

"It should be quite adequate, I would think, ma'am. Most of the guest rooms remain closed up as Margate does not often see visitors."

The housekeeper spoke with a neutral tone, but her words held a bite Viv could not avoid. Margate Hall did not see visitors because the duke and the duchess were never in residence together.

Until now that was.

Ryder usually floated from one country house party to the next, and Viv spent her summers at one of her family's homes. She'd come to Margate only once in the time of their separation for the summer, and it was immediately after she'd seen Eliza wed.

Eliza had given her something to think over, and Viv did her best thinking away from the demands of her family.

It was hard to believe that Eliza and Dax had encountered disaster immediately after their marriage, but it was at her worst that Eliza had said something to Viv that had upset her belief that her marriage could ever be saved.

Eliza had asked her if Viv had ever spoken to Ryder about what she wanted their marriage to be like.

The thought had honestly never occurred to her. She'd been wildly in love with Ryder from the moment he'd asked her to dance at the Merriweather ball. Her debut had been delayed by her father's death, and she'd thought herself older and wiser than the other debutantes. She couldn't possibly fall for Margate's roguish charms.

But she had.

She'd fallen hard.

They were wed before the end of the season, and she was proud to be seen on Ryder's arm. She'd thought that's what it meant to be loved, to be put on display like that. She hadn't realized it wasn't love at all. It was merely ostentatiousness.

Ryder had been showing her off. He hadn't been in love with her.

She'd never thought to speak to him about what she wanted from a marriage. At such a painfully young age, she couldn't have said what she wanted. But she knew now. She not only knew what she wanted, she had other things she wanted from him. Things that required him to have a civil conversation with her.

She'd doubted him capable of such a thing. He was always the quickest wit. But the previous morning in his bedchamber, he'd given her the very reason to doubt.

He'd revealed a flaw.

Ryder never admitted to any deficiency of any kind, but he'd said he had been in the company of too many frivolous people, and it may have affected his manner. She wanted to chalk it up to an excuse well played, but it was the look in his eyes when he'd said it that bothered her.

It was as if he'd found fault with himself.

Ryder was a bastion of confidence, a near god among men. He'd never once shown an ounce of indecision, a modicum of doubt. He was the Rogue Duke of the *ton*.

But not that morning.

That morning he had turned his gaze inward and found something lacking.

It rattled her. It had her questioning everything she had believed about her marriage during those four long, lonely years.

Could she simply talk to Ryder?

He had suggested, too, that his reputation was largely a matter of *ton* gossip, and its sizable nature had no merit in truth. The topic had not come up again, and she would not be the one to raise it. Therefore, it left her with further questions and an even greater sense of indecision.

Could she have the conversation she had imagined time and again and dismissed because of her husband's hedonistic attitude?

Perhaps she could.

The holidays had given way to the icy cold of January, and the sea wind had taken a sharp turn. The gardens were dormant even though the sun was bright in the winter sky. But there was something about its bleakness that gave her hope.

What was it about the possibilities found in a new beginning? She'd never thought of it before, but maybe now it might just apply to her.

Her thoughts were shattered by the opening of the guest

room door. She and Mrs. Olds had made their way to the opposite end of the east wing from the family rooms, and she had considered it progress until she could no longer count the pillowcases in her hands.

She turned to see which maid or footman was returning from a task she'd sent them on when she found no servant at all.

Instead she found Ryder's leg.

At least, she assumed it was his leg as it was a solid block of plaster pushing its way through the door. She dropped the last of the pillowcases, not noticing where they landed as she made her way to the door. She thought she might have spoken his name, but she couldn't be sure. Her heart raced at the sight of the bright white plaster, suspended in the air by a —well, she didn't know what it was.

The leg proceeded to float into the room until it was followed by the rest of her husband, sitting comfortably in the contraption that held his leg aloft.

"Hello, wife," he said with exuberance. "I thought I would visit you on your duties for the day."

She blinked.

While she could have anticipated he'd try something to get out of the sickroom, she had not imagined this.

"Whatever are you doing?" She pointed an accusatory finger. "And what is that?"

"Daniel made it for me. Isn't it brilliant?"

"It's not brilliant at all. It's entirely reckless. I should think you might not have a care for yourself, but you could at least think of—"

Me.

She stopped the telling word before it could trip from her mouth.

She swallowed. "What is it?" she asked again.

Ryder's expression had dimmed somewhat from the

exuberance it had displayed when he'd entered the room, and he watched her carefully now. She could feel the heat at her cheeks and willed herself not to pull at the suddenly tight collar of her gown.

Seeing him in that contraption seemed to have sparked a rush of concern for her husband that was entirely unwarranted. She shouldn't care about his person as he so clearly didn't care about himself, and yet—

She swallowed and fixed her gaze on him, settling her hands at her hips to still their shaking.

"It's a modified Bath chair. I asked Daniel to build it for me."

She studied the elaborate device in which he was ensconced. "It looks like one of those velocipedes."

He sat between two large wheels, his hands firmly affixed to flat, rectangular pedals that seemed to be connected to the front wheels through a series of gears and chains. His broken leg sat perfectly snug in a wooden channel built between the two front wheels.

She forced her eyes to his. "And who the hell is Daniel?"

A small smile played at the corners of his lips, but she didn't care.

"Daniel Stoker. He's apparently the village blacksmith, but I knew him as a boy. He was the hops manager's son here on the estate."

"I don't care if he's the Archbishop of Canterbury. He obviously has no regard for your health either if he thought to—"

"He was doing a favor for an old friend."

His voice had gone soft and careful, and it had the effect of forcing her gaze to steady on his. She felt a hypnotizing wave of calm wash over her as if he were putting her into a trance.

She wasn't sure how long she held his gaze, but it was the

most intimate thing she'd done with her husband in four years. Slowly, her heart returned to a normal beat, and she relaxed her hands from her hips.

"How did you get into that thing?"

"My skilled and competent bevy of footmen. They are getting rather good at moving a grown man from one seated position to another."

His eyes cast downward to his broken leg, and for the first time, Viv felt a spike of remorse. She swallowed again and looked about them, suddenly realizing they were alone. Mrs. Olds must have slipped out when Ryder had arrived, leaving the two of them to some privacy.

"I see." She didn't like how her throat had suddenly grown tight. "I trust the bath worked out to your liking."

She spoke the words before she realized what she was about and immediately regretted it.

His smile was slow and carried with it just enough heat to let her know he was letting her off easy. "The bath accomplished its task. Although I can say the experience could have been more…pleasurable."

His words were just on the right side of sultry, and she didn't like how they poked at her defenses.

"I'm sure I can summon one of your mistresses to provide you with a better experience should you wish."

Silence sparked between them, so deep and profound she thought her ears would ring with it forever.

Never had she spoken so boldly to him. His infidelities were something mentioned only in analogies and euphemisms. She had not once mentioned the existence of his lovers as simple fact.

Now that the words were out, something shifted between them. It was as though reality hadn't been quite what it should have been and with the truth spoken, the world righted itself to its proper footing.

Confidence coursed through as the ringing silence receded, and Viv folded her hands calmly in front of her.

Ryder looked down, fiddling with the tie of his banyan.

"That won't be necessary." His tone was neither defensive nor sardonic. It was simply honest.

She recalled the previous morning when his honesty had unnerved her, and she worried at her lower lip, wondering what was transpiring between them. It was as though the past four years vanished, and in its place was nothing but a blank void on which they could build a new foundation.

She didn't trust it.

"Viv, I owe you an apology." He didn't look up as he said the words, but she could see where the corners of his mouth had tightened, as though what he was about to say required a great deal of strength. "I had no right to question your affairs. Your personal relationships are yours alone." Finally, he looked up and the starkness in his gaze captured her breath. "I gave up my right to your loyalty years ago."

The silence rang back in her ears, flooding her senses while she tried to regain her breath.

Thankfully, he continued, saving her the need to find words in her jumbled thoughts.

"I actually came here to ask you to sup with me in my rooms. I know it's nothing so extravagant as partaking of our meal in the dining room, but I find I should very much enjoy the pleasure of your company."

She remembered exactly what he had looked like the first time he had bowed to her. He wore all black, so crisp and severe, and yet she thought him so dashing. There hadn't been the fine lines that bracketed his eyes now, nor the crease along one side of his mouth, evidence of his one-sided smile. His brow had been unworried and his smile genuine. She might have fallen in love with him at that very moment.

Now as she stood before him, covered in dust in her

oldest gown, he in the contraption that allowed him some form of mobility, his black hair a tumbled mess about his battered face, she knew she could fall in love with him again.

And it frightened her.

"Yes, I should think that can be arranged." Her tone was as formal as his, and she waited for him to make his usual sarcastic comment, but nothing came.

He only smiled at her with a softness that warmed her heart. She licked her lips, willing her defenses to hold.

He gave a nod then. "I shall look forward to it."

He turned himself about using the hand pedals of his chair and wheeled silently from the room, leaving her to wonder why her heart was racing.

CHAPTER 7

*H*e should not have done that.

His arms ached with the effort it had taken to pedal the chair down the corridor to the opposite end of the east wing. That should have been enough. When would he ever learn not to push it?

He'd left Viv with the intent to practice with the chair in the vast corridors of Margate Hall, but he couldn't stop the ghost of a thought from controlling his actions. No matter how he tried, he couldn't push what Daniel had told him from his mind. And after consuming the swill that passed for the house ale, he knew something wasn't right with the hops.

He should have simply called on Reynolds to see how the hops were being managed. He trusted his steward, and he knew the man wouldn't attempt to cover up any misdeeds. But it was more that Ryder needed to see it for himself.

So he'd summoned his bevy of footmen to carry him down to the drive so he could pedal his way over to the barracks where the hops workers stayed when the crop was harvested.

Mrs. Olds had fussed over him, wrapping him in extra

woolen blankets and putting a warming stone in for good measure.

He'd found the barracks in the condition Daniel had described.

It was almost more than he could take in. The hops had been the largest crop for the estate, the harvest almost the most magical of times during his childhood.

Ryder's father had taken pride in providing the best accommodations for the workers, and in return, the workers performed better. He hadn't known at the time that his father was paying those same workers well above the average rate for the hops harvester, and now Ryder understood a little more why the workers were so loyal to his father.

The sight of the dilapidated barracks was enough to freeze the air in his lungs.

He'd only had enough energy to make it to the barracks and back to the house. His arms were trembling by the time he returned to his rooms and ordered another bath. He shook with cold even as the sweat soaked his shirt, and he worried the fever had returned.

Viv would have his head.

He washed quickly, wanting nothing more than to wrap himself in a blanket and warm up by the fire. He was better at leaning over the basin to rinse his hair, but the effort left him nearly sapped of what little energy he had remaining.

Dr. Malcolm was right. He would need to exercise. Being forced to remain in his chair was taxing his other muscles.

He toweled off his hair only enough to make it back to the bed to retrieve a blanket. He hadn't counted on how difficult it was to maneuver with the chair in the close quarters of his rooms, and trying to retrieve the blanket expended the last of his strength.

By the time he reached the fireside, bumping into the chairs that remained in front of it, the blanket covered only half his body, the towel left forgotten on his head where he'd attempted to dry his hair. He was asleep before he could right any of it.

He awoke to voices although he couldn't have said if the voices were real or a part of the disordered dreams he was having.

He dreamt of Viv, of course. She wore that blue gown with the worn cuffs, but her vibrant hair was loose about her shoulders. She looked so beautiful it had hurt his chest even in his dream. He tried to go to her, reaching out his arms toward her, but he couldn't move.

He looked down to find himself in a chair, both legs covered in plaster now hanging limply to the ground. He tried to call to her to come to him, but she only smiled and faded away.

"He wasn't to be stopped, ma'am."

"I'm sure he wasn't, Mrs. Olds. I know precisely where the fault lies."

He awoke fully at the sound of Viv's outrage and knew for certain poor Mrs. Olds was getting an earful because Ryder wasn't conscious to receive his own scolding.

He tried to speak to clarify the matter, but his throat had gone tight with sleep.

"He could have died, the fool."

Was there a note of concern in her voice? Was she truly worried he might have succumbed to the chill being outside had caused him?

The thought had him opening his eyes and forcing his hand to raise to catch her attention.

Instead, he smacked her in the face.

She reared back but the impact did nothing to remove the scowl from her features.

He couldn't have known she was that close to him, and yet he felt an apology springing to his lips. It too got stuck in his dry mouth, and he licked his lips furiously. But his eyes were sliding shut again.

"Leave the food. I'll tend to him."

He heard rustling and the sound of a door closing, but sleep was beckoning to him again.

"Ryder. Ryder, you must stay with me a little longer. I need your help to get you dressed."

No, he didn't want to dress. He wanted to be naked. With her. That was by far superior.

"Ryder."

Perhaps this time when he dreamed of her, he could finally catch her in his arms...

The lips that touched his were soft and warm, tentative and shy. His senses soared from sleepy to high alert in an instant, but he wasn't about to give any indication of such. He let her find her place against his mouth, her lips coaxing now, building pressure.

Only when she had settled firmly against his mouth did he come away from the chair, his hands going into her hair and pinning her to him. He tilted her head and deepened the kiss, ravaging her mouth with all the pent-up desire his frustrating dream had caused.

He would have left it at that until she moaned, and she shifted against him, her chest coming against his until he could feel every curve of her.

God, he'd forgotten what it was like to kiss her. He felt the pins in her hair loosen as his fingers explored, the soft waves of her hair falling over his hands as he destroyed her coiffure. He slipped a hand lower, cradling her cheek as he nibbled the corner of her mouth, sucked her lower lip between both of his.

Her hands were on his shoulders now, and he wondered if she knew how tightly she held him. It was his turn to moan now as he shifted, moving one hand to rest against her back, tracing the line of her spine through her gown.

She pulled away from him so quickly he sat forward in the chair.

"No, Ryder, we need to get you dressed." Her face was flushed, the light of the fire behind her mixing with the fire of her hair in a disorienting illusion.

She stood, and his hands involuntarily chased her, hoping to catch her before she shattered the moment. He dropped his empty hands to his lap and realized he was quite naked. The blanket had slipped off his lap at some point, and something invaded his vision on his right side. He reached up to find the towel now soaked with the water from his hair. He tossed it aside.

"I much preferred the kissing. We can continue to do that if you wish."

There was more rustling behind him, and he moved to turn the pedal to pivot the chair but even that effort had his arm shaking.

When she came back into his line of sight, her lips were firm.

"The kissing was to get you awake so I could dress you properly." She shoved a nightshirt over his head before he was prepared for her to do so.

"How odd," he said once his head popped free of the shirt. "I always found kissing to be much more pleasurable when one was undressed."

He turned a heated gaze on her, but she only fisted her hands against her hips.

"And how do you intend to do that if you catch your death of chill?"

"I didn't catch my death of chill. I—"

"Ryder."

She spoke only his name, but her tone carried a legion of

frustration. His hands stilled where he'd been tying the front of his nightshirt, and slowly, he raised his gaze to hers.

The heat that shot back at him had his heart racing. She was trying to remain so perfectly composed that she radiated with the effort of it. He could see it in the whiteness of her knuckles where her fists remained at her hips, at the lines that bracketed her mouth.

Realization came over him like a tidal wave, swamping him with its truth.

Viv cared about him.

For years now, he'd lived his life in a string of house parties, balls, and galas. He was the life of a dinner party and the lover of lonely society wives. His lovers might have pouted when he left them, but he was only ever an object, easily replaced by the next rogue who stumbled into her bedroom.

He was merely a spot of frivolity in an otherwise dull life.

But not to Viv.

He didn't know how he'd neglected to see it. Earlier she had told him she wanted to have a civil conversation with him, but that wasn't the heart of the matter. It was only a symptom.

Viv wanted a real conversation with him because she cared about him. She wanted to see him, to talk to him, to know him, and the realization left him speechless.

He studied her face, but it remained unchanged. The frustration sang from her tight jaw and her pinched gaze.

He continued tying the strings of his shirt.

"I didn't catch my death of chill," he continued more softly now. "I was going to see the state of the hops workers' barracks. I had received some upsetting news about their condition, and I wanted to see it for myself." He tied off the last string and moved his gaze to her. "I thought as long as I am in residence, I could try to address some issues that seem to have arisen in my absence."

He knew he mimicked words she had only recently said to him, and he watched as her hands relaxed, sliding down until her arms hung at her sides.

Her tone was softer when next she spoke. "Perhaps you could go about it in a more prudent fashion."

"How would that be?" He raised his arms to indicate the chair. "I'm stuck in this contraption for the foreseeable future."

"Maybe I could help you." He wondered if he imagined the hesitancy in her voice, but he thought it real.

She was offering herself to him, making herself vulnerable. Suddenly he recalled that first time he opened his eyes to her after the accident, remembered the stark pain in her voice as she'd spoken her feelings.

You hurt me.

And yet she would offer to help him. He wasn't at all surprised by this. She was nothing if not loyal to her duties. It left a sour taste in his mouth. He didn't want her misplaced sense of loyalty. He wanted her, all of her. He wanted her loyalty, her trust, her...forgiveness.

Was that what he needed? Would that end the torment of restlessness that plagued him?

He was suddenly tired again, and something must have shown on his face because Viv moved. More rustling occurred, and then she returned with his banyan held between both her hands.

"Lean forward and I'll help you get this on."

She smelled of soap and vanilla, and he leaned forward more than was necessary to get the banyan on if only to take in her scent, bring his face so utterly close to where he wanted to bury it in the soft space along her collarbone.

"How does this thing work? We need to get you into a

more comfortable spot." She tugged at the wheels, and he had presence of mind enough to point out the brakes.

She toyed with the lever along the wheels until the brakes came free, and she wheeled him over to the settee by the windows.

"I can't lift you into bed, but I think you can slide onto the settee. Do you think you have the strength for it?"

He opened one eye. The span between the chair and the settee might as well have been an ocean for all he thought he could cross it. But he put his hands to the wheel and levered himself up like Daniel had shown him. The trough with his plastered leg in it swiveled with his movement, allowing him to slide onto the settee.

Viv was there, pushing the banyan around his legs so he was more comfortable as he slid into place along the head-rest of the settee. He didn't know what else happened as he could no longer keep his eyes open. But he felt the weight of blankets on his legs, heard the chair roll away from the settee, the rustle of skirts as she moved past him.

He reached out and caught her hand, suddenly gripped by a startling fear.

"Stay with me," he whispered, but he didn't open his eyes.

Instead he could only picture how she looked, gazing down at him, and in his mind, she was as beautiful as always.

If only she would stay with him...

"I'll just get a chair—"

Now he did force his eyes open.

"No. Here. Stay here with me." He slid over on the settee, making space for her alongside him.

She eyed the spot as if it were a snake readying itself to strike.

"Please, Viv."

Her eyes met his, and a stillness passed over her. His heart fell as he prepared for her rejection, but she didn't do it. She picked up her skirts and slipped onto the settee beside him, curling her body against his.

Warmth spread over him in a rush, and he was so overcome, words seized in his throat, his heart raced, and his lungs felt tight.

She laid her head on his shoulder as he wrapped his arm around her, holding her tight to him.

Only then did he let sleep take him.

* * *

SHE LISTENED to the sound of his heartbeat.

If she concentrated on only that, she wouldn't think about what she was doing. She wouldn't think about how it felt to be curled against her husband's body. How it felt natural. How it felt comfortable. How her insides seemed to calm and settle whenever she felt his touch.

She wouldn't think about that if she concentrated on something as mundane as the beat of his heart.

She had come to Margate with a sense of purpose and a clear plan, but now she wasn't sure where to step.

He hadn't been the husband she expected to find.

Pieces of the old Ryder she remembered slipped through. His inability to resist humor. His disregard for his own safety. Even now as she lay there, she could smell the lingering scent of his favorite butterscotches in the air and knew a bowl of them must be somewhere nearby.

But there was so much more to him that was unexpected. He'd gone out into the January chill with a broken leg to see the hops workers' barracks because someone had told him concerning news about them. That was not like the Ryder she knew. The Ryder she knew would have delegated the task to a footman to report back to the steward. He would not have gone out to see them for himself.

And the way he sometimes quieted himself with merely a look from her. In the past, she had thought him fun and carefree, but such a cavalier attitude had been her destruction. She didn't enjoy it so much anymore.

But there was something off about him. As if the untroubled Ryder she had married was somehow worn at the edges, leaving his manner inconsistent. He surprised her at every turn. When she expected sarcasm, he was serious. When she expected hedonism, he was responsible.

Her clear plan and focus were not so any longer. Now she wondered who this man was that she'd married. A part of her even worried Ryder was somehow…broken.

Not just physically. Emotionally and maybe mentally.

Something was not right, and yet she couldn't have said what it was.

That he would have taken advantage of her kiss earlier was exactly like the man she had married. That he would catch her hand and ask her to stay with him was not.

Ryder needed no one, especially her, but this Ryder was different. And she feared she wouldn't be able to resist him.

Would that be so bad?

She could still feel the heat of his kiss on her lips. Something inside of her awakened when he touched her. Something she had thought either long dormant or worse: something she feared she never had at all. But when Ryder touched her, when he so much as looked at her with longing, it came to life, soft and fragile. But she knew with a little coaxing, it would come to stay.

And maybe then she would no longer feel like a woman in limbo. Maybe then she could have the life she wanted with children and a family.

But no, that wasn't true.

Because she would never have Ryder.

The pain was quieter than it normally was when it pulsed

through her, and she drew a deep breath, willing her treacherous thoughts to vanish.

But they continued to needle her as she listened to her husband's even breathing.

Ryder clearly wanted her, and at least for the next few weeks, he was trapped here with her. She could take what she wanted, and that could mean the start of a family.

But could she survive the heartbreak when he left?

For he *would* leave. It was inevitable. When the plaster was removed and he regained his feet, Ryder would hitch up and race off as soon as he was able, leaving her once again all alone.

She squeezed her eyes shut against the image.

But she wouldn't be all alone now. If she were lucky, she would find herself with child. A small flame flared inside of her, a flame of hope, a flame of excitement. For the first time, her future didn't loom before her with such darkness and despair.

If only she could endure the fleeting attentions of her husband.

It was some moments before she realized Ryder's breathing was no longer so steady, his heart picking up pace. She lifted her head and saw his face tight with pain. She raised her head from his shoulder, immediately worried she was hurting him. But no, his lips were moving as if he were speaking to someone.

He was having a nightmare.

She sat up and studied his face, considering whether or not to wake him. He needed rest, but this was not rest. She reached to shake his shoulder and wake him, but now words were forming and spilling from his lips.

"No." She heard the word quite clearly even though his voice was low and foggy with sleep.

"No. Stay. Please."

She canted her head and placed the hand she thought to wake him with lightly on his chest, feeling the contours of muscle through his nightshirt and banyan.

Was he dreaming of her?

The thought sent a thrill so acute racing through her, her skin pimpled with goose flesh. She waited, holding her breath as if to hear him better should he say anything more.

He turned his head against the back of the settee as if he were looking for something, and for a second, she thought he had awakened and caught her watching him. But no, his eyes were still shut, the corners puckered as if in concern.

"You're so beautiful."

She snatched her hand away involuntarily at his words, pressing it to her stomach where her insides roiled.

He couldn't be speaking of her. Not like that. He wouldn't call her beautiful. Would he?

"But I want…" His hand twitched as if he were reaching for something in his dream.

He wasn't talking about her.

The thrill that had raced through her turned to ice and stabbed her directly through the heart.

He'd never spoken those words to her, and she knew someone to whom he might have. The writer of the wet loins. A coldness so complete passed over, she felt an instant chill. She rubbed at her arms and slipped from the settee, leaving him with his dreams.

They were supposed to dine together that evening, and Mrs. Olds had left the food trays on a table by the windows that opened up to the back gardens. Earlier, the expanse had been lit in beautiful oranges and purples as the sun had set behind the house, casting the last of its rays over Margate and the fields beyond. Now the windows were nothing but unrelenting black, and she caught her reflection in one of them.

Her hair was loosened with one strand falling along her cheek and resting in a curl against her collarbone. She had put on a new gown she'd had made for the Christmas gathering at Ashbourne Manor, and when she'd first donned it, the green velvet had made her feel pretty and festive. Now it just made her feel washed out and empty.

She poured herself some wine from the bottle that had been left on the table and while she wanted to swallow all of it in one go, she refrained, taking only a strong gulp before allowing her gaze to travel back to the blackened window.

"Viv."

She spun about, the wine sloshing in the glass.

Ryder's eyes were open, his gaze focused on her.

The tension had gone from his face, and a soft smile was on his lips. His arm still curved as if he held her, and she swallowed painfully.

"You should try to eat something if you're feeling up to it."

She went back to the trays of food without waiting for his response. Setting aside her own glass of wine, she tore a piece of pudding to accompany a slice of the now cold beef roast. She placed both on a small plate then filled another glass with wine. Walking over to Ryder, she perched on the edge of the settee and handed him the glass of wine first.

"You really shouldn't be traipsing through the country-side in the middle of January with a broken leg. I would ask that you consider your actions more carefully in future." She kept her tone light, knowing the reasons for his reckless behavior but still wishing he'd be more careful.

She expected him to try to brush her fingers with his when she handed him the glass, but instead, he closed his hand over hers, holding her captive until she met his gaze.

"I didn't take you for a coward."

His voice was low and molten, and she was helpless to stop the responding flame that sparked low in her belly.

"I'm sorry?"

"You didn't stay." He released her hand and took the wine glass from her.

She drew a steadying breath. "You were dreaming. I thought I might be hurting you."

It was partly the truth, but he needn't know that.

If she hadn't been watching him so closely, she would have missed the look of guilt that whispered across his face. He averted his gaze, suddenly overcome with a great interest in his wine.

Disappointment flooded her, but she could hardly be surprised. He was still the Ryder she had married, and the Ryder she had married was a rogue.

She took the wine glass from him and handed him the plate of morsels. He tore at the pudding and popped a piece into his mouth, chewing methodically, his gaze on his food.

"You said someone had given you word of the hops workers' barracks. Who might that have been?"

"Daniel," he said between bites.

"The same Daniel of this contraption?" She gestured to the mechanized chair.

"The same." He swallowed some beef and motioned for his wine. She handed it to him as he said, "Daniel is the son of the former of hops manager, Mr. Thomas Stoker. We were of an age here on the estate and practically grew up together."

Both of Ryder's parents had passed before she had met him, and as he was an only child, she knew little of his extended family beyond a handful of cousins. Hearing him speak of someone who had shared his childhood with him was almost like hearing a ghostly tale. It was nearly too much to believe.

"You grew up together?"

Ryder pumped his eyebrows mischievously as he took another bite of pudding.

"I see why he would be a willing accomplice in this then." Again, she gestured to the chair.

"No," Ryder said as he shook his head. "For that I just offered him a lot of money."

She couldn't stop the laugh his remark elicited, and the sound startled her. He wasn't being sarcastic or witty; he was simply being funny. It had a wholesome feeling to it, which made her wary.

"You said he was the hops manager's son. He didn't choose to go into agricultural management like his father."

Ryder shook his head. "That was the first thing to tip me off. Stoker showed up here as the blacksmith. He apparently apprenticed under the village's former blacksmith. His father had been dismissed, and all that was left for Daniel was to take to an apprenticeship."

"That must have been awful not to be given the choice to follow in his father's footsteps."

Ryder gestured with a bit of pudding. "And he would have, too. Daniel loved the harvest as much as I did."

He stopped mid-chew, a small bulge of food resting in one cheek as if whatever thought had struck took his entire focus just then.

She waited, wondering what it was that plagued him. Eventually he resumed chewing, but his focus was no longer on her. He pushed the remaining food on his plate around as if he were shuffling his thoughts with every movement.

Finally, she took the plate from him and handed him the remainder of his wine.

"I think you should get some sleep. Shall I call for the footmen to help you into bed?"

His grimace was swift. "I shall lose all dignity if that bevy of boys should lift me again on this day." He patted the settee. "Please just leave me."

She considered this as she knew a night in bed would be far more restorative, but he did look rather comfortable.

"Are you sure? You've had quite the taxing day. I should think a good night's sleep—"

"Please, Viv."

She could deny him nothing when he spoke to her like that, wielded those two simple words like that.

"All right." She pushed to her feet. "But I'm going to leave the connecting door open, and if you have need of anything, you can call for me."

She expected a brash comment at her statement, but none came, leaving her perplexed and somehow…waiting.

He only smiled, but sleep was already pulling at his eyelids.

She placed the plate and wine glass on the table with the rest of the food and wiped her hands on a napkin tucked beneath the edge of one plate. When she turned about, his eyes were already shut.

She padded over and pulled the blanket higher up on his chest. She smoothed it down, and her hands lingered as she studied him in sleep.

So many questions paraded through her mind, and as she watched him fall deeper into sleep, she felt her resolve grow.

She would get her answers from him, and perhaps… something more.

She tiptoed to the connecting door and glanced back one more time to ensure he slept. Satisfied he was all right, she slipped through the door, leaving it open as she'd promised.

CHAPTER 8

"Do you know what it is you're looking for?"

He balanced the bulky ledger on his lap, using his elevated leg to hold the book in place.

"I want to see the profits from the hops crops over the past twenty years. If it's truly declining as the state of the barracks would suggest, I want to see it in ink."

He flipped through the pages of the ledger as Viv worked the shelves behind him.

After great maneuvering of both himself and the chair by several footmen, they had made it to the duke's study. It was difficult for Ryder to think of it as his study even though his father had been dead for more than ten years. He could still picture the old man hunched over his desk, meticulously penciling in notes along the ledgers' neat columns. He ran his fingers over a marking on the page now, outlining his father's crisp handwriting.

His father had been much older when Ryder was born, and although there was a significant age difference, his father had not ignored him. It wasn't exactly a close relationship, but neither was Ryder neglected. The previous duke ensured that Ryder knew what to expect when he inherited the title one day and how to manage the various accounts, the tenants, and the crops.

Still, it was odd to be sitting there now, going back through the very ledgers his father had so carefully kept. He didn't know why he was suddenly compelled to uncover the state of the hops crops. But then, Ryder didn't know what to expect from himself these days. His attempt to escape the restlessness that plagued him had ended in near disaster, and he knew, somehow, that he could never return to the life he had been living.

He looked up as Viv moved down the shelf she was currently scanning. She wore the blue gown again. He was coming to find the image of her in her work gown, dust sleeves affixed to her forearms, strangely comforting. It was as if the sight of her dressed for work signaled safety. The restlessness couldn't get him as long as Viv was there to keep him distracted.

"This one is from the twenties. I can't tell if that last number is a six or an eight, though." She tugged a bulky ledger from the shelf, sending up a cloud of dust as she pulled the tome from the bookcase that spanned the wall behind the duke's desk.

They both watched the dust settle before exchanging a glance.

"I'll be sure to speak with Mrs. Olds about having the room aired."

While her tone was neutral, he couldn't help but hear a telling ring to it.

"Mrs. Olds likely hasn't bothered to have this room aired because I am never in residence." He said what he knew she must be thinking.

"It would be a more efficient use of the staff." Her smile was nothing more than a flash of tight teeth.

He couldn't stop a laugh.

"I would be offended by such boldness, but in this case, it's rather the truth." He thumbed through more pages. "I should inform Mrs. Olds, however, that I intend to be in residence going forward and this room should be regularly cleaned."

Viv's skirts rustled madly as she turned to him, suspending her perusal of the shelves so abruptly she laid out a hand to steady herself against the bookcase.

"You're going to be in residence? Whatever for?"

He lifted his gaze from the ledgers. "Because I live here."

She pursed her lips. "You, in fact, live at whatever house party is currently the most attractive. Why ever would you stay at Margate?"

He placed a finger along the column he had been studying so as not to lose his place, but it also bought him time to study his wife. Her lips were slightly parted, and he couldn't help but remember the kiss from the previous night. It had felt so right to kiss her, so perfect. Surely that was a sign that he had been right. She did hold the power to quiet whatever it was that haunted him.

"I find myself growing tired of house parties. They all seem to be rather the same. I don't care for such tedium and repetition any longer. There are other things in this life that warrant attention."

Namely her, but he didn't think she would be agreeable to that conversation as of yet.

She studied him, and he felt naked under her gaze. He hadn't told anyone of the restlessness that consumed him. If he were frank, there wasn't anyone to tell. The acquaintances he made in society were just that. He would never go so far as to suggest they were friends. Therefore, he had no one in whom he could confide.

As he regarded his wife now, however, he wondered if he might confide in her.

The thought had never occurred to him. In fact, he had never before considered what their marriage would be like. He had assumed that his marriage would be like much of society's unions. It would be an arrangement of sorts, mutually beneficial and serving to fulfill the needs of the title. He hadn't before thought he might be friends with his wife.

"Such as?"

He hadn't expected her to continue along that line of thought, and her question had him pausing.

He didn't know.

He knew there was something else out there he should be seeking, but he could not have given it a name if it were a matter of life and death.

He closed the ledger, his hand holding his place.

"Do you know you can take a steam-powered paddler across the Atlantic now? They say soon we'll be able to reach America in a week's time." He pointed out the window as if she could see what he envisioned in his mind. "Explorers have reached an entirely new land in the Southern Hemisphere. An entirely new land yet to be discovered even today." He dropped his hand and shook his head. "House parties seem so frivolous at a time like this."

She did nothing more than blink at him, leaving him feeling vulnerable and exposed.

He cleared his throat. "Haven't you ever thought about things like that?"

"No." She did not speak the word harshly, and somehow he thought he might have startled her more than anything.

He shrugged again. "I do. And sometimes I wonder what more there is out there to be found."

He met her gaze, and he knew she understood he didn't speak of discovering new lands or inventing new technology.

Something passed between them in the silence then, and somehow it was as though they were starting over. But that wasn't true. He still lived with the pain of knowing he'd hurt her, and he always would.

But something was different now. Perhaps she viewed him a little less critically. Perhaps he saw her as more than the wife society demanded he take. He couldn't name it, but then he didn't want to. He simply enjoyed the feelings that simmered between them.

"My sister—Eliza—makes little books for children." The words were loud in the quiet of the study, and Viv's eyes had gone wide as if she were putting forth a great deal of effort. "They are quite popular. I never would have thought my quiet little sister would hold such a revered place beyond our family."

He couldn't stop the smile that tripped to his lips. "I always knew there was more to Eliza than she was letting us see."

Viv shifted then, and he realized she had had a death grip on the bookcase behind her during their conversation. He made note of it. If his kisses held no power over her, his words certainly seemed to.

He decided to save her by opening the ledger in his lap once more and finding his place along the column of numbers. He heard her pull the next ledger from the bookcase, and she set it on the duke's desk. He had positioned his chair close enough to the desk that he caught a whiff of her vanilla scent as she sat.

"Are you finding what you need?"

He looked up. "I believe I am. I'd like to compile the yearly profits for the hops crop over the past ten years."

Before he could say more, she began rummaging in the desk, pulling forth a sheet of paper and an old quill. She rattled a bottle of ink over the desk.

"Do you suppose luck is with us that this hasn't dried out?" Her smile was almost mischievous, and he was struck by how the playfulness seemed to transform her features.

She had always been the strong one of her sisters. Slightly taller and with that mane of captivating red-gold hair, he could see how people were easily intimidated by her. But not him. He reveled in her strength, marveled at her prowess.

He held out a hand.

"I'm due for a spot of good luck."

She placed the ink bottle in his hand. He closed his fingers around it and gave it a good shake before carefully pulling the lid free. He handed it gently back to her, and she placed it on the desk as she gathered her quill.

He didn't know why he should find this game so amusing, or more, so consuming, but perhaps it was because it was Viv, and for once in so long, he didn't feel the monotony that dogged him.

The quill emerged from the bottle glistening with indigo ink, and she cast him a wry smirk.

"It would seem your luck is changing, Your Grace."

He raised his chin to a haughty angle and returned her smirk with a pompous grin of his own. "Oh, very good, ma'am."

Her laugh was light and airy, and he was mesmerized by the way it softened her face.

Others might find her brash, a towering vixen, but to him, she was like a mystical water sprite, glittering with magic and possibility.

He swallowed, not daring to cast so much hope on this.

"When you're ready," she said, gesturing with the quill.

He picked up the ledger and read off the date and the yearly profit for the hops crop. They continued like that: she finding the correct ledger, he searching for the proper column so she could transpose it on the compiled list.

He only wished to catalog the last ten years from before the passing of the public house bill until present day, but it seemed hours passed by them without notice.

There was an entire block in the early thirties for which they could find no ledger, only to discover them shoved behind some piano samplers. Margate Hall did not even contain a piano. Viv muttered about setting the room to rights before heaving the ledgers free.

Finally, when the windows beyond the study had turned black with night, she handed him the compiled list. He studied the single piece of paper as his heart sank.

The hops crop was failing.

Each year showed a steady dwindling of profits, yes, but more than that, it showed a smaller crop was harvested. His steward must have diverted funds to other more plentiful crops, leaving the hops to languish.

He looked up from the list to find Viv studying him, her eyebrows raised in question.

"It's not good."

"Worse than you expected?"

He could only nod.

Something unexpected happened then. She placed her hand on his forearm, curving her fingers about him and squeezing in comfort. He watched the gesture, heat and anticipation coursing through him, but another feeling overcame them.

Tranquility.

Her very touch had the power to still the roiling thoughts inside of him. The feel of her skin against his sent a shock wave through him that willed his very being to settle and be easy. The sensation was hypnotic, and he never wanted her to stop.

"I'm sorry. Is there anything that can be done?"

It was a moment before he could collect his thoughts

enough to answer. "I'd like to speak with Mr. Stoker. If there is a solution to this, he would know of it."

She squeezed his arm again, and regrettably, let go to put away the ink and quill.

It was only much later as he lay on the settee in his rooms, staring out the windows at the stars that dotted the night sky, that he realized he had felt the restlessness not once that day.

* * *

IT HAD SNOWED in the night, and her booted feet crunched across the grass as she moved in the direction of the hops workers' barracks.

She had awoken that morning in a surreal state of uncertainty. She no longer had such a firm grip on her resolve to get answers from her husband, and instead, found herself with more questions. Especially after yesterday.

She had no idea he was interested in steam paddlers or explorers, and yet he spoke of them so fervently. Did he wish to explore? Was wandering the entire width and berth of England no longer enough for him?

But no, that wasn't right. He had said he planned to spend more time at Margate Hall. What could that possibly mean? Did he intend to assume a more direct role in the running of the estate? Would he take his seat in Parliament?

Would he want to start a family?

Her heart thudded at the thought.

None of this made sense, and she was in a trickier quagmire than when she'd left Ashbourne at Christmas. This was not at all the way she'd anticipated things would transpire, and she needed to get a better handle on the situation. It was time to confront Ryder with her questions and gain a better understanding of what he meant for the future.

Because it was her future, too.

She rounded the corner of the horse paddocks, and the workers' barracks sprang into view. From this distance, they appeared no more than forlorn huts settled into the slightly uneven landscape of the fields. The snow had coated its roof with a blanket of white, and dead and dried plant life clung to the outside as if the yard had not been kept in good repair during the summer and weeds had been left to grow.

She picked up her skirts and kept going, the wind lifting the tie of her bonnet as she pressed into the crisp winter morning.

As she drew nearer, details emerged that could only paint a grim tale. Most of the doors hung at odd angles, their leather hinges having long ago stretched and warped until the portals were no longer sealed against the elements. Shattered glass like jagged teeth were all that remained in most of the windows, and at the far end, a great hole in the roof loomed black against the fresh snow.

What had happened?

She wanted to blame Ryder, but that was an easy excuse. His absence should not have led to this if his steward had been reliable. She'd met Reynolds once, and she didn't think it was his fault either. The man was pragmatic and sensible. This deterioration was a result of simple math.

The hops crop didn't bring the profit necessary to maintain the barracks. It was as simple as that.

She wasn't sure why she felt a pang of sadness at the thought. There were plenty of estates in Kent that harvested hops. Surely there was a surplus in supply. Or what had Ryder said? There was some sort of bill that had passed that had affected the market.

None of that mattered. All she could see before her was a shattered way of life that may never regain its footing.

She wrapped her arms around herself as if to hold off the

cold, but it wasn't the winter wind she felt. It was the passage of time. Something she knew only too well.

A noise from behind her startled her into turning, and she saw that a horse had been released into the paddock off the stable. The horse trotted away, its clever hoofs sending up a dusting of snow wherever it trod. It shook its mane as if delighting in the morning sun, pillowy bursts of breath rising from its nostrils.

The sight was a splendid one, and she found herself at the stable door before she realized she was moving.

The stables were a flurry of movement that morning. Some lads shoveled out stalls while others dragged bales of hay along the main corridor. They seemed to be singing to one another, a sort of call and response that brought a kind of dance to the work.

"Your Grace!"

She turned at the exclamation to find Geoffrey standing behind her, his arms wrapped snuggly around a harness.

"Hello, Geoffrey," she said with a smile, but it did nothing to lessen the astonishment on his face. "I never did get to properly thank you for your expedition through the night. I hope you know how incredible it was, what you did. I thank you for it, and I hope to count on your service for many years to come."

Geoffrey's surprised face remained unchanged except his lips may have parted farther apart.

"Thank you," he finally stammered. "Your Grace, if I may, but…what are you doing here?"

He looked around them as though she had wandered into something far more debauched, like a gaming hell.

"I saw the horse in the paddock." She gestured back the way she had come. "I was wondering if I may see His Grace's horses. The ones driving the phaeton that day."

The mention of the horses involved in the accident

seemed to break the spell, and Geoffrey turned, setting the harness on a pile of hay bales off to the side.

"Ve and Vili, you mean." Geoffrey rubbed his hands together, and she wasn't sure if it was to remove any detritus that may be on them or to warm them in the chilly air.

He nodded his head for her to follow. They made their way down the main corridor to the other end of the stable where there wasn't so much bustle. Most of the stalls were empty at this end, although she noted they were a great deal larger.

When they reached the very end, she saw that the last two stalls were occupied. She couldn't make out much more than a great, towering blackness swaying softly inside of them.

"Here they are, ma'am. Two of the finest horses in England."

Geoffrey plucked a carrot from a sack leaning against one of the empty stalls. He approached the stall on the left first.

"Here ye go, boy." He was careful to keep his hand flat as a massive horse appeared at the bars. His thick lips wiggled as his teeth emerged, sucking the carrot into his mouth with a grace that belied such massive jaws.

"This one here is Vili. A beautiful horse, isn't he, ma'am?"

She only vaguely heard what Geoffrey had said, so transfixed was she by the glittering dark eyes of the horse. He was entirely black except for a small white patch on his chest. She wasn't sure how long she studied him, but it must have been long enough because Geoffrey actually touched her arm.

"Ma'am, are you all right?"

She started and forced a smile, unsure of why the horse had unsettled her.

"Yes, quite. It's just…he's a beautiful horse."

Geoffrey's smile was exaggerated in obvious delight. "Oh, that he is. But you haven't seen Ve yet."

He moved to the opposite stall, snatching another carrot

as he went. The horse that moved to the bars was identical to the other, but Geoffrey was right. There was something different about this horse. It was almost as though he could read her thoughts by merely looking at her.

"His Grace was worried they were injured in the crash."

Geoffrey shook his head. "No, ma'am. They came trotting back to the barn looking for their oat bags. That's the thing about horses. They always know where the food is."

He rubbed at Ve's snout as the animal chomped the last of his carrot.

Geoffrey sobered suddenly, and Viv found herself leaning in to hear him. "Poor Ve, though, was still attached to the pole." He gestured with his hand to indicate the pole that ran between the horses and connected to their harnesses through thick straps so the animals could stop the vehicle behind them. "It does say something about His Grace's dedication to his horses. He never lets anyone else inspect the traces nor hitch up his horses, even if he was in a hurry that day."

She had reached out a hand to nuzzle Ve's nose, but she stopped at Geoffrey's words.

"His Grace was in a hurry?"

"Oh, that he was, ma'am. He'd come tearing into the yard not a handful of hours earlier, said to ready his phaeton team. He had to be off."

Suspicion and dread pierced through her like twin lightning bolts.

"Did he say where he must go?"

Geoffrey shook his head. "There wasn't time. His Grace was ready to leave just as soon as we had the phaeton ready and the horses brought round." He scratched at Ve's nose now. "Like I said, only His Grace does all his own hitching. Doesn't trust another soul to do it." He turned his gaze on her then, and she was struck by the seriousness such a young face could carry. "It likely saved his life, it did. His Grace is nothing but methodical and ardent about how he takes care of his horses."

She'd heard Geoffrey, she was sure she had, but the thoughts rattled about in her head. Where had Ryder been going that was so urgent? Did it have something to do with the writer of the letter? She swallowed the bile that rose up at the thought.

Had she been waiting for him? Had they planned a lover's tryst?

Why did it matter?

She had spent four years as the scorned wife, betrayed by an unfaithful husband. He had not begged her forgiveness then, had not followed her in the hopes of convincing her to stay. The life he had led since then had not been celibate. She'd heard the rumors. All of society had heard them.

Ryder Maxen, the Rogue Duke, and bedder of widows and lonely wives.

It was almost a rite of passage for neglected wives.

Have you had the Rogue Duke yet?

She'd heard the scandalous whispers more than once in ballrooms across London. She knew of whom they spoke, and they knew who she was. It needn't matter, though. It was clear theirs was not a marriage of faith and fidelity, and those who wished to share a bed with her husband were not so discreet as to whisper their scandalous thoughts where she couldn't hear them.

And yet, for some strange reason, the writer of the letter haunted her more than any of the whispering widows and wives before her.

A coldness seeped through as she grew used to the feelings of betrayal and suspicion. This was how it always was when she heard tales of the Rogue Duke's conquest. But even as the familiarity of being the scorned wife fell over her, it somehow didn't fit as comfortably as it once did. Because

Ryder didn't fit the picture she'd drawn of him the way he once had.

"So His Grace was headed out of Margate when the accident happened?" she asked now.

She wasn't sure why, but she'd always assumed Ryder had been driving toward Margate when he'd crashed the phaeton. She'd never spent a holiday season at Margate, and it was very likely her husband hosted a house party there for the season. Perhaps he'd left for a few days for a sumptuous rendezvous with another widow somewhere in Kent and was returning in haste to the debauchery he'd left behind.

But if he'd been leaving Margate instead...

Well, where was he going?

"Yes, he was, ma'am. Just as quick as could be."

"Did he say anything when the rescuers found him? Anything to suggest where he might have been going?"

Geoffrey scratched at his chin. "Well, not so much as that, ma'am. As I told you when you I found you in Glenhaven, His Grace was only saying one thing."

She wrapped her arms around herself once more, bracing for what she knew not.

"And what was that?"

He pushed back the brim of his wool hat. "Well, he was asking for you and only you."

"Did he ask for me or did he merely speak my name?"

"Begging your pardon, ma'am?" he asked, screwing up his face in question.

"When he was speaking, did he ask someone to send for me? Or did he merely say my name?"

A look of understanding lit his eyes then, and he snapped his fingers. "Ah, I see your meaning, ma'am." He shook his head. "No, it wasn't so grand as all that. He merely spoke your name over and over. Almost as if he was saying his prayers."

CHAPTER 9

"*W*ill this hurt?"

"A great deal likely."

Ryder eyed the doctor. "I thank you for coming anyway." He moved his gaze beyond the doctor to where Viv paced in front of the windows. "While I'm quite certain my wife could have achieved the same results, I find her level of agitation unnerving. What if she should slip and poke me in the eye?"

She stopped at this suggestion and turned her glower on him.

Dr. Malcolm was smart enough to refrain from laughing.

"I assure you it's no trouble at all. I am happy to remove the stitches." He took a pair of slim, hooked scissors from his bag. "I wished to observe the progress on your leg, and this was a nice enough excuse for me to do so. Has the leg been troubling you?"

He couldn't properly chase after his wife, so the answer would be *yes*, it was troubling him a great deal.

"It appears to be fine. Aches now and then, and the itching is enough to consume a lesser man."

The doctor nodded as he tugged at the first stitch in Ryder's shoulder.

"I can imagine the itching must be damnable. It would be one thing to have your skin irritated by the plaster but another to suffer it so in the dryer conditions of winter."

"Do you know my wife makes a lovely potion for that?"

The doctor shifted his gaze from his work to meet Ryder's eye.

"What kind of potion?" he said with a skeptical tone.

Ryder waved off his suspicion. "Oh, it's nothing like that. It's a wonderful mixture of tallow and honey and peppermint. It does the trick, though, let me assure you."

"Is that so?" The doctor moved his focus back to the stitches in the shoulder before moving to the laceration on Ryder's face.

The skin had tightened further over the last several days, and with every tug by the doctor, a white hot flash of pain pierced Ryder's skull and drove directly into the base of his head. The good doctor might as well have taken a hot ember from the fire and driven it through his eye socket.

He studied his irritated wife to keep his mind distracted. Something was different about her today. He'd rather enjoyed their evening together even if he had slept through most of it, and their day in the duke's study was more than pleasant. If he'd had his feet, he knew he would have made far greater progress by now. But handicapped the way he was, he would take whatever boons he could muster.

He felt the first tickle of the restlessness at the back of his neck like a ghost. He swallowed and willed it away. He was working on it. It wouldn't gain a foothold in him again. He was sure of that.

Meanwhile, he could figure out what had happened to his wife. She was always rather annoyed with him, but the past few days had been, well, calm. Almost as if a truce had been called, and he wasn't aware of it.

But now she must have acquired some information that had put a bend in matters. He watched her pace from one side of the room to the other, her skirts rustling as she pivoted. The day was sleeting beyond the windows, and they cast an appropriately cold and icy backdrop to her progress.

His abilities only extended to his deftness with his chair. How could he possibly have accomplished something to cause her this much grief?

You hurt me.

The words rang over and over again in his head, and he closed his eyes against them now.

Why had he thought this would be easy?

Why had he never considered how Viv would feel about his return?

Because he hadn't seen anything wrong in what he'd done.

He blinked his eyes open, catching her as she spun back the way she'd come, a beautiful fury of green and red gold.

Gentlemen in society took lovers all the time. He hadn't thought he was doing any different when he'd brought the woman to his chambers.

Was she an opera singer or a ballet dancer? He couldn't remember anymore.

"There it is." Dr. Malcolm sat back, placing the small scissors back in his bag. "I'm sure that will help you to feel more like yourself now."

"There are more than twenty kilograms of plaster wrapped around my leg. I'm not sure I'll be feeling myself until you break the thing off." His smile was lopsided, and the doctor's lips may have actually twitched in response.

"I'll be back in six weeks to have a look at it. In the meantime, continue to rest." He snapped his bag shut.

Ryder thought the man would bid them good day then, but instead of heading for the door, he took a step back and studied Ryder's chair.

"Wherever did you acquire a contraption like that?"

Ryder straightened his shoulders with pride as if he'd had anything to do with the chair's design. "Daniel Stoker. The blacksmith in the village. It's his creation."

"Stoker did this?" Dr. Malcolm pointed at the chair as if discovering a lost masterpiece. "You don't say."

Ryder nodded. "I told him what I wanted, and he adapted the workings of a velocipede to make it happen."

The other man pointed at the set of chains driving the wheels and how they connected to the hand pedals.

"This mechanism is what makes it move?"

Ryder nodded and pushed down on one of the pedals to move the chair slightly forward. The doctor rocked back as the chair rolled.

"Well, I'll say," he muttered, scratching his chin. "I might just need to pay Mr. Stoker a visit." He looked up and for the first time, Ryder might have described the man's expression as cheery.

He picked up his case and with a small bow to Viv left them with a farewell.

"Would you now like to tell me what it is I've done to upset you or would you like to continue to wear a hole in my carpet until you fall through into the room below?"

She stopped so abruptly, her skirts swished around her legs.

"Where were you going?"

He took a moment to let that question settle as he hadn't expected her to ask something so ridiculous.

He motioned to his broken leg. "I'm not sure if you realize, but I haven't gone anywhere of late."

She strode toward him, her face tight, and he put up both of his hands.

"I apologize," he spoke quickly and quietly. "I'm sorry. I understand you asked a question with a certain degree of seriousness, and I made a childish retort." He waited, his hands still in the air as he watched her decide if his apology was enough.

She nodded and made a noise he took to mean he should continue.

"I haven't gone anywhere in weeks as I've been confined to this chair and to the settee. Please explain what you are asking."

"You were leaving Margate when you had the accident. Where were you going in such a hurry?"

He blinked. "You care to know where I was going?"

"Yes."

The single word had the power of a cannon behind it.

He opened his mouth to tell her exactly what he had been about, but he stopped as he saw her hands tremble where she held them in front of her.

"Where do you think I was going?"

"I—" Her lips trembled now, too. Her body practically vibrated with some pent-up emotion so strong, he feared it.

He pointed to the low table that sat in front of the settee. It was covered in discarded newspapers, the odd periodical, and his half-empty bowl of butterscotch candies. But beneath it was a clump of distorted, nearly unreadable correspondence a maid had delivered with his tea the previous week.

"Have you been reading my letters?"

Her face turned instantly scarlet.

"What?" she blurted, and her eyes darted to the table.

"You have been reading my letters." He folded his hands across his abdomen, enjoying watching her grow uncomfortable with every sentence. "Tell me. Did you find anything interesting?"

Her jaw nearly snapped in two before she surged forward as if coming to a sudden decision. "It was one letter and only because I was trying to dry it out before it was ruined. Who the hell would write about wet loins?"

He wasn't sure who was more shocked by her outburst. She took a tottering step back, her hand flying to her mouth, and he tried very hard to stop the laugh that bubbled up to his lips. God, she was beautiful when she was angry. Not that he wished to make her so angry so frequently, but he would enjoy the look of her.

He wondered if she looked this amazing when she was aroused.

The thought dampened his mood because he honestly couldn't remember. Four years was a long time, and even then, he wasn't with Viv the way he was with his lovers. Viv was a woman to be respected and revered. Something had always been stilted between them because of it, he feared.

But as he looked at her now, there was nothing polished or reverential about her. She was all woman, and she was furious.

"Viv, I don't remember who she is."

The words were like a dousing of cold water.

"What?" Her features went loose as her hands fidgeted with her skirts.

"The woman who wrote that. I don't remember who she is." He gave a shrug. "I can't say that another way, and yes, you should believe all that it would suggest."

Her mouth worked, open and closed, but no words emerged.

He pushed his chair closer to her. "Viv, I haven't led a virtuous life, you know that. But I think there's a misunderstanding here." He was close enough now that he could reach out and grab her hand. He worried that she let him do it, but he clasped her hand between both of his, afraid she might spook and run at any moment. "Viv, I don't remember any of these women. I think you believe all of my infidelities are some kind of grand love affairs, but I'm telling you they're not. They're just lonely wives and widows looking for pleasure, and I give it to them. It's shallow and despicable, but that's it. I never did any of it to purposely hurt you."

At this, she tugged her hand away, holding it against her chest with her opposite hand as if it were burned.

"Then why does it feel that way?" Her voice had gone low and hard, and it stabbed him in the gut.

"I think because you thought ours a love match when it wasn't." The words were the truth, but he saw how they hurt her as the pain was riddled across her face. "It's my fault, Viv. I convinced you that you were in love with me, but we were so young then. You had just come out, and I was the only man you ever knew. Viv, please, believe me. I'm the Rogue Duke, aren't I?" He laughed but he felt no humor.

Her eyes searched his face as if looking for the truth she wanted and not the one he gave her.

She guarded her hands, but he had to touch her. He gripped her skirts just below her waist as it was the only thing he could reach and tugged. It drew her close enough for him to grip her hips, holding her in place.

"Please, Viv. You must understand I never did this to hurt you. I did it because I didn't know anything else. I thought this was how society marriages worked. My father had scores of lovers—"

"Your mother died when you were a child."

Her words stopped him. They were spoken with a coldness that couldn't have come from her, and he felt the hope he'd nurtured inside of him dying.

"Viv."

She wrenched free of his grip and made for the door. He didn't know how far she made it because he couldn't bear to turn and look.

Instead, he spoke to the windows when he said, "Viv, I was going to find you."

The scurry of footsteps ceased.

"I was going to find you in London when I crashed my phaeton."

* * *

IT WAS as though time suddenly stopped.

It wasn't the stuff of fairy tales and novels. It was crueler than that, raw and painful. His words sliced through her, robbing her of breath, throwing her heart into a pounding frenzy.

He was coming for *her*?

It was four years too late but…

She spun about. "What do you mean?"

She asked the question of the back of his head, but she couldn't force her feet to move. She thought she couldn't feel anything more, but when she laid her eyes upon him, she discovered his head bent, his fingers massaging the bridge of his nose.

She had never once seen Ryder exhibit a modicum of frustration, and yet…

He had held on to her so tightly.

She could still feel the echoes of his grip on her hips, feel the imprint of his anguish. God, it was exhilarating and heartbreaking all at once.

She swallowed. "What do you mean you were coming for me?"

He stopped massaging the bridge of his nose and dropped his hand to the armrest of the chair, straightening his head.

He didn't move for several seconds, and she wondered if he'd heard her.

But, of course, he had. Was he taking his time to conjure more lies?

She hated herself the moment the thought popped into her mind. Ryder was not a liar. He had done nothing but tell her the truth. If he had lied to her, they would still be living as man and wife.

"I thought you would be in London with your family for the holidays. I had to…" His voice dropped away.

He had to…what?

She crossed the distance between them and took the back of his chair in her hands to turn him so he faced her. It wasn't enough, though, and she leaned closer, willing him to answer. But his expression was blank, almost as if he were lost in his own emotions.

"You had to what?"

He studied her face, his eyes going back and forth, and she felt the tension low in her belly grow as he took her in. She'd never been scrutinized like that before. Oh, she'd been coveted when she first debuted, even admired by a few leering old men. But this was something different.

Ryder looked at her as if he were surprised to find her there.

With him.

He reached out a hand and with a single finger stroked the line of her cheek, the curve of her jaw. The touch was light, and if she hadn't been watching him, she would have thought she imagined it.

In those few seconds, though, she felt…cherished.

Precious.

And maybe even…loved.

She wasn't shocked when his lips touched hers seconds later nor when his hand slipped lower, pulling her toward him. She fell into his lap and caught the arms of the chair in her palms.

She wrenched away from him, her chest heaving with sudden exhilaration.

"Am I hurting you?" She was whispering, but she didn't know why.

His smile was slow and steamy, and his eyes remained half closed. "It depends on what you mean."

He pulled her head down to resume the kiss, and fire sparked through her at his touch. His hand cupped the back of her head, kneading the muscles there until she relaxed in his hands.

A pulsing began low in her stomach, growing stronger and hotter with every stroke of his tongue against her lips. Somewhere in the back of her mind, she thought she shouldn't be doing this. But four years of clawing loneliness drowned out the voice, and she plunged her hands through his hair, deepening the kiss.

"Viv," he moaned against her lips.

Something, perhaps the sound of her name like an oath, exploded inside of her and kissing suddenly wasn't enough. She used the arms of the chair to push herself up, tugging her skirts free until she could straddle him.

She had to break the kiss in order to do it, and his eyes fluttered open. His face was sleepy and pleasured, and she wondered at her ability to do that. To push him from one extreme emotion to the other.

Holding onto that feeling of power, she reached up and closed her fingers around the buttons of her shirt. His eyes flashed wide, and his hands gripped her thighs. She'd never been so glad in her choice to wear her riding outfit to the stables that morning.

"Viv." It was no longer a moan. Now it was a question and a promise all at once.

She slipped the first button free. Then the next and the next. Before she could lose her nerve, she undid all of the buttons to where they stopped at the middle of her torso. The fabric fell away, revealing her corset and chemise, and of course, her bosom neatly on display at his eye level.

But his eyes never moved from her face.

Her confidence slipped, and she bit her lower lip. She wanted to cover herself back up, but her hands wouldn't cooperate, fluttering uselessly in front of her until he grabbed hold of them in both of his.

"Viv, you don't have to do this. I don't want you to think you must do this to prove some silly point. I only want you to do this if *you* want to do this."

Her voice trembled but finally she said, "I don't know."

She wished to take back the words as soon as she spoke them, and she tried to remove herself from his lap but he held her hands fast.

"Why don't you know?" His voice was even and calm, and it soothed her.

She kept her eyes focused on his while she searched for the answer.

"I don't know," she said again, but the words were softer now as she explored her thoughts. "I just...I just..." The words wouldn't come until finally she just said what was boiling inside of her. "I'm just so lonely."

Finally, he broke his gaze from hers, but it was only to close his eyes. His face pinched with what she thought was pain, and she tried again to get off his lap, but he held her tight.

"I'm hurting you." Again, she was whispering.

His laugh was soft. "Yes, but not how you think."

When he opened his eyes, they'd gone soft and wondering.

"I don't want to hurt you again," he whispered now.

Something inside of her broke open at his words, and four years of pent-up emotions poured out of her. The want she had tried to ignore, the desire she denied, it all came to the fore in a splendid rush.

"Ryder." She spoke his name, the only thing she could do as feelings poured over her. "Ryder, I want this."

She didn't know if that were true. She tried to remember what it had been like when they were together before, but it was so long ago. She couldn't remember it ever being like the writer of that letter had suggested, but suddenly...suddenly...

"I want you to make love to me like you do to those women."

She wasn't sure which of them was more surprised by her words. This time when his mouth opened without sound emerging, she didn't let it strike her confidence. Instead, she took his mouth in a hot kiss, searing his lips with hers.

She didn't really know what she was doing, but she knew he liked it by the way his hands tightened on hers. When she had captured his attention, she tugged her hands free from his suddenly loosened grip and plunged her fingers beneath the lapels of his banyan, feeling the heat of his skin through his nightshirt against her palms.

She moaned against his mouth, delirious with the feel of him beneath her hands. His chest was strong with muscle, and she followed the fine bones of his collar like a trail.

Now free, his hands cupped her waist and slid upward until they perched beneath her breasts, held up by the confines of her corset. Even with so many layers between them, she could feel his heat, and it made her inhibitions slip even further.

"Ryder," she moaned against his lips.

His hands slipped around to her back beneath her shirt, and seconds later she felt her corset loosen. He broke free of the kiss, and with a low guttural moan, he yanked the corset free. No longer confined, her heavy breasts sank, and she watched as his eyes darkened at the sight of them.

Power and confidence surged through her. She did this to him. She had the power to make his eyes go dark like that, to make his speech turn to nothing more than base sounds.

Emboldened, she sat up and grabbing the hem of the shirt, pulled it over her head. Her hair had come undone at some point, and when she cast the shirt aside, her red-gold locks fell in a curtain around her shoulders. His lips parted, no sound emerging as he studied her.

But she wasn't done.

She placed her hands where he had held her along her waist, pressed her palms against the soft mound of her stomach and ran them upward. The cool air pierced the thin fabric of her chemise, and she knew he could see her nipples now, straining through the cloth in dusky peaks.

He licked his lips, and she couldn't stop the slow smile that came to her own.

She inched her hands upward, achingly slow, until they cupped her breasts. She held them for a moment before she squeezed, massaging the mounds in both hands. An involuntary moan escaped her lips, and she realized with a jolt that it felt good.

She'd never touched herself like this before. She hadn't known. Ryder's eyes grew round, and he lifted his hands as if to cover hers, but she batted them away.

She *liked* this. She wasn't going to let him steal it for himself.

Finally, she slid her hands around and covered her nipples. The fabric of the chemise was rough against the sensitive skin, and she cried out, throwing her head back at the sensation.

Now she did let him take her hands, prying them from her body as he leaned forward and sucked one nipple into his mouth through the gauze of her chemise. She grasped his head, his name spilling from her lips like an oath.

Pure pleasure spiraled through her to that secret place between her legs that suddenly ached.

God, was this what it was supposed to be like?

Was it supposed to be such pleasure? Such desire coiling through her?

Without knowing what she was doing, her hips began to move, thrusting softly against him. The movement brought her closer against him, and she slid against his hardness.

She gasped, pulling her hips back, but he caught her with both of his hands at her waist.

"God, Viv, are you trying to kill me?"

She'd never heard his voice in such a tone, low and pained.

She did it again, sliding her hips forward against the strength of his hands, moving deeper this time until she rode directly against him.

He ripped his mouth from her nipple.

"You are trying to kill me," he muttered before taking her other nipple into his mouth.

Pure sensation spiked through her, and she forgot to torment him with her hips, instead plunging her fingers through his hair to hold his mouth against her. Heat coursed through her, and she throbbed for him.

"Ryder, I need...I...well..." She didn't know what to ask for.

He relinquished her nipple, only to slide his hands up her sides and cup her breasts like she had. The pressure was enough to have her arching until her breasts were pressed fully into his palms.

"I know, darling. I know."

One hand disappeared, and she gave a small cry for its absence. But soon she felt him pushing at her skirts. She looked down, mesmerized by the sight of his hand slipping beneath her skirt, exploring, delving, probing.

He found the slit in her pantalettes, and when his fingers first touched her most intimate place, she gasped, her hands going to his shoulders to hold on.

"Ryder," she breathed.

With stunning dexterity, his fingers slipped through her folds, caressing her core, and she bucked against him. He captured her mouth, his fingers moving deeper, until a single finger slipped inside of her.

She moaned at the exquisite intrusion.

"Ah, my sweet, you're so very wet for me."

The words were like the sleeting rain on the fields, and she jerked away from him, the words of the letter writer spiraling viciously through her mind.

Suddenly she saw him. With her. Not someone specific. It was a parade of faceless lovers, his conquests.

All the women who weren't her because he didn't love her.

She fell more than got off of him, her skirts tangling around her legs. She found her shirt and corset, pressing them to her chest. Was that her own hiccupping breathing? He reached for her, and he was saying something but she couldn't hear him.

She bolted for the connecting door. Only when she was on the other side of it did she let the tears come.

CHAPTER 10

"Why aren't you eating? Are you feeling unwell?"

If she stood any farther away from him she'd be in another room.

He crossed his arms over his chest and settled back into his chair.

"So that's what it takes. A threat to my well-being, and the little wife comes to the rescue." He knew his words were harsh, but he wasn't feeling particularly pleasant just then.

She'd avoided him for over a week.

A week.

How this was possible as they slept in rooms that *connected*, he wasn't sure. He hadn't heard her retire to her rooms in the evening nor did he hear her leave in the morning. She was like a phantom. He knew she was somewhere in the house, but where he didn't know. The mere existence of her presence haunted him.

"Your sense of duty overwhelms you at times, doesn't it?" He didn't know why he taunted her like that, but he thought very much he was feeling hurt. Like a petulant child, he goaded her with words he didn't mean but which he knew would cause the most damage.

She folded her hands primly in front of her as if his words held little consequence. She wore a gown of dark green he'd never seen before, but he didn't miss how the buttons marched directly up the front, closing in her magnificent bosom from any and all onlookers.

He could still recall the taste of her. Hell, he could *feel* her in his mouth.

Why had she run? Had he done something wrong? Had he frightened her? He'd never treated her with the passion he did his lovers, yes, but he'd thought…

Well, he'd thought she wanted it. She'd been a step ahead of him the entire way, and yet he somehow felt as though he'd missed something and hurt her all over again.

He'd tried finding her, zipping up and down the corridors in his chair, poking into every room to see where she might be hiding. But his searches had proven fruitless. It appeared she wasn't above going where he could not reach in his chair.

He had, of course, requested her presence, and each request had been properly denied. She'd manufactured every manner of excuse, and poor Mrs. Olds was left to deliver them.

But there was one thing he knew she could not deny.

Duty.

So he'd simply stopped eating.

He'd refused all food, claiming he just wasn't up for it. His stomach was raw with hunger now, but it only matched the sick feeling he got when he thought of hurting her again.

"Are you feeling ill? Shall I send for the doctor?"

"I don't need a doctor, and you know it." He tried to keep his voice even, but the worry gnawed at him.

She raised her chin. "Then I don't see why you feel the

need to act so childish. You must eat to regain your strength and to allow your leg to heal."

"Mrs. Olds said just the same thing. It must be intolerable if you have finally come." He adjusted the blanket over his plastered leg, feeling the fight drain out of him with a suddenness that surprised him. "You know very well there is nothing wrong, Viv. I simply wanted to see you, and I didn't know how else to gain your attention."

"I'm terribly sorry, but I'm very busy. There's much to be done before I leave in a month's time."

Her words sliced through him like a dagger.

"You're still planning to leave?"

"Of course. Those were the terms of our agreement. I must be back in London before the start of the season. Johanna is another year older, and it will be more difficult—"

"Johanna has no wish to wed. You know that as well as I do, and yet you use her as an excuse. Are you that terribly afraid of me?"

Something flashed in her eyes, and her knuckles turned white as though she were holding herself together.

"Afraid of you?" She gave a bark of laughter. "Hardly. It's only I prefer the company of nearly anyone else to you."

Her words took him aback. While she had not been friendly when he'd first awoken after the accident, she had not been mean.

She seemed to register the same as she closed her eyes briefly. When she reopened them, he saw nothing there. Her countenance was completely empty of feeling as though she were a mere shell of what she was supposed to be.

His chest tightened, and for one small moment, he feared he'd lost her completely. The restlessness roared up, but he shoved it back down. He wasn't done with her yet.

He pushed the pedals of the chair until he was closer to

her. She didn't retreat, and from that, he held a measure of hope.

"Viv." She brought her gaze to his. "I need you to tell me what happened. What did I do to upset you?"

Now she did take a step back, and that damnable chin went up.

"It's nothing. You mustn't worry. I simply made an error, and it shan't happen again."

Her proper tone needled him, and before he could think better of it, he snatched her hand and pulled. The motion was so unexpected it worked to set her off her balance. He tugged again, and she fell.

He caught her neatly about the waist, turning her so she landed in his lap where he could wrap both arms around her. He gripped her chin and forced her to look at him.

"I deserve to know what happened. You owe me that. And then I will leave you alone if that is your wish."

She watched him, her eyes wary and alert, but she didn't struggle. He didn't like it. His Viv was all fire and fight. The woman in his arms was defeated and empty.

"I simply made a mistake," she said again.

"Don't lie to me—"

"I'm not lying," she cut him off, her voice sprinkled with the heat he was used to. "I really did make a mistake. I thought—" She stopped, her eyes focused on his.

"You thought what?"

She shook her head, and he released her chin. She looked down to where his arm came around her.

"I thought it was enough, but it's not." When she looked up, there was a starkness to her gaze now. "I don't know that I can trust you again. There are too many other women between us."

He cupped her cheek, bringing her gaze back to him when she tried to look away.

"I have apologized for what I did. I can't—"

"I know you've apologized. It isn't that."

"Then what is it?" he pressed.

She met his gaze directly. "There's too much between us. The rumors, the—" She choked. "God, Ryder, I saw you in bed with *her*." Her voice faltered on the word as though she might be sick, and there was a resounding stab in his gut at the hurt he saw on her face, the hurt he'd put there. "That will always be there, and I don't know how to do this without so much haunting me."

He wanted to make it all go away. If only he could kiss her until she forgot, if only he could make love to her until he banished the past that plagued them.

But it didn't work like that.

He cradled her face now in the palms of his hands and leaned his forehead against hers. "I can't erase the past, Viv. But I can promise you my whole future. All of it. It's yours if only you'll have it."

She grasped his wrists, her palms hot against the fine bones there.

"It's not the future I'm worried about. It's what's happened that I can't escape."

Fear so acute he thought it would rob him of all breath scoured his lungs, tightened his chest, and turned his mouth to a desert. This couldn't happen. Viv was his answer; she was his savior. He had to convince her to give him a chance.

His lips found hers without him realizing he wanted to kiss her, but in that moment, he could do nothing else. She hesitated, and he pulled back, not wanting to force her. But then she leaned into him, deepening the connection. He groaned and slipped a hand around to the back of her neck to hold her in place so she might never escape him again.

He didn't try anything else. This wasn't about that. This

was telling her he was here now, and she was the only woman he wanted.

The truth rang in his head like an echo, and he realized it had been the truth all along.

Viv was the only woman for him. He could see it plainly now. All those years ago, he'd made the right choice, and almost just as quickly, ruined any chance he might have had at turning it into something real.

Like love.

The thought was a lightning bolt cutting through his consciousness, and he pulled back just enough, letting the kiss linger until he broke it entirely.

He was breathing heavily, and his thoughts scrambled at its sudden discovery. He'd never considered love before, and it wasn't as if he were considering it now. It was only…

If he were to love someone, it would only be her.

She blinked as she seemed to come into herself. When she finally met his gaze, he swallowed and gave it everything he had left.

"I want to make a bargain with you."

Her mouth tipped up on one side. "I thought my being here was already a bargain."

"Well, then a bargain within a bargain, I suppose. While you remain here, I want you to believe as though the rest never happened. Right now it's just the two of us. Here in this moment. It's just us surrounded by the frozen fields of Margate, and no one else can reach us."

He saw her eyes light at the idea, and he pressed on.

"For the next four weeks, it's only us. No past and no future, only now. When the first of March comes, you're free to return to London, and I shan't try to stop you."

She considered this, her eyes searching his face as she was prone to do, and he tried very hard not to squirm under the scrutiny.

He would let her go. He was a man of his word, and yet he hoped to God that day would never come. But if he were to succeed at this at all, she must have an open mind and forget the past that lay scattered between them like a scarred battlefield.

If he'd ever wished for a second chance, it was now, and she held all the power to grant it or deny it. Never before had he put so much of himself in the hands of another.

"Just you and me? Until March when I must return to London?"

A line had appeared between her brow, and he wanted nothing more than to press his thumb against it, forcing the tension from her face.

"Yes, just us. No letters, no recriminations, no accusations, and God, no rumors. Let me show you who I really am, Viv. Please."

Her features relaxed at last, her eyes widening with some decision.

"I will agree to your proposal, but only on one condition."

"Name your price." He wasn't sure when but at some point, he'd slipped his hand into hers and now he laced their fingers together and pulled their connected hands to his chest.

"I want you to answer a question."

"Ask it." The words flew from his lips, desperation gnawing at him to get her acceptance of their bargain.

She swallowed and looked down as though gathering her thoughts. Finally, she looked up, and what he saw now in her face, had his assurance slipping.

"Why?" she asked.

"Why the bargain? Because I want you to—"

She shook her head. "Not the bargain. Well, yes, the bargain. But it's more—why? Why do you want this? Why do

you want me to know who you really are? And more impor-
tantly, why now?"

Guilt swamped him. She didn't know of the restlessness
that ate at him, that had driven him to near destruction on
the road outside Canterbury. She didn't know of his selfish
reasons for making her stay.

And he couldn't tell her.

"I—"

The knock at the door rescued him from further words.
Viv slid from his lap without another second passing and
brushed her skirts swiftly as though she were the picture of
propriety.

"Yes?" she called when she finished.

He watched her, his heart hammering in his chest. Would
she remember that he hadn't answered her?

Mrs. Olds stepped into the room. "The visitors are here,
ma'am."

* * *

SHE HAD NEVER WITNESSED the four footmen it took to move
her husband down the stairs actually attempt the maneuver.

And she wished she never had.

She closed her eyes as they made their way around the
bend of the landing and down to the floor below where the
Stokers were waiting in the green drawing room.

She was already still flustered from her encounter earlier.
She ran a hand along the back of her neck, hoping what had
just transpired did not reflect anywhere on her person. She
trailed her fingers over her lips when she thought no one was
watching as the footmen navigated the particularly difficult
task of setting Ryder back in his chair, which had its own
bevy of footmen.

He hadn't answered her question.

She'd finally had the opportunity to ask him one, and it wasn't even one to which she longed to have the answer. It was simply a product of the moment.

Why was he so adamant in winning her affection?

She dare not use the word *love*. She'd fallen into that trap once, and she wasn't bound to do so again.

And yet...

It felt a lot like love.

But wasn't that something all the rumors whispered of?

She'd heard it time and time again.

I thought he was in love with me.

Viv had thought he was once in love with her, too.

She watched him now as the footmen carefully laid his plastered leg in the trough that held it suspended between the wheels.

Could she agree to his bargain?

Four weeks didn't seem like an awful long time. She was trapped here anyway until Ryder regained his feet. What harm would it do to indulge him?

It might irreparably break her heart.

She swallowed and took the last few steps down to stand beside her husband. The green drawing room was opposite the landing, and the open door revealed Mrs. Olds directing the placement of a teacart.

She wasn't sure what she'd expected, but Mr. Stoker senior did not appear at all ready to give up the harvest. He was a tall man and thick through the chest and arms. His cheeks had gone saggy somewhat beneath his whiskers, but it was the only sign of age on his person. His suit was simple and neatly pressed, if showing telltale signs of wear at the cuffs and along the buttonholes. His shoes were exquisitely polished, and he stood straight and proud as she and Ryder came into the room.

"Mr. Stoker, you will forgive me for not standing to greet you," Ryder said.

Mr. Stoker gave the appropriate bow as did his son. Viv eyed the younger Mr. Stoker.

"Mr. Stoker, I believe it is you I have to blame for this contraption," Viv said by way of greeting to the younger man.

He lit up with pride, not at all cowed by her tone. "I am," he said to her before turning to Ryder. "Are you finding it to your liking, Your Grace?"

"It's enough to give me a semblance of freedom, and for that, I cannot thank you enough."

The elder Mr. Stoker pressed his hands together in concern.

"The missus and I were right worried when we heard of your accident, Your Grace. She asked me to tell you, you were in her prayers right from the start."

Ryder's face sobered as he studied the older man.

"Thank you, Mr. Stoker. I greatly appreciate that. I would appreciate it more if you brought some of her shortbread with you."

A twinkle came to Mr. Stoker's eye as he turned and picked up a tin from the table behind him. Handing it to Ryder with a great deal of pride in his smile, he exclaimed, "Fresh this morning."

The tin was faded, but Viv could just make out the advertisement for Barlye's Tea, a cut-rate tea known for its cheap price and not for its taste. The tin was well scrubbed and free of dents. Ryder accepted it as though he were being handed the Crown Jewels.

He considered the tin in his lap for some time, and when he looked up, Viv swore there was a dampness to his gaze.

"Please tell Mrs. Stoker this has helped me feel a great deal better."

Viv's chest tightened at the sound of gratitude in Ryder's voice. Ryder had come to her alone without parents or family, and there'd been no one on whom his past reflected for her to see. There was no one to tell the stories of his childhood or hint at old traditions. But it was clear now these people were a part of Ryder's past. A beloved part, if she were to judge.

She shook herself from her observations and invited the Stokers to sit as she busied herself with the tea things.

"I understand you grew up with my husband, Mr. Stoker," she said as she indicated the sugar cubes.

"Two please, ma'am. And Daniel, please. It will grow confusing otherwise." His smile was cute and not without mirth as he moved his gaze to her husband. "And I did have the pleasure of growing up with your husband. I'm afraid I shan't be able to tell you any stories, though. We swore ourselves to secrecy."

Ryder laughed, and the sound was so full and startling it drew her attention. His face was free of the tension that had been etched into the lines of his brow and the brackets around his mouth that he'd carried for the past several weeks. She'd almost say he looked like the man she had married.

"It's not my wife I'm worried about. I don't believe we're too old for the switch, are we, Mr. Stoker?"

The older man's laugh was rich and gravelly. "You will never be too old for a good discipline, I'm afraid."

"Were they naughty children, Mr. Stoker?"

She wasn't sure why she asked the question, but the idea of Ryder as a young boy suddenly struck her as odd. He'd always been a man to her and a rather spectacular one. It was hard for her to imagine him racing about as a lad, seeking out trouble at every turn.

"Well, now, I can't say I am one to divulge a person's past, but I will tell you, ma'am, I have been sleeping a lot better since these two matured."

Viv joined them in laughing now, and she wondered why Ryder had never mentioned them before. Her mirth was dampened by the thought, and she picked up her cup of tea to hide her fading smile.

"Mr. Stoker, I assume Daniel told you why I wanted to see you." Ryder held his teacup in between both of his hands as the chair did not allow him to reach the table.

Mr. Stoker set down his own cup, his expression suddenly grave. "He did, Your Grace. I'm only too happy to help if I can. I've been tending hops since well before you and Danny here started racing through them."

Ryder sat forward in his chair. "What I don't understand, sir, is why the quality of the harvest has fallen. The new law should be driving demand for hops, which logically would force the price up. The quality of the hops would move in parallel. A better quality hops for a better price. But instead the hops are not fit for consumption, and we're selling off the harvest at detrimental prices. What have you to say about this?"

Mr. Stoker pushed his teacup between his fingers, his brow furrowed as he seemed to consider his answer.

"Well, I've had some time to think on this now, Your Grace, and I think what it comes down to is not what price the demand can drive but rather what price the consumers can afford to pay."

"What do you mean?"

Mr. Stoker looked up, his eyes soft and troubled. "We all thought with the new law allowing anyone to make and sell ale, the demand for hops would go wild. We started planting more than usual. But come harvest time, no one could pay the market price. While they were making and selling ale, they were trying to keep their costs down. They went across Kent looking for the cheapest price."

"Bartering swill in one pub after another then," Daniel murmured, his eyes on his teacup.

"They can't keep customers with such a poor product, can they?" Viv couldn't help but ask, suddenly feeling the weight of the situation.

She had thought Ryder had merely wished to find distraction from his confinement, but now she saw he truly cared about the crop. Looking at the two men seated opposite her, she realized just how much deeper Ryder went than she gave him credit for.

She shifted in her seat, feeling her world tilt once again. There was too much she had been so certain of that she now wasn't certain at all about.

"Tired and poor men don't care what they're drinking, ma'am. Begging your pardon," Mr. Stoker said, hiding his eyes as though he were bashful of speaking of such things to a duchess.

"So it's the pubs that won't pay for the better quality hops." Ryder's gaze moved between the two men.

"The passing of the bill had a lot of small shops opening up. Pubs thinking they could brew their own ale and save the cost of having to purchase it from a brewer," Daniel said.

"And the brewers?" Ryder asked.

Mr. Stoker scoffed. "They're hurting even more than we are. Suddenly anyone can make and sell ale, and no one wants to pay a fee for something they can do on their own."

"How do we change their minds?" Ryder asked and oddly enough, his gaze swung to Viv as if she might have the answer.

Startled by his direct gaze, she answered without thinking. "I wouldn't drink it. I don't care how cheaply it was made."

Mr. Stoker set down his cup across from her forcefully enough to set the china to ringing.

"Do you know I hadn't thought of that?" He pointed at her as though she had unraveled a particularly perplexing problem. He shifted his gaze to Ryder. "There must be gents—and ladies—" Again, he pointed at her. "—who do not care for such stuff. Why aren't we selling the hops to them?"

Daniel shook his head. "That kind of clientele wouldn't care for the rubbish Margate is producing now." He slid a glance at Ryder. "Begging your pardon," he muttered.

Ryder waved him off. "I'd be the first to call it rubbish. It would be a great risk to invest in a better harvest. What would it take to bring back the quality of hops Margate was once known for?"

Mr. Stoker shook his head, twirling his now empty teacup between his fingers. "I'm afraid the strands we used to plant have long since gone. There aren't any more seed plants from what was once here. You would need to find another grower willing to sell you some of their crop. And then you wouldn't have control over the quality of plants you'd get."

"So you're saying the risk is mighty?"

Mr. Stoker's focus was sharp when he looked up. "I'm saying it would take a mighty fool to attempt it."

Ryder considered his tea, which she noticed he hadn't drunk at all, and her stomach turned at the sight of it. He was truly worried—not just for the crop, but what it would mean for Margate, its tenants, and the crop workers who came from London every season.

So much weight on his shoulders she'd never known he would carry. She had always pictured him racing from one party to the next, showered in the accolades of the ladies who most wanted to be his next lover, and accepting the congratulations of the gentlemen whom he'd bested in some sort of test of strength, wit, or speed.

But just then, he wasn't that Ryder at all. He was a man trying to save the livelihood of so many people. And doing it all handicapped by the confines of a Bath chair and a plastered leg.

"Would you advise against me attempting such a thing?" Ryder finally asked, but his voice lacked the strength it had at the beginning of the conversation.

Mr. Stoker released a great sigh. "I'll tell you what, Your Grace. Let me put a few questions about to my old contacts at the neighboring estates. Maybe someone might just be as crazy as you seem to be."

CHAPTER 11

*I*t was late before the Stokers left.

Once they had finished their conversation about the hops, he couldn't quite bid them good day. He'd tumbled into asking of Daniel's work and Mrs. Stoker's attempt to make the finest strawberry jam in all of Kent. Ryder had been subjected to so much taste-testing of strawberry jam as a child he never ate the stuff since.

He smiled now at the memory as he sat staring at the blackness that filled the windows of his room. He was once more on the settee he found himself abandoned on all too often, but he'd had the presence of mind to ask the footmen to turn the settee first, so now at least, he had a nice view when he laid his head back.

Except the candles in the room prevented him from seeing anything but his own reflection.

He closed his eyes.

The weight of the day pressed down on him, and he scratched absently at the spot just above his knee where the edge of the plaster tormented him.

Only four weeks until the bugger came off. Only four weeks to convince Viv to stay.

And then what?

He pushed the question aside. He couldn't think of that. He only knew he had to keep her with him. When she was there, the restlessness stayed away. He only had to convince her...of what?

He pinched the bridge of his nose.

She wanted to return to London to see her sister safely wed. Women had very few choices, he knew that, and a good match would ensure Johanna's future. Was he selfish enough to keep Viv from that? To keep her for himself?

He didn't know anymore.

Just that day he'd asked her to strike a bargain with him, a bargain to consider only their present and never their pasts. But how could he ask her not to look at his past when he still questioned hers?

He had thought he could ignore the question of whether or not she had taken lovers during their estrangement, but after her actions the previous week, he was fairly certain she had not been chaste in his absence.

The way she so wantonly unbuttoned her shirt, cupped her own breasts and held them out to him like an offering. God, he'd kill the man she'd first done that with.

A sharp knock at the door had him lifting his head. He expected to see Mrs. Olds bringing him his dinner tray, but instead, it was Viv, pushing a cart laden with foodstuffs.

She'd changed from earlier, wearing a simple soft gown of lavender, the collar undone at her throat, her hair down at her shoulder in a thick braid. His heart sped up at the sight of her, and he tightened the sash of his banyan in some weak attempt at keeping his composure.

"I thought you might be hungry."

She had no idea.

She stopped just inside the door and looked up. He didn't know what expression was on his face, but it must have been telling because her features folded in concern.

"What is it?"

He shook his head, not wishing to worry her. "It's just been a long day is all."

He watched her for a few seconds more before an idea formed in his head.

"Blow out the candles."

She moved as if to instantly carry out his request but stopped and sent him a look.

"Are we to eat in the dark?"

He smirked. "Trust me."

Her laugh was soft as she moved about the room extinguishing the candles. The fire had burned down low, and its soft glow hardly crept into the room. By the time Viv was finished, the blackness had lifted from the windows, and he could just make out the tall oaks that bordered the gardens, their empty branches reaching into the darkness.

It was snowing.

Snow was rare here on the coast, and as a child, he'd marveled at its existence. There was never enough to take out his toboggan, but he never failed to give it a try. Now he stared, enraptured, as the stuff fell from the night sky like something from a fairy tale.

He heard Viv's soft intake of breath as she caught sight of it and without thinking, he reached out a hand.

"Come here."

She padded over to him and took his hand.

"How do you feel about a picnic?"

He could just make out her smile in the soft light.

She bent to the cart of food as he pushed himself over on the settee making room for her. When he expected her to take the seat next to him, she stopped, her feet shuffling against the carpet.

She was taking off her slippers.

He didn't know why the thought thrilled him, but it did. She slipped onto the settee, handing him a filled plate. When she curled her feet under her, the domestic sight of it nearly had him choking on his pudding.

"I used to play in the snow all the time as a child."

He looked sharply at her. "You played in the snow?"

She nodded as she took a bite of pork. "The Darby country seat is north of Leeds. It would often get cold enough in winter to give us some snow. Johanna always made the messiest snow angels." She laughed and picked up a piece of pudding, growing suddenly quiet. "I'm sorry you didn't have siblings to grow up with."

He laughed as he broke off a piece of pudding. "Hardly. I had Daniel. We were enough for each other."

He watched her as she chewed, considering what he'd said.

"You're very close with the Stokers."

He swallowed his food and nodded. "I don't really remember my mother. She died when I was still so young. My father was a great deal older, and I simply never knew him well. He never beat me or anything horrid like that. It was just different."

She nodded. "Our father was older, but he took great care of us after our mother died. It was as though he thought our mother was watching from somewhere in heaven, and he didn't want to make a mistake should she haunt him as a ghost."

She laughed, and he could almost picture her poor father attempting to manage raising four girls.

"You must miss them."

"My parents? I suppose I do—"

"Your sisters," he interrupted.

Her smile faded. "Yes, I miss them a great deal." She set aside her plate on the low table by the settee. "But two of them are married now. It's hardly the same."

The pudding in his mouth turned to ash, and he set his plate on the table at his elbow.

"Three."

"I beg your pardon?" she asked.

"Three of the Darby sisters are married."

"Oh…right." Her smile was sheepish.

"Am I so forgettable then?" He made his tone light, but his stomach clenched at the thought that she so easily dismissed him.

But he hadn't been a part of her life for four years. Of course, he would be so easily forgotten.

"No." Her voice was anything but playful, and the way she looked at him made his mouth water.

He lay back, resting his head against the settee, and placed his arm along the back of it.

"Come here." He nodded at the window. At this angle, he could see some of the inky night sky and the white flakes a blaze of brightness against it.

She turned her head to the window, a soft smile coming to her lips as she leaned back, resting her head on the pillow of his shoulder.

They lay like that for several minutes, the crackle of the fire sporadic as the flames burned lower. It was only the two of them and the softly falling snow, but he couldn't help but feel the weight of the remaining four weeks he had with her.

Would she really leave?

What would he do then?

He tried to think of something to say to her, but the silence only rang in his ears.

159

"It was nice having the Stokers to visit today. I should like to meet Mrs. Stoker one day. Perhaps I can have her to tea."

"Ask her to bring her strawberry jam." He closed his eyes and turned his head just enough to catch her scent.

Vanilla.

He would never think of vanilla the same way again.

"Oh? Does she truly make the finest strawberry jam in all of Kent?"

He laughed. "She makes great quantities of it. I'm sure she'd have some to spare."

She turned her head, and he could feel her quizzical stare on him. He reluctantly opened his eyes and met her gaze. A thousand emotions rushed at him from that single look, and he swallowed, feeling the importance of the moment wrap around him.

He couldn't make a mistake this time.

He lifted his hand and traced the curve of her cheek until he dipped lower, and his finger came off the curve of her jaw.

He smiled and studied her face, memorizing each valley and crest. She could be gone again in four weeks' time, and he wanted to remember her face.

Fear gripped him, suddenly and powerfully, and in that moment, he would do anything to keep her from leaving. Without her, he would succumb to the restlessness that dogged him, and he would finally go mad from it.

He bent his head, capturing her lips in a kiss that he meant to be passionate and fervent, but once his lips touched hers a different sensation passed over him.

Peace.

Rightness.

Calm.

His fear abated at the first touch of her kiss, and he gentled his lips against hers, savoring instead of taking, caressing instead of plundering. For the first time, he was not kissing a woman to entice her into bed, to drive her into a frenzied passion, to make her beg him for more.

He was simply kissing his wife.

And it was wondrous.

He'd never taken a breath to consider the exquisiteness of such a simple act. He'd been racing through life seeking anything that would spark his emotions, and with each new encounter, he grew more immune to the wonders the world had to offer.

But he'd missed this.

He'd missed the uncomplicated act of kissing his wife in the dark while snow fell outside.

Her hand touched his chest first, lying there softly and unmoving as she tilted her head to allow him to deepen the kiss. But within moments, her fingers began to explore, slipping beneath the lapel of his banyan. He groaned against her mouth, but flashes of the week before doused his growing ardor, and he pulled back.

"Viv, I don't want—"

She placed a single finger against his lips, stopping his words.

"You said four weeks. Do you still mean that?" Her eyes never strayed from his, and he felt the intensity of her words as she slipped her finger from his mouth.

"Four weeks. That's all I'm asking." He couldn't bring himself to say he'd let her go in four weeks. His throat burned with the words, and he just couldn't let them go.

Because he couldn't let her go.

He bent his head to resume their kiss, but she stopped him with that finger against his lips again.

"And in four weeks, I am free to return to London if I wish."

He stilled. This was the first time she intimated a possibility of not returning to London. Of not leaving him.

He swallowed and thought about what he would say carefully. "Yes, of course. You are always free to choose what you want."

Something flickered in her eyes, and his stomach clenched, wondering what she could be thinking.

"I am free to choose what I want." She whispered the words back to him like an incantation.

"What do you choose, Viv?" Never before had a question taken all of his energy to speak it.

Now he waited, the breathing seizing in his lungs as he waited for her answer.

But she didn't give one.

Instead, she slipped her hand around his neck and pulled him to her for a kiss.

* * *

SHE DIDN'T WANT to give this up.

Kissing him, touching him, *being* with him.

She didn't want to give any of it up.

But must she?

Yes.

The thought sent a shiver through her. She still didn't know why he was suddenly so adamant about this arrangement, why he was showering her with attention and kindness. All she could think was that heartbreak lay at the end of it.

He'd hurt her once when she believed he was in love with her. Would he hurt her again?

He was right. They had been young and naive. She had thought him in love, and he had thought them to have a society marriage of indifference. They were both foolish. Maybe this time it could be different.

She shoved at the lapels of his banyan, frantic suddenly to

feel the heat of his skin. She reached for the tie of his robe and found his hands already there, pulling the garment from his body. He shifted to toss the robe aside, and when he came back to her, bent over her. He nibbled kisses along the line of her jaw and up to her ear where he pressed a hot, wet kiss to the sensitive spot where her neck met jaw.

Her hips came up off the settee, and her fingers dug into his back as sensation roiled through her.

"Ryder." It was the only thing she could say, and in his name, she poured everything.

Was this lust? Was this passion? She didn't know. She'd never felt anything like it before. When they were first married, their coupling had been sweet and always in the dark. She didn't know she was meant to feel something.

But now she did.

With the banyan removed, she trailed her fingers down his back, searching for the edge of his nightshirt. She tugged at the fabric until she felt bare flesh beneath her fingertips.

Heat.

So much heat.

She plunged her hands beneath the shirt and explored the ridges of his spine, the muscles of his back.

Her head fell back as he discovered the line of her throat, that small spot nestled between her collarbones. Her dress got in the way, though.

"Ryder, please," she moaned.

He reached up and yanked the dress apart. Vaguely, she heard fabric rip and buttons striking some hard surface, but she didn't care. His mouth continued its wandering path to the edge of her chemise.

"God, your underthings will be the death of me," he muttered against her skin.

He sat up, pulling all the delicious heat from her, and she whimpered. But he took her hand and pulled her up with him. More carefully this time, he separated the remaining buttons at the front of her gown until he could push the fabric from her shoulders. She tugged her hands free from the long sleeves as he went to work on her corset. The relief was nearly as delicious as his kisses when the garment finally sprang free, and he tore it from her body.

He didn't stop. Gently, he leaned her back on the settee, and she let him, marveling in the way his gaze burned with hunger as he studied her.

She should have felt wanton and exposed, but instead she felt…desired. Heat began to pool between her legs, and she thought of what he'd done, putting his fingers down there, stroking. Her knees tried to come together, but her skirts prevented her from doing so.

He leaned over her now, using one hand to stroke the edge of her chemise.

"Do you like it when I touch you like this?"

She looked down, fascinated by the blunt finger that caressed her delicate flesh.

"Yes," she heard herself say.

His fingers dipped lower, beneath the edge of the garment, and her back arched, willing him to touch her like he had before. He nudged her sleeve over her shoulder until the chemise fell. Cool air struck her skin, but it was soon replaced with glorious heat as his lips replaced his fingers. He trailed kisses along the curve of her breast, lower and lower, until—

"Oh, God, Ryder." She bucked as his lips closed over her nipple.

Her hands were in his hair, but it wasn't enough. She wanted to feel more of him.

Just as he'd pushed the chemise from her shoulder, she tugged at his shirt until he sat up enough for her to pull the garment over his head.

He was naked, perched above her, his chest heaving with exertion. She could make out every detail of him in the soft glow from the fire, and she knew there would never be enough time to learn all of him.

He was magnificent.

And right now, he was hers.

His smile was devilish as he leaned over her.

"Like what you see?"

"Mmm, very much. But weren't you doing something earlier that I may have interrupted?"

He dipped his head, and she thought he might kiss her, but then he kept going until his lips met her collarbone again. His fingers played with the sleeve of her chemise that remained on her shoulder.

"God, please, Ryder, just push it off."

His laugh vibrated against her chest. "So impatient, darling."

But he did as she bid and soon her other breast was exposed to the cool air. She felt her nipple tighten instantly, and she arched, yearning for the feel of his mouth on her. He obliged, sucking her nipple into his mouth while he massaged her other breast.

God, how had she never known this?

She had been so stupid to think her marriage had been adequate when passion had never been a part of it.

In an instant, her desire was replaced with a flood of realization. Ryder had always been attentive to her and kind, but it hadn't been love. She knew that now, understood her own folly in the destruction of her marriage.

An image of her sisters round with child flashed in her mind, and realization dawned again. They were so quickly with child because their husbands loved them. Because their husbands did *this* to them.

Oh God, she'd been so stupid.

Hers had not been a love match at all. She had been deluded by Ryder's attention, blinded by his kindness. That was all.

Because she had been so desperate for someone to love her.

She'd been so desperate to prove the whispering mamas and the leering debutantes who thought her unnatural to be wrong. She had wanted to show them she could be loved, so she'd believed it when Ryder had smiled at her, asked her for a dance.

It wasn't love.

The realization freed something in her chest, and years of remorse and regret and hurt slipped away to be replaced by yearning and curiosity and expectation.

She reached up and gripped his shoulders with both hands. It wasn't love then. But maybe now it was different. Maybe now she had a *chance* to be loved.

His hand left her breast to trip down her torso, plunging into the folds of her skirt. She wished she'd worn something more alluring than wool stockings, but she hadn't known he would be seeing beneath her skirts when she'd changed earlier to bring him dinner.

His fingers found the wool stockings, but he never hesitated, his hand moving up the inside of her leg to the bare spot just above her ties. Her leg jerked from the touch, and he rose up to take her mouth in a devastating kiss.

"I want to touch you," he whispered against her mouth. "I want to touch you here."

Her legs fell open of their own accord, and she expected to feel shame, but she didn't. This felt right. This felt like something she'd been waiting for, for so long.

His fingers moved higher. She'd forgone the pantalettes she normally wore during the day, and his fingers found her exposed flesh quickly enough.

He raised his head. "Were you planning to be seduced this evening, Your Grace?"

His smile was wicked in the dimness.

"Are you so certain I didn't plan to be the seducer?"

His eyes blanked at her words, his mouth slackening, and she took pity on him, pulling his head back down to capture his lips with hers.

His hand remained against the soft skin of her inner thigh, and the heat was almost too much to bear. She thrust her hips upward, encouraging his exploration.

He laughed against her lips. "Still so impatient."

He broke the kiss to lean over her. She met his gaze but felt an instant stab of vulnerability.

"I want to watch you."

She didn't understand his words, but his hand finally began to move again, exploring the curve of her thigh until he found her most sensitive flesh. She prepared herself for his fingers to slip between her folds. The throbbing there was nearly unbearable now, and she didn't understand how he could touch her and make it better.

A single finger caressed her intimate folds, and she closed her eyes against the sensation. It was as if her body knew what was coming even if she didn't. The pulsing grew stronger, and her hips thrust against his palm.

"Do you want me to touch you?"

She grasped his wrist. "Please," she nearly begged.

She expected his fingers to slip inside of her, but instead they traveled higher, leaving her opening wet and throbbing. He placed his thumb against her sensitive nub, and her hips came up off the settee.

"Ryder," she groaned and turned her face to bury it against his chest.

"Shhh," he whispered against her ear. "Trust me."

His thumb moved in slow circles, the tension in her body

coiling with every stroke. She was going to come undone if he didn't stop, but she thought she might die if he did.

The strokes came faster now, the pressure more acute. She held onto him as her body continued to coil and then—

When she exploded on a wave of light and sound, a noise came from her lips she had never heard before, a groan of pleasure, and she knew she'd never be the same again.

This was so much…more. This was so much better than those few nights of their marriage spent hidden under the covers while he touched her. This was magnificent.

She scrambled to recover, her head coming up to find him watching her.

"What…what happened?"

His smile was just as wicked, but it held a note of confusion. "You climaxed, darling. Have you never climaxed before?"

She blinked, his words making very little sense.

"I what?"

His expression changed then. Even in the near darkness, she watched the heat in his eyes be replaced with something deeper, something priceless, and she wondered if he'd just discovered something about her he hadn't known before.

He didn't answer her. He rolled onto his back, his strong arm coming around her to roll her on top of him. He shoved her skirts up her legs until she could straddle him.

Only then did she become aware of how aroused he was.

"Oh." Her hand moved instinctively to the spot between her legs where his penis rested, thick and hard.

"Don't."

The word was harsh, and it brought her gaze quickly to his.

"I mean—" He gestured weakly before covering his eyes with his hands. "I mean, not right now." He peeked at her from between his fingers. "I would love for you to touch me at any time. Just not right now. I very much want to be inside you."

She knew only a little of what that meant. She knew he would want to place his penis inside her, but what about the touching part? If she touched him like he touched her, would it feel just as good to him? She marveled at the idea and quite simply couldn't stop herself.

She touched him.

He hissed in a breath as her fingers closed around him.

"Vivianna. Please. Stop." He spoke the words through gritted teeth.

She wanted to stroke him as he'd stroked her, but instead, she lifted herself and carefully placed him at her entrance. She held his gaze as she slowly, so very slowly, lowered herself, her body so wet it slipped around him with little resistance. But she wasn't used to such intrusion any longer, and her muscles tightened.

He grabbed her hips. "God, you're killing me."

She didn't let his grip stop her, and she lowered herself farther until she was fully seated atop him.

His eyes were closed, his head flung back, silent and still. She raised her hips and lowered them. His eyes opened, his gaze pinning her with heat and desire and lust.

That feeling of power spiked through her.

She did this to him. She had the ability to harness his attentions.

She did it again.

Oddly, the throbbing started once more. She looked down to where he was inside her, perplexed by the sudden building sensation within.

Could she…did she…was she supposed to enjoy this, too?

Compelled by curiosity, she thrust her hips more quickly, bringing herself up only to let her hips come down fully atop him. Again and again and again. Faster and faster.

The tension came back, coiling stronger and deeper inside of her. Her nipples throbbed for attention, and she threw her head back, her body a battlefield of emotion and sensation.

He sat up. She brought her head forward, her eyes springing open as his arms came around her, his mouth once more closing on her aching nipple. He groaned, his hands traveling down her back to grip her buttocks. Now when she came down, his hips thrust upward and pure sensation spiraled through her.

A cry sprang from her lips, and her hips pounded against him. One hand left her buttocks to slide up her torso, cup her breast, slip down her stomach, and—

When he touched her, she came undone, the climax tearing through her body as she convulsed around him. His cries of ecstasy mixed with her own as she tried to hold onto him.

He fell back against the settee, bringing her with him.

It was only as she drifted into sleep that she heard him shift, heard the whisper of the blanket coming off his chair, felt him wrap it around her, tasted one more fleeting kiss against her lips.

CHAPTER 12

*S*leep came quickly, but it didn't stay.

He awoke sometime in the night, cold and with a deep ache in his plastered leg.

He hadn't had real pain there since the first week of the accident, and he felt a flicker of concern. He had, after all, just made rather acrobatic love to his wife.

The thought of it had his body responding, rousing out of sleep with a rush, but he tamped it down. If he had truly caused harm to his leg, engaging in another round of the activity that had caused said problem was ill advised.

But perhaps if he did compromise the healing of the leg, the plaster could not come off at the end of the month, and Viv would feel compelled to stay out of duty. The notion no longer held the appeal it once did. He didn't want her to stay because she felt she must. He wanted her to stay because, well, she wished to.

The very thought stilled him. He blinked at the ceiling, wondering where such an idea had sprung. Through the whole of this, his intent had always been to keep the restlessness at bay, but something had changed in the past month.

He enjoyed spending time with her.

It was as though he were just discovering her for the first time. When he'd proposed, he had seen a lady perfectly suited to fulfill the role of duchess. Now he saw a woman. A woman who made him laugh, who made him feel frustrated, who made him want things he didn't know he could want.

A woman who indulged her husband's whims and picnics in the dark on a settee to watch the snow fall. A woman who made messy snow angels with her little sisters when they were children.

A woman who would ride horseback across the frozen fields to reach the husband she believed to be dying, even when that husband had no right to expect her loyalty.

A flutter in his chest had him pressing his hand to it.

Was this what love felt like?

He'd never given it any thought before. It never concerned him nor elated him. He had simply thought love was a construct for fairy tales and poems. He didn't realize anyone might actually feel the emotion.

He turned his head to where she slept beside him. She curled herself against his side facing away from him, so her sensuous round buttocks pressed into his hip. Damn her.

Her red-gold hair fell across her cheek. She'd stolen the blanket entirely, and now it was wrapped around both her hands, tucked under her chin.

Did he love his wife? *Could* he love her?

He didn't know.

The realization that she had not taken a lover in his absence had struck him in a way he hadn't thought it could. Lovers meant nothing to him, and he meant nothing to them. They were equal parts distraction to one another, but the idea that Viv should betray him like that…

He suddenly felt how she had felt, and he thought himself the worst kind of person. But on top of the thought, he vowed never to make her feel like that again. He vowed never to have so little respect for a person, including himself, ever again.

He wanted nothing more than to wake her with a kiss now and continue on where they'd left off, but the pain in his leg was concerning, and if someone did not build up the fire soon, they would be frozen by morning.

He leaned over and pressed his lips to the pale, soft skin of her shoulder that just peeked out from under the blanket.

She stirred, one hand coming up to brush the hair from her face. She seemed to come awake all at once and quickly twisted her head, nearly colliding with him in the dark.

"Shh, it's all right," he whispered. "It's only I find I must grovel at your feet for assistance, Your Grace."

"S'matter?" she murmured.

He smiled at the sleepy tone in her voice. "The fire has nearly gone out. It needs more coal if we are to make it through the night."

This brought her eyes open, and she blinked as if taking in her surroundings for the first time. He saw the moment she realized where she was and more likely, realized she was rather undressed, but her cheeks heated with a lovely blush.

"I'll tend to it." She sat up, the blanket firmly clutched to her chest. She made to swing her legs over the side of the settee and stopped, peering over her shoulder at him. "I'd ask that you look over there, Your Grace."

He laid back on the settee with his hands folded behind his head.

"Why? I've already seen everything."

She eyed him, her lips tipping up on one side. "Is that so?"

She stood then, and when he thought she'd keep the blanket as a shield, she left it on the settee. Once standing, she shed what remained of her clothes until she stood before him completely and utterly naked.

His throat went dry.

He couldn't see much in the near dark, but that didn't stop his imagination from filling in the gaps. From the curve of her breasts to the delicate roundness of her stomach to the delectable line of her thighs, he knew every bit of her, even if he couldn't make it all out.

She padded over to the fireplace, still utterly naked, and pulled the poker from its place on the brass stand. She poked at the remaining coals until they flared up. Only then did she add a scoop of coals from the bucket kept beside it. Once the fire was going again, she carefully moved the bucket of extra coals away from the flames and stood.

With the fire at her back, he could see her silhouette in its entirety.

His leg throbbed as if knowing where his thoughts were straying, and he sent up a string of curses for bad luck. Perhaps it wouldn't hurt too much to—

She made her way to the basin and pitcher in the corner, washing the coal dust from her hands before drying them on the towel that hung from the stand.

"Are you in need of refreshment? I realize it's quite late, but one must remember to care for oneself after such exercise."

She tossed him a smile before filling one of the glasses on the dinner cart with the wine she'd brought earlier.

He took the glass she offered him, downing the contents in a single gulp. The alcohol rushed to his head, and he willed his body to think of anything else besides his gorgeous wife's naked body.

She took a drink from her own glass of wine before setting it aside to wander over to the bed. He watched her go, her buttocks bouncing with every step.

Dear God, save him from perky buttocks.

She pulled another blanket from the bed along with two pillows and returned to the settee.

Without a word, she placed the pillow behind him and covered him with the blanket from the chair before adding the extra blanket on top. Only then did she slip beneath the covers herself, tucking back against his side like she'd been when he'd awoken.

She was cool now against his side, and he turned just enough to wrap an arm around her and pull her closer. Vanilla invaded his nostrils, and he closed his eyes against it.

He wasn't sure how long they lay like that, and he was almost certain she'd fallen back asleep, but she surprised him by asking, "What do you think you'll do about the hops?"

In one of those odd moments that sometimes occur between night and day, he'd forgotten about the Stokers' visit. It came flooding back to him, and with it, the painful reality of the hops crop. It wasn't as though Margate needed the income from the hops. He could replace it with another crop that was perhaps more marketable.

But he couldn't let go of the hops. All six Margate dukes before him had likely grown hops on the estate, and Ryder would not be the first one to break the tradition.

But it wasn't up to him to make such a decision, and it wasn't only the tradition of the Margate dukes at jeopardy. He had to ensure that his tenant farmers made not just enough to live; he wanted them to thrive.

He buried his nose in her hair.

"I must do what is best for the tenants."

"Which is what exactly?"

He opened his eyes and watched the fire for several moments before answering. "I think the only viable option we have is to see if new strands of hops can be procured. We'll need to differentiate Margate from the other hops growers if we are to appeal to a more lucrative clientele."

She stilled beneath his arm. He felt her breath grow ragged with a hitch.

"What is it?"

She shook her head, her hair crackling against his cheek.

"It's only that you keep surprising me. I thought I knew who you were, and yet I find you're nothing like I thought."

Her words were compelling enough that he tugged on her shoulder until she turned flat on her back, and he could study her face.

"What do you mean?"

Her eyes passed back and forth over his face. "Well, it's just that the Rogue Duke carries with him a certain reputation. I had no reason to refute any of the claims I'd heard over the years, and so I took them as, if not fact, then some embellishment of the truth."

"What sort of claims?"

He thought she would try to avoid the situation and turn away from him, but instead, she launched headlong into it.

"Lynwood's youngest daughter, Hillary. She claims you took her on her mother's sewing table in the middle of a ball at Lynwood House."

He considered her. "I do not know any woman named Hillary. What on earth are you talking about?"

"She isn't the only one to claim such an assignation. The dowager Countess of Kingsley says you took her not once but twice on a piano directly under her dead husband's portrait. This was all during her daughter's coming-out ball last season. She said it was quite exhilarating to have the dead earl leering down on them while you—what was the phrasing she chose?—oh yes, while you pounded into her."

"Who the hell is Kingsley?" His heart was picking up pace as her accusations grew more sordid.

Had he truly done any of those things and simply not

remembered? He knew he had been rather enthusiastic in his hedonistic ways in the last couple of years, but this...

"She said you pounded her so hard, they had to restring the middle *C*."

"I would be flattered by such an accusation if it were truly I who had done the deed." He paused and thought about her words. "They had to restring the middle *C*?"

She nodded, her eyebrows lifting as if to assure him of just the thing.

He lay back on the settee, casting his eyes toward the ceiling as he released a sigh. "God help me from such outlandish gossips."

She came up on one elbow to lean over him, her hand coming to lie on his chest. "Do you mean to tell me it isn't true? I had rather hoped it was. The piano bit was most fascinating. Although I did wonder how Lady Kingsley didn't hurt her back with such vigorous attentions."

He raised an eyebrow. "Are you suggesting I wouldn't take care in such an assignation?"

Her laugh was soft. "I would never make such a horrid suggestion." She looked down to where her fingers traced his breastbone. He caught her fingers in his, drawing her attention back to him. "Well, I did wonder if it were true, and with everything else—" She shrugged. "I didn't have anything to make me not believe it."

The wistfulness in her voice sent a spike of sadness through him. Sadness, remorse, regret, everything. In that single moment, he felt like the greatest cad and the worst bastard for hurting her.

And not just that, for not realizing the depths to which he'd caused her pain. For not doing something about it. For not begging for forgiveness then and there.

For not going after her when she ran.

He squeezed her hand. "Viv, I've had lovers, and I won't

deny it, but I assure you my depravity is not what rumors might suggest. And—" He licked his lips. "I'm sorry, Viv. I'm sorry I hurt you—"

She tugged her fingers free and placed one against his lips.

"You've already apologized for that. You mustn't continue to apologize for the rest of your life."

He took her finger away from his mouth and wrapped her hand in his. "I will apologize for as long as it takes me to feel better about it."

Her brow furrowed. "I don't think you'll ever feel better about it. Once I might have thought you didn't care, but that wasn't true at all. You care deeply for the things you—"

She didn't finish the sentence. It was as though her tongue simply became stuck on the word she'd meant to say.

"For the things I what?" he asked.

But she only shook her head. "It's nothing."

He released her hand to cup her cheek, pulling her attention back to him.

He studied her eyes, glass pools in the moonlight from the windows. "For the things I love?"

She watched him so carefully he may have been the prey in a hunter's sights. He knew what she wished for him to say. He could feel the words burning in his throat.

But in the end he couldn't say them.

So he drew her head down for a kiss, pouring everything into it that he didn't understand.

Maybe she could find what she was looking for if only in his kiss.

* * *

SHE WANTED to say the next four weeks were the stuff of romantic poems and everything young girls dreamed about at night.

However, it was, in fact, a great deal more tedious.

She hadn't been prepared for the kind of courtship she read of in novels. But love affairs did tend to be rather concerning when the gentleman in question was to be seeing to the healing of his broken leg.

It became clear after their exhibition on the settee that Ryder was not at all prepared for such physical exertion, the limitations of the cast notwithstanding. When his leg had swollen about the plaster, she'd sent for the doctor.

And there was no better way to kill the passion of a newly rediscovered affair than by bringing in a medical professional.

Dr. Malcolm ordered bed rest until the plaster was to be removed, and Ryder threatened to have the man's head removed in turn. Malcolm in no way responded to such bodily threats.

"What could he possibly know about broken legs?" Ryder fumed from where he was ensconced on his bed with every pillow she was able to sequester.

He looked rather like he'd been plopped into a vat of cotton, and it was more than difficult to take him seriously.

"I assure you, he knows a great deal." She shifted the ledger she had been scanning to bring the columns on the kitchen accounts closer for her inspection. "Do you know I believe the scullery maids may be helping themselves a bit?"

His eyes sharpened, and he stopped spewing nonsense about doctors and bed rest. "What did you say?"

She looked up from the ledger. "You've spent nearly a hundred pounds on lye this year alone. Whatever are you doing that requires quite so much lye?"

He crossed his arms over his chest.

"I would very much like to know the same."

She traced her finger down the line of neatly written numbers. "They always hide it in the lye purchase. I think they don't expect a duchess to actually read the ledger books."

She shook her head. "I must speak with Mrs. Olds."

She moved to stand, but Ryder's expression stopped her. "What is it?"

He looked as though his puppy were being taken away.

"If you leave, I'm stuck here all alone."

Perhaps just more like a petulant child.

She placed her hands on her hips. "Do you really expect me to spend all day in here with you?"

She regretted the words as soon as she spoke them.

"I'm expected to spend all day in here."

She crossed her arms over her chest. "Yes, but that's because you're being punished."

"There were two people involved in the lovemaking if I'm not mistaken. What is your punishment?"

His voice dropped at the end, and his sensual tone had her stomach clenching.

"I don't believe I'm deserving of a punishment. I was the innocent victim in all of this."

His laugh was quick. "I'd hardly call you innocent."

"Ryder Maxen, if you're trying to get me into bed with you—"

"Yes, please."

Her mouth was still open without words coming out.

"Unless you don't trust yourself." He raised his eyebrow as if daring her to contradict him.

"I do trust myself." She marched over to the side of the bed to better scold him. "But I do not trust you, and Dr. Malcolm said strict bed rest until the plaster is off. You've been doing too much with that blasted chair."

She threw her hand in the direction of the windows where the chair had been abandoned behind the settee. Her heart pounded every time she saw the settee and remembered what they had done on it. She hadn't known what lovemaking was until then.

And now she truly was curious about Lady Kingsley's claims with the piano. She turned back to her husband. "There is more to making love than what we've done, isn't there?"

"Ah, yes, yes, there is," he stammered. "A great deal more."

"Is there something you could show me that wouldn't be violating the doctor's orders?"

He swallowed hard and licked his lips. "I can think of one or two things."

Delicious anticipation coursed through her at the disbelieving expression on her husband's face. He was the one who had taunted her. It would do him good to get a dose of his own medicine.

She went to the door and turned the key in the lock, the small sound echoing through the room. She turned toward the bed, noting how his eyes followed her, and at just the last moment, she changed direction for the windows.

One by one she pulled the drapes aside. The day beyond was overcast, and the grayness lent a coziness to the room. It was as if they were the only two people in the world as long as they stayed inside this room.

Wasn't that what this was about?

There was no past and no future, just them here and now?

She couldn't help the pang of anxiety that came at the thought of how quickly the month was passing. What happened when March arrived? Would she go to London? Would he ask her to stay?

She didn't want to think about that now.

Right now, she only wanted to take.

She made her way back to the bed, slowly, her eyes locked on his.

"We never did finish our game of backgammon, Your Grace," she said as she stepped from one slipper and then the other.

"No, we didn't." His voice was soft as his eyes absorbed her every move.

She picked up her skirts as she climbed on the bed. He swallowed again as she made her way over to him on her knees. The mattress dipped beneath her, and soon her knees were against his thighs.

She grabbed one end of the tie of his robe and gave a small tug.

"You appear to be overdressed."

His eyes had gone unfocused with desire. "I do? How terribly inconsiderate of me."

She tugged again and the sash came free of its loose knot. She unwound it and pushed the fabric aside as she ran her hands up his muscled chest. He reached up and teased the sleeve of her gown.

"But wouldn't that mean you're overdressed, Your Grace?"

She leaned against him, her hands plastered to his chest as she drew her mouth painfully close to his.

"Not for what I have in mind."

She captured his mouth in a kiss before he could respond. She hadn't known how intricate kissing a man could be. She had thought it all lips and tongue, but there was so much more to it. She stroked the fullness of his lower lip with her tongue, nibbled her way to the corner of his mouth until he groaned, his hand catching the nape of her neck to pull her closer.

She let him take command of the kiss. The sensation was

heady and exhilarating. For too long, she'd wanted this. For too long, she'd allowed loneliness and pride to keep her from this.

What if she had gone back to him? What if she had demanded this four years ago?

She didn't know what this was though.

Would he return to his roguish ways once his leg had healed? Would he hitch Ve and Vili to a new phaeton and tear off across England, leaving her once more to consider her own worth?

She sounded pitiful when she thought of it that way and shoved her thoughts aside. For now, he was hers, and maybe, just maybe, they would make a child while they were together. Even if it were only for this brief time, she would have something of him.

He just had to get that damned plaster off.

She tore her lips from his and moved lower, sucking at his neck, the bones of his collar. His fingers plunged into her hair, and she felt the chignon her maid had styled it in loosen.

"Viv, I think—"

She came up on her knees before him, pulling his hands from her hair.

"I think you think entirely too much, Your Grace." She ran her hands up his wrists, capturing his fingers in hers. "I think you should stop thinking for now."

His eyes went wide at the sight of their interlocked hands, as she moved them up and away from her and back behind his head. She didn't stop until his knuckles hit the headboard behind him. She released his fingers to carefully turn his hands, bend his fingers over the headboard.

She cupped his cheeks then, caressing the stubble of his chin ever so delicately as she leaned close once more.

"Your Grace, I've heard tell of your prowess. Are you prepared to prove your valor in a most arduous task?"

His lips moved as if anticipating her kiss, but she kept herself just out of reach.

"Yes." The word was hardly more than a noise.

She shifted, bringing her lips to his ear before whispering, "No touching."

She felt more than saw his eyes fly open as he exclaimed, "What?"

But she was already moving, sliding down his body as she yanked up his nightshirt at the same time. She found him already hard and before he could utter a single protest, she took him in her hand.

"Viv." His voice was strained and demanding, his sleepy senses suddenly alert it would seem.

His hands came away from the headboard, and she held up her free hand.

"Uh- uh. I said no touching." His hands froze in midair where he'd been about to grab her shoulders. She pointed to the headboard. "Back."

He studied her as if weighing the seriousness of her command, and slowly, he placed his hands back on the headboard.

She swallowed, perhaps realizing she was really going to do this. She'd heard the maids talk about it with embarrassing laughs, but it sounded as though their men enjoyed what she was about to attempt. And as she couldn't very well do what she'd done that night on the settee without hurting him further, this was all she had left to her. So she thought anyway.

When she took him into her mouth, she realized he might not fit, and doubt swamped her.

But his responding groan was unlike any other she had elicited from him yet, and it bolstered her courage. She moved deeper, drawing him into her mouth, and his hips came up off the mattress.

"Viv, you…I…it's…" The string of words remained incomplete, and she drew her mouth slowly along the ridges of his penis until she sucked against his tip.

"Christ." His hands came around her head, frantic and tight, and she wanted to admonish him for touching, but the power that raced through her at his reaction was too savory to relinquish.

She sucked him into her mouth again, but this time she moved the hand she had wrapped around his length in the same direction as her mouth.

"Oh God, Viv. I can't…" His voice was pleading now, and she knew she must be doing it right.

She stroked him, sucking him in and out of her mouth, and she didn't think it possible but he grew harder, fuller, his penis pulsing against her lips.

His hands hadn't moved against her head, but his hips lifted ever so slightly off the mattress every time she stroked him, every time she sucked him. The motion was erotic, and she felt a coiling deep inside of her. She thought this would be about pleasuring him. She didn't know she would find it so appealing.

"Viv," he said again, pleading in his tone now. "Viv, please let me give you some pleasure, too."

She lifted her head at this. How could he know she grew aroused? Her look must have given her away because his hands moved to her skirts, tugging them from under her knees with little finesse until his fingers found what they sought.

She was wet. She could feel it in the way his fingers slid over her nub, and she reached out her free hand to brace herself against his shoulder.

"Ryder."

She bent her forehead to his, unable to hold herself steady as he stroked her. She did the same to him, wrapping her hand fully around him and mimicking the motion she had been doing with her mouth.

She came within moments, the cry flying from her lips before she could stop it, and only then did he let himself go to her ministrations.

She collapsed against his shoulder, her chest heaving.

"I told you no touching," she said, but he only laughed.

CHAPTER 13

*H*e knew exactly what he wished to do when the good doctor finished removing the plaster.

He was going to take his wife for a walk in the gardens.

The thought surprised him. Only months ago, his first thought would likely have been something more carnal, but not anymore.

The day was the kind that made one believe spring would really return at any moment, and he itched to get out there in the sunshine, feel its warmth on his shoulders and its promise in the breeze.

And he wanted to hold his wife's hand.

The thought should have seemed absurd, considering what they had done over the past couple of weeks while he'd been on bed rest. Their activities had been far more scandalous than the holding of hands. But whereas before he would have seen the month as a spree of debauchery, it was anything but.

He'd spent the month learning his wife.

He'd explored her body, yes, but he'd also discovered her tastes, learned of her interests, studied her manners.

The Duchess of Margate was extraordinary.

He'd known it all along, but the past several weeks had proven his point. She was loyal and kind, astute and conscientious. Her family was the most precious thing to her, and madly, he hoped he was included in it. Duty had sent her across the icy roads to him, but he wished and prayed that it was something more that kept her here after the first of March.

He knew he couldn't be so fortunate. He didn't deserve her attentions or her company. But maybe, just maybe, she would think differently of him now.

The wrenching of breaking plaster brought his thoughts to the present as Dr. Malcolm tore the first piece of material from around Ryder's ankle. He flexed his foot immediately, feeling the sting of unused muscles attempting to work.

"Easy, Your Grace," Dr. Malcolm cautioned. "Your body will not be used to such mechanics. You'll need to progress slowly."

Slowly? He hadn't the time for it. March was only days away now, and he must convince Viv to stay. He was running out of time.

With some more chiseling, the plaster cracked, a line running clean up his leg to his knee. More ripping ensued and finally, gloriously, the plaster came free. He moved to straighten the leg, but Dr. Malcolm stopped him with a hand.

"We must ensure it's properly healed before you attempt to move it."

"Should it not have healed?" He hadn't considered what would happen if he didn't heal properly. He wanted to be free of the cast to woo his wife suitably. He couldn't face a setback now.

"There's no reason to believe it might have been hampered in its healing, but it's better to be sure of these things."

The doctor bent over his lower leg, massaging at points along his shin. Carefully, he continued his exam deeper into the tissue of the calf muscle. The skin there was prickly as it came back to life, and the sensation of the doctor's probes felt oddly disconnected from Ryder's body. It was as though the good doctor were examining another patient entirely.

"My leg feels as though it's been detached," he found himself saying.

Dr. Malcolm straightened. "That's to be expected. The nerves in your leg are deadened from so much time inside the plaster. You will need to be careful as the feeling comes back."

The doctor moved to his bag and removed a small device with a rounded head. He tapped the device against Ryder's knee and on both sides of his ankle. Ryder could see nothing in response, but the doctor seemed satisfied.

"Your muscles are responding to sensation. I must say, Your Grace, you appear to have recovered."

Viv's exhalation was loud enough to draw his attention. She stood nearly across the room, her back to the bank of windows there, and he couldn't see her face clearly for the shadows.

But the sound of her relief had his chest tightening.

He watched her and wished to God he could see her face better.

Did she care that he had healed? Or was it only that she saw this as a release from her duty?

"Can he walk on it, Dr. Malcolm?"

"Yes, but he should be careful. Might you have a cane on hand? He may require support until he can regain the strength in that leg."

Ryder bristled. "*He* is perfectly capable of walking on his own."

The doctor returned his instruments to his bag. "Your

Grace, it is not a slight against your capabilities but rather a function of biology. The muscles in your leg have not been properly used for nearly two months. They will have weakened. You must work to recondition them."

"Recondition them? You mean exercise."

The doctor buckled his bag. "Yes, exactly." He turned to the windows. "Today would be a fine day to attempt walking outside, I should think."

Ryder found himself smiling at the doctor's suggestion.

Malcolm picked up his bag. "With a cane, of course."

Ryder's smile dropped.

"You do not wish to undo all of the hard work your body has been doing these last several weeks, do you?"

Ryder couldn't prevent his gaze from sliding to Viv, who pointedly looked away, one hand going up to cover her mouth as if hiding a knowing smile.

"No, I shudder at the thought."

The doctor gave a neat bow before heading to the door. "Then I recommend moving slowly and with assistance. Should you experience any setback at all, do not hesitate to send for me." The man gave no goodbye and simply slipped from the room.

Viv removed the hand from her mouth as she said, "If you had a valet, you could dress more quickly."

He growled in response. "Were you ever taught how impolite it is to point out one's shortcomings?"

"Shortcomings? I was merely making a practical suggestion."

He frowned. "I'll keep that in mind."

She moved away from the windows, and he could finally see her face clearly.

"May I make another suggestion?"

His body tightened at her words. "What kind of suggestion?"

Delicately, she touched only the tips of her fingers to his newly freed leg as she drew near enough.

"Your Grace, I believe you require a thorough bathing."

Her touch was better than the first sip of the finest liquor.

"I have a salve you can put on your leg here. Do you see how the plaster has dried out the skin? It will require extra attention to heal."

He could think of just what kind of attention would do it good. When she rolled his leg, however, they both saw the destruction the phaeton accident had caused. A jagged red scar burned its way up his calf.

She said nothing, only stroked the angry skin with her delicate touch. He couldn't prove it, but he was dead certain her touch could heal anything.

He wanted her to stay, to keep touching him, but she moved away before he could catch her. She went to the bell pull in the corner.

"I'll have Mrs. Olds arrange a bath for you so you may dress."

"Will my lovely wife be assisting me with this bath?"

She turned a narrowed eye on him.

"The good doctor did say I should not move about unsupported." He plied her with his most seductive grin.

"The good doctor did say that, didn't he?" She crossed her arms. "But how about this? You work on the bath, and I shall find a cane for you."

He perked up at her words, almost feeling the sunshine on his shoulders.

"I should think that a marvelous compromise."

Mrs. Olds arrived quickly, and a bath was arranged. The footmen who had helped him in the past weeks arrived to remove the chair Daniel had made for him.

"Wait," Ryder said as they tried to wheel it from the room. "I think I should like to keep it."

"For what?" Viv asked as she gathered up bits of the plaster on the bed. "Please do not tell me you are thinking of getting in another accident with your phaeton?"

He laughed. "Surely not. But don't you think with some tuning it might be a fine instrument for racing?"

She dropped the pieces of plaster she had gathered.

He smiled devilishly before instructing the footmen to carry the chair to the barns for storage.

The tub arrived next with a bevy of maids with buckets of steaming water. He practically salivated at the thought of a warm bath, the heat encapsulating his tired muscles.

A bath and exercise would do him good.

He clasped Viv's hand as she moved to dispose of the plaster.

"Please, I beg of you. I must stand or I will simply expire from the agony."

Her smile was soft and knowing, and she laid aside the bundle of plaster, offering him her arm.

He dropped his legs over the side of the bed, the rush of blood to his newly healed leg sending a tingle from his thigh to his toes. Gently, he placed his foot on the carpet as Viv slipped her arm beneath his, securing herself on that side as extra support.

He concentrated on placing both feet on the ground and only when he had a sure footing did he attempt to stand.

And immediately sat back down.

The room swam around him, the light from the windows suddenly harsh and puncturing.

He covered his eyes with his hand.

"Ryder? What is it? What's wrong?" Viv's voice was frantic, and he covered her hand with his own.

"I'm fine. I simply haven't stood in near two months."

He opened his eyes to find his words had not at all calmed her.

He attempted to stand again, and this time actually made it upright.

He held onto Viv, his legs almost like water beneath him. The tub seemed so very far away, but he wanted nothing more than to slip inside it. He gave Viv a playful tug in that direction.

"Are you sure?" Her voice held a note of humor.

"Do you think me incapable?"

She eyed the bed where he had only recently sat. "Not incapable, Your Grace. Rather out of practice I should think."

"I fear you are correct." He stumbled his way toward the bath, but with Viv's help, every step seemed more solid, a little more sure.

Until they reached the tub.

"Do you think you can stand on one leg long enough to lower yourself in?"

He eyed the rim of the copper tub. "Perhaps."

She helped him slip off his banyan and pulled the night-shirt over his head. She wrapped her arms about his waist as he bent forward and placed a hand on either side of the tub.

"Ready?" he asked, although he wasn't sure of whom he was pondering such a state.

Her grip around his waist tightened. "Yes. Do be careful please."

His arms had grown stronger with the need to pedal the chair about, but with the last three weeks of ordered bed rest, he had felt his body turn to little more than fluff. He drew a deep breath and willed his muscles to work. Quickly, he slipped his good leg over the edge of the tub and plunged it into the water, removing the weight from his newly healed leg as quickly as possible and relying on his arms to hold him up.

The warm water was sheer bliss. He sank into it, his head going back to the rim as he closed his eyes in ecstasy.

Only to have his euphoria interrupted by snickering.

He opened only a single eye. His wife leaned on the edge of the tub, her body shaking with mirth.

"I will demand retributions for your insolence later, Your Grace." He snapped the eye shut. "For now, I shall indulge myself."

Her lips were soft against his, and the kiss startled him. Before he could deepen it, she slipped away.

"I shall go in search of your cane, Your Grace. Please do not use this time to concoct some new water sport."

He opened a single eye again. "Bathtub racing? I'm sure it's been done already."

He sank into the water while her laugh faded as she left the room. He allowed himself several moments to simply soak, letting the warm water bring his sadly underused muscles back to life. Then he picked up the soap Mrs. Olds had left and went to work.

It was only minutes later that he dumped the final pitcher of fresh water over his head, rinsing himself of the remaining suds.

Viv was right, however. This really would be easier with a valet. Perhaps it was time he hired one.

Once again relying on his arms for most of his strength, he pushed himself from the tub. He used the stool Mrs. Olds had set the towels on to brace himself while he dried.

Already, he could feel how much improved his leg was. The short walk from the bed and the healing qualities of a hot bath were just the thing. He padded about the room, marveling at the wonder of walking on his own feet. He would never take such a thing for granted again.

He tugged on clothes, fastened buttons, and tied ties, his fingers flying with anticipation.

A small knock came at the door just as he finished tying his cravat. It was rather overdone for the country, but he didn't care. He was rather compelled to look good for his wife on their promenade, even if there was no one there to witness it.

Viv strode in, her hands clutched around a bright purple monstrosity.

"It appears, Your Grace, the only cane in residence was last used in 1796." She held the thing out to him, her smile wicked.

"No man would select such a thing." He backed away from her offering.

"It wasn't a man who selected it, Your Grace. It was the fourth *duchess* who did so."

* * *

OF COURSE, the Rogue Duke could make even the ugliest of walking sticks appear perfectly acceptable.

The gardens were bleak this time of year, but he seemed not to notice or care. He plunged out onto the terrace that bordered this edge of the back gardens, his walking stick clicking against the stones.

He stopped at the edge of the stairs that led down amongst the flower beds, and she paused, watching him. He held his chin high as he drew a deep breath, and she realized this was the first time he'd been out of doors since his fateful trip to see the hops workers' barracks the previous month.

Had it really been so long ago now?

The early spring air had a bite to it that was likely refreshing to him, having been cooped up in the house for so long. She found herself copying him, drawing in a much deeper breath, filling her lungs with the newness of the coming spring.

Calm swept over her as her lungs expanded, and she followed his gaze out to the very end of the gardens where, in summer, the roses disappeared into the rolling fields that led to the sea.

Peace.

She felt peace.

For the first time in four years, the niggling sense of unfinished business no longer plagued her. She studied her husband now, knowing more than ever that she had been wrong.

They had been wrong.

She had believed herself in love, and he had believed they were in a typical society marriage in which both partners did as they pleased. How could they have been so stupid?

Eliza was right. Perhaps it was all a matter of misunderstanding. Words truly were so powerful.

But what did that mean for the future?

When she'd come to Margate, she had only expected to bury her husband. She had prepared herself for widowhood.

She'd never considered what might happen should he live.

That she might get another chance to love him.

"Do you smell that?" he asked now.

She gave the air a good sniff. Margate was quite close to the channel, and the air always carried a slightly musty scent, thick with the tang of salt.

"The ocean?" She tilted her head, wondering what he might be going on about.

He turned, a grin on his lips and a concerning narrowness to his eyes. "Freedom," he whispered.

"Ryder." She did not feel at all guilty at the sternness in her voice as he took the stairs down into the gardens at a mad clip.

She chased after him, picking up her skirts to keep from tripping.

He'd made it to the first small fountain set amongst the

slumbering flower beds and stopped to see if she were following. She paused, catching his watchful gaze.

"Are you going to ensure I keep to the path, Your Grace? I shan't wish to be scolded."

She swallowed at the way he said *scolded,* like he was offering her the chance to lick chocolate from his body.

She put fisted hands to her hips. "I shan't care if you fall into the fountain, Your Grace."

His grin faltered, and if she hadn't been looking at him, she might have missed it. He said nothing further, and instead, turned back in the direction he had been frolicking. She wondered why her mention of the fountain should cause him such grief but trotted after him before he could get much farther ahead of her.

He turned off the main path and onto one of the smaller side paths as he made his way into what, come spring, would be the house vegetable garden. The neat rectangular beds were dark with rich soil, resting until it was time to plant once more.

He had stopped at the head of one such bed, his arms crossed, the walking stick dangling from his fingers.

She came up beside him and followed his gaze to where he studied the quiet garden.

"Do you think Mr. Stoker can convince the other estates to give us some of their hops?"

She was surprised by his question. When they were first married, he'd asked little more of her than the condition of her health and if she thought this ball or that soiree was truly necessary to attend. She was left slightly unbalanced by his talk of something far more important.

"I think if anyone were capable of the feat, it would be Mr. Stoker. He seems to have a manner about him that all but forces one to do his bidding." She pulled her wrap tighter around her shoulders. The afternoon sun did not reach this corner of the garden as it lay too far from the beds, and a chill bit at her arms. "And I would assume he has a reputation in this area as the former hops manager at Margate."

Ryder scratched his chin at this. "I suppose he does."

She nodded. "There you have it. I don't see why there is cause to worry until there is cause to worry."

His laugh was soft. "I've never heard you say that before."

His words hung in the air between them as they both realized why he might not have heard her say it. It wasn't as though they had spent a great deal of time in one another's company over the past several years.

She rubbed her hands together. There was no sense dawdling in the past.

"I say a great many things, Your Grace. I find not everyone listens."

His laugh was richer this time. "That is something on which we can agree."

"Do you mind moving a bit into the sun? It's rather cold over here."

He stirred and set the walking stick to the ground, looking over his shoulder at her as if seeing her for the first time.

"Your Grace, should you like to promenade with me?" he said, a twinkle in his eye that gave her a moment's hesitation.

"Promenade? I hardly see how that's relevant as there's no one here to see us do so."

"You're here," he pointed out. "And I'm here. Isn't that enough?"

She shrugged again. "I suppose it will have to do."

She took his proffered arm, and he led her back into the warm afternoon sun. She turned her face up to it, letting the rays make their way under the rim of her bonnet.

"Ah, that feels rather splendid after so many weeks of ice and rain." She watched him through the flutter of her lashes as she squinted against the light. He, too, had turned his face up to the sky, his features awash in the warm sunshine.

He looked younger.

She could almost see the man she had married in there.

She didn't want to hope. She didn't want to believe that he had changed or maybe he'd just stayed the same and they only realized who they really were just then.

Either way, it caused her a great deal of apprehension. There was so much unknown, but it all would suggest a level of vulnerability she wasn't sure she was ready to accept.

He'd broken her heart. Was she stupid enough to let him do it again?

Was she stupid enough not to give love a second chance?

She gave herself a mental shake.

He'd not said anything of love. He'd spoken of forgiveness and moving on. He'd asked her to stay for reasons she still did not fully know.

But love?

That was her own imagining, and she would do best not to let her mind get carried away. He was still the Rogue Duke, and even if he no longer sought the warm bed of a willing woman, he still sought the thrill of the race and the danger of the chase.

Who was to say he wouldn't leave her when the time came?

She focused on the feel of her arm in his and the heat that radiated from his body. These were the things of the present, and of that, she could be certain.

"I daresay, have we resorted to speaking of the weather? I find myself cringing at the thought."

She laughed. "I hardly meant it like that. I am only remarking that it was a rather deplorable winter, and I am glad to see the other side of it."

"I didn't realize having to spend time with your husband was such a terrible fate."

She elbowed him in the ribs. "You know perfectly well that's not what I meant. Although it wouldn't have been so terrible to not be forced to ride hell for leather across two counties in the rain and ice, but that is a topic for another time."

"You wound me."

"I do no such thing." They drew short as they reached the main garden path once more. "I think you've had enough exercise for one day, wouldn't you agree? It's not as though you should attempt to walk to Canterbury on your first day."

His frown held a hint of resignation. "I suppose I shan't."

He allowed her to turn them back toward the house.

"When must the hops be planted, should Mr. Stoker secure them?" she asked as they made their way back to the house.

"As soon as the ground is ready. Likely sometime in middle to late March, although we could push it as late as April. I should think we would need a sample crop first to test the theory."

"A sample crop?" She had never before believed hops to be very interesting, but Ryder's enthusiasm was catching.

He nodded. "I'll want to grow some for my own brewing to test their quality. I can't attempt to sell something I haven't tried myself."

The statement rang with a sincerity she was coming to expect from him. The thought had that sense of hope ringing once more in her chest, and she swallowed against it.

Just because Ryder was far more mature and sensible than she had believed him to be did not mean he was interested in anything to do with love and commitment.

He stopped at one of the stone benches along the walk and drew her down upon it.

"I don't want to go in just yet," he said, turning his face to the sun.

He looked almost boyish, and her heart swelled at the image.

She tucked her hands into the folds of her wrap.

He must have noticed the gesture because he asked, "Are you cold?" He was already moving to take off his jacket, and she stopped him with a hand.

"Just a bit chilly, but it feels marvelous after the heat of the fires all winter."

He put his arm around her anyway, drawing her against his side. She fell into him, the intimacy of the moment overwhelmed by the domesticity of it. Sharing a bench in the garden on a spring afternoon. Never would she have thought to find herself in such a place. Not with Ryder. And certainly not feeling so at peace with it.

"How is your inventorying of the house going?" he asked.

She glanced briefly up at him. "I hadn't realized you were paying attention."

"You kept flitting into the room with those atrocious dust covers on your sleeves. I wasn't sure if you were cleaning up or preparing for surgery. Either was concerning."

She smiled as she said, "It has gone quite well. The linen cupboards are back to rights as is the silver and china. I should say, Margate may even be prepared to a host a ball come summer."

As soon as the words were out she regretted them. They hadn't spoken of the future. It was supposed to be only them, now, and here for this month alone. She worried very much that she had ruined everything, but if one such silly comment had the power to destroy the peace they had found, then what good was such peace?

"A ball?" He scoffed. "I should think we'd host a house party and do all those obnoxious things like croquet and charades." He looked down at her. "I bet you're diabolical at charades."

She raised an eyebrow. "I could certainly best you if your backgammon prowess is any suggestion."

"She wounds me again," he muttered.

She laughed and pulled away from him, making to stand and take them back to the house to warm up, but he kept his arm snug about her.

"Not yet," he said. "I'm resting."

"You've been in bed for three weeks. What could you possibly be resting for?"

"I have plans for this evening."

Her chest tightened at this. Had he invited guests, knowing the plaster was to be removed?

"Oh?" she asked carefully.

When he looked down at her again, his grin was absolutely naughty.

"I plan to make love to my wife." He leaned down, his lips so close to hers. "A lot," he whispered just before he kissed her.

CHAPTER 14

*H*e would not be a gentleman if he did not keep his promises, and he had every intention of keeping the one he'd made to his wife in the garden that day.

Standing in front of the windows of his bedchamber, he was afforded a view he had not seen in the two months he'd been recovering in the same room. The rear gardens stretched down and away from the house as though someone had unrolled a carpet from the terrace steps.

The thing that bothered him about the hops was the fact of the sample harvest. He couldn't ask a tenant to give up precious land for the experiment. His tenants desperately needed the money their fields brought to support their families. He'd never ask them to give it up.

So how was he to test his theory should Mr. Stoker secure the samples?

His thoughts were interrupted when the connecting door opened. He turned, a smile already on his lips that vanished at the sight of his wife.

She wore a robe of blue silk that turned her hair more gold than red as it hung loose around her shoulders, and it was as if he were seeing her for the first time. Her feet were bare, and he found himself absurdly fascinated with how they looked against the Aubusson carpet.

Her return smile was soft and knowing. "I believe a statement was made earlier, Your Grace. A statement that requires verification at this time."

The bold accusation required a pithy retort, but he found himself swallowing around a sudden lump in his throat.

"You're beautiful," he breathed.

Her smile faded, and she looked nervously at the floor. He strode over to her and using two fingers under her chin, lifted her gaze to his.

"Don't hide from me, wife," he growled playfully and leaned down for a swift kiss. "Now was this statement something of a grandiose nature?"

"Most grandiose," she said as if they were discussing a subject of some gravity.

He stepped back to survey her. "And are you prepared to see this investigation through?"

Instead of answering him, she reached for the tie of her robe and in a single tug, the sash fell free, the edges of the robe separating.

He sucked in a breath. "Your Grace, I believe you've forgotten your clothing."

Her smile turned devilish as she shrugged the robe from her shoulders, and it fell to her feet in a pool of blue silk.

He swallowed, sending a silent prayer to any god that might be listening to save him from his wife for clearly she was a siren of mythic lore.

She stood before him completely naked, and he couldn't stop himself from running his eyes up her long legs to the soft roundness of her stomach, the heavy globes of her breasts, the delicate lines of her collarbones, the full lips and arched cheekbones.

She really was beautiful.

But it wasn't her beauty that struck him. It was her boldness, her confidence. He'd had lovers. Not as many as his reputation had claimed, but it was still enough, and never had a woman been so sure of herself to present her body as the wonder that it was.

He knew he should have swept her off her feet just then, carried her to bed, and ravished her, but he needed to tell her something first.

"Vivianna Darby," he said, taking her hands in his as her smile vanished and a slightly wary note came to her eyes. "Do you know why I asked you to marry me?"

She swallowed and shook her head.

"You were the only debutante brave enough to speak to me." He laughed, recalling that season so long ago, the stuffy ballroom and the line of debutantes that looked as fragile as porcelain dolls. "Your aunt introduced us and told me to waltz with you. Do you remember?"

Her lips parted slightly as she studied his face, but she remained silent, watching him.

"And you said you hoped I was as good a dancer as the lover my reputation suggested."

Her face flushed at his words, and she dropped her gaze again.

"Viv." He nudged her chin up once more. When her eyes finally met his, he said, "I'm lucky you're so brazen or I wouldn't be standing here right now. With you."

Even though he had spoken the words, their truth rocked him.

He was lucky to be standing there. He was lucky to have her as his wife. Why had it taken him so long to see it?

She blinked, her lips opening on a soundless word, and he didn't hesitate. He bent and scooped her into his arms and carried her to the bed. He laid her down gently, letting his hands slip slowly over her body as he released her.

He wasted no time in shedding his own clothes before returning to the bed. He stretched out next to her and pulled her into his arms.

"Do you know what I'm most looking forward to?" he whispered, stroking the line of her cheek.

She smiled. "What would that be, Your Grace?"

"Being on top."

He smothered her laugh with a kiss, capturing her mouth with all that he had. He traced the outline of her lips with his tongue before nibbling softly at the corner of her mouth.

Not wishing to waste a moment, he pivoted, rolling her beneath him so he came above her on his elbows. He grinned down at her.

"Yes, this is most exquisite," he said as he cast his gaze down the length of her.

Her fingers dug into his shoulders. "Are you just going to look or are you going to do something, Your Grace?"

"You're rather saucy. Has anyone told you thus?"

"Only you." She pulled his head down but instead of kissing him, she arched her head to give him access to her neck.

Who was he to refuse to her? He kissed and licked his way down her neck to her collarbone to her breasts. God, she had amazing breasts. They filled his hands, and their nipples formed yearning peaks ready for his mouth. He sucked one, lapping at the stiffened peak until she came up off the mattress.

"Oh God, Ryder," she moaned.

He released her only to carve his way lower, sampling as he went until he reached the soft pale skin of her inner thigh. He ran his hands down her legs, marveling at the softness of her skin, at the way her knees involuntarily came together as though she was unable to endure.

"So beautiful," he whispered as he traced the line of her knee.

He looked up and found her watching him, pure anticipation in her gaze.

He smiled just before he dipped his head and placed his mouth against her hot core. She bucked, pushing her mound into him, but he only continued his assault, his tongue insistent against her sensitive nub.

"Oh, Ryder," she cried, and he grabbed her hips in both hands, trying to hold her still.

Her fingernails bit into his shoulders, and he groaned against her, his body straining with desire. He sucked and nibbled until she writhed, her hips pushing against the cage of his hands. His arousal throbbed, aching to be inside her, to feel her pulsing around him, but he wanted to give her this first, needed to give her pleasure before taking his own.

As she climaxed, her hips came entirely off the mattress, and she dug her fingers into his scalp, holding him against her. When she collapsed, her hands falling to her sides, he came up and in one swift motion entered her.

She cried out, her eyes flying open, her hands reaching for him.

"Easy, my brazen siren. I've got you," he whispered against her lips.

He pushed inside of her, filling her until her muscles contracted around him. He moaned her name and withdrew only to slam into her again. Her legs came around his hips, and she stroked her hands down his back.

He leaned his forehead against hers, struggling for breath.

"My God, woman, I believe you will be my destruction."

"That is not my intent, I assure you," she said as she

moved her hips, matching his thrusts so he went deeper inside her.

He groaned and pumped into her faster and harder.

"Ryder." Her voice was pleading now, and he bent his head, kissing her with a ferocity he hadn't known.

"Tell me what you want," he breathed, sliding in and out of her. "Tell me."

She shook her head against the pillows, her hair crackling like fire.

"I want you," she groaned.

He pumped hard into her. "Tell me. What do you want me to do?"

"I want…" she gasped, her words trailing away. "I want…"

He sat up, pulling her with him, and her legs tightened around his hips. Her eyes flew open, startled, as she brushed the hair from her face.

"Take it," he said and leaned back on his hands, so she fit snugly against him.

"But you wanted—"

"I want to give you pleasure, my darling," he said, thrusting softly against her. "Now take it."

She hesitated for a moment before positioning her hands against his shoulders. When she began to move, he felt his strength dwindle by half. He couldn't take much more of this, but God, he wanted it all.

She lifted her hips and sank so slowly against him. He held his breath, watching and gritting his teeth against his building climax. He wanted this to go on forever. He never wanted to let her go.

"Ryder." The pressure must have been building for her, too, because now she slammed into him, lifting her hips up to drive harder against him.

Her breasts bounced, full and magnificent, and she threw her head back, his bold, beautiful siren.

When she came it was like an explosion around him, and his own climax ripped through him without mercy. He sank against the bed, pulling her with him until she sprawled across his chest.

His muscles had turned to water, and his heart thundered in his chest.

He could feel her heart beating against him, and her breath came in fitful gasps against his chest.

It was some time before she slid off him, coming up on her elbow to lean over him.

He had thought her beautiful before, but as she leaned over him, her wild hair creating a cocoon around them, he was lost.

"I have learned my lesson, Your Grace," she said as she traced circles on his chest.

"What lesson is that?"

Her smile lifted on one side. "I shall never again accuse you of being boastful."

He growled as he rolled her into his arms, coming above her.

"See that you don't, wife." He kissed her before she could scold him.

* * *

It was easy to fall under the spell of routine after that.

Their days were filled with walks in the garden while he exercised his leg, his strength growing every day. Their nights were filled with passionate lovemaking.

She knew she should have guarded her heart against it. She knew she should have been reasonable. She should have asked questions and demanded answers.

But it was easier to simply love him.

And she did.

Love him.

She loved him. Whether it was again or for the first time, she'd never know.

The first of March came and went, and she knew she must return to London. She had responsibilities waiting for her there, but she never seemed to gather the strength to address them.

Ryder walked with the fluid assurance she remembered now, long strides with his head held high. The cane did little to deter him. He took in the gardens around them, his eyes scanning the trees as if searching for the first signs of spring.

"I never realized before how much these trees block the view of the gardens from the house when they're full."

"You've spent a great deal of time looking out those windows when you've never done so before now."

"I shall ask the gardener to see them properly trimmed in time."

The comment gave her pause, and she found her step slowed unconsciously. "Will you be here to see them when their branches are heavy with green leaves?"

He looked at her sharply. "I should think so. Why ever would I not?"

She stopped and turned to face him.

"Well, it's just that in these past few weeks you've never failed to remind me of what I should do come March, but you've failed to mention your own intentions."

While her wording was sterile in its politeness, she knew he understood her much deeper meaning as his eyes shifted away from her face.

His gaze drifted to the far end of the gardens where the manicured spaces melted into the wildness of the fields that tumbled ever closer to the edge of the sea.

She didn't think he would answer her, and she turned to

continue their walk, but then he stopped her with a hand on her arm.

"I should like to see the hops crop planted with new strands. Margate land was meant for hops, and I know if we can only produce the finest quality, I can attract the kind of clientele that will desire them."

He spoke with such a passion she could hardly believe it was the Rogue Duke who stood beside her.

"What of your racing? Your fellow competitors are sure to miss you."

He laughed. "I hardly think so. It matters not who they race against, only that they feel the thrill of the competition."

His voice held a note of derision that surprised her.

"But you've never stayed at Margate for very long."

Again, she couched her words in politeness, but he knew very well what she meant.

The Rogue Duke's reputation required him to traipse from house party to house party, from one widow's bed to that of a lonely wife.

She swallowed, afraid she might be suddenly sick at the thought.

She hadn't been fooling herself the past several weeks. She knew very well that he was giving of his body but not of his mind or heart. She would take what he offered. Not because she thought herself deserving of so little, but rather because she was trapped.

She was trapped in this marriage, yes, but it was more than that.

She was trapped in her love for him.

For try as she might, she could not deny it. She'd loved him then, and she loved him still, but it was different now. It wasn't a boisterous thing. It wasn't a thing of trumpets and heralding. It was something quiet, something born of a shared history.

As she stood beside him now, she could see that.

When she had married him, she'd been in young love, the blush of a first romance. Only it hadn't been love. Not really. She had been infatuated with the idea of him when she had never bothered to see the reality of him.

Now that she knew the truth of him, her love grew deeper and more complex, more unyielding.

The way his first words upon waking from the accident were not for himself but for his horses. The way he lit up with memory when speaking with the Stokers. The way he held her in the cold of the night.

The way he asked for her forgiveness.

She blinked, looking away from him as tears threatened her eyes.

But he put a hand to her chin, turning her back to him.

His eyes were solemn as he said, "What are you really asking, Viv?"

She held his gaze for what seemed like an eternity but what must have been not more than a breath. She couldn't find the words. The whispers of the *ton* came back to her in a flurry, and instead of the gentle spring breeze, she could only hear their recriminations.

Bold.

Brash.

Too much.

She was too much surely.

Hadn't he pointed it out himself? What woman—what *lady*—would ride horseback across the icy English roads to get to her husband's side in his time of need?

She might have been born beautiful and titled, but she was not born a lady.

The familiar pain spread through her, robbing her of air and words. She pulled her chin from his grasp, forcing a smile to her lips.

"It's exactly as I said." She nodded back in the direction of the house. "You've never stayed long at Margate. I should think there are a great many things that require your attention."

She took a step as though to move them once more along the garden path, but he stopped her again with a hand on her arm.

"Like my marriage requires my attention."

His forthright words struck her deep in the chest, and the tears burned at her eyes anew.

"Your marriage?" She felt herself backing away from him, afraid and yet yearning for what he might say.

He let her go, and she stumbled against a bench set along the garden path. She sank, her legs no longer able to hold her up. The wind held a bit of a chill for early spring, and the stone of the bench was cold against the backs of her legs.

But she felt none of it.

She stared at Ryder as he studied her, his gaze so intense, her fate lying in his hands. He moved over to her, taking a seat beside her.

She couldn't bear to look at him. Would he tell her to leave? That he'd changed his mind and she wasn't for him after all? He would go back to his lovers?

For weeks now she had managed not to think of the writer of the letters, but now those haunting words came sailing back to her.

And then he took her hand.

It was such a simple gesture, and she stared down where their fingers intertwined on her knee.

"Viv, I will spend the rest of my life apologizing to you for what I did, and I can never hope that it will be enough."

She looked at him, the tears brimming in her eyes. "It is enough," she said, her voice raspy with emotion, and she swallowed, willing herself to stay composed. "It is enough,

Ryder. We were young, and we both had ideas of what a marriage meant. Our only mistake was in not speaking to the other about them."

He cleared his throat, and she wondered at what emotion gripped him as well. She'd never seen him so overcome before. Her heart picked up pace, and for one silly moment, hope soared through her.

But she reminded herself that it was March. He knew as well as she that her time here was coming to an end. Might he be feeling the urgency of it as well?

"I wish I could feel the same as you do, but I think I should always carry some guilt with me." He turned his gaze to her now. "I will never forgive myself for hurting you."

The sincerity in his voice had her stomach clenching. Surely if he felt that way, he must feel...other things as well.

She squeezed his hand. "You mustn't, Ryder. It's in the past, and we know better now than to assume what the other might be thinking or feeling. Have the past few weeks shown you nothing?"

He laughed. "The past few weeks have shown me entirely too much." His eyes turned dark, and she wondered what he was thinking.

Had she been too bold? Had she taken too much? Her face warmed with memories of the past weeks. The way his naked body felt against hers, the way his mouth could—

"My duchess, are you thinking unholy thoughts?"

She eyed him. "Only because you suggested it."

He plucked his hand from hers only to wrap his arm around her and draw her against his side. "I can suggest a great many things," he murmured before pressing his lips to hers.

His kiss was soft and exploring, and even when she thought she knew every bit of his kiss, she found it somehow different, found something new to enjoy and discover.

She wanted this. Always. She wanted the chance to keep discovering him, to keep learning him. She wanted a chance at a life with him.

When he pulled away, she let her eyes flutter open at the last possible moment, wanting to hold onto his kiss for as long as possible. To remember the feel of the sun on her cheeks, the way the breeze lifted the edge of her wrap. The way he smelled of the soap Mrs. Olds made, and the way the stubble of his chin brushed against her cheek when his lips trailed over her skin.

She wanted to remember all of it, because somehow, painfully, she knew he was about to tell her goodbye.

"Stay."

The word had her eyes popping open, her world shifting on its axis. She put a hand out, the cold of the bench beside her traveling straight through her thin gloves.

"What?" She studied his face, her eyes searching.

Had he just asked her to stay?

He had said the same numerous times in recent weeks, but this time it was different. The tone of his voice was firm and unyielding and at the same time, it held a note of pleading. He wasn't asking her to stay to help him recover.

He was asking her to stay.

Forever.

"Stay with me," he said, his voice growing more urgent. "Stay with me here. At Margate." He reached up and cupped her face, running his thumb along the arch of her cheek so she tilted her head into the warmth of his palm without thinking.

"I want you by my side as we resurrect Margate. I want you to be with me. Forever." His voice changed on the last word, and in it, she heard years of regret. Of time missed. Of things sacrificed. Of things never before known.

But what she saw in his eyes broke her.

This was not the Rogue Duke she had prepared herself to face. This was Ryder, her husband.

She'd been wrong about so many things. They had been wrong together, and now they were faced with a chance to change it all.

She had changed, and she knew Ryder had, too. She could tell in the way he longed for something else, for something permanent and steady. He had said it himself. The parties no longer held the allure they might once have, the races no longer a pull.

It was truly happening.

Her very future was coming true, and it was sitting right beside her. Her smile came first, slow and almost disbelieving, and then she threw her arms around his neck and held on, kissing him over and over again.

"Yes," she said between kisses. "Yes, I'll stay. Of course I'll stay."

A hint of a smile curved his lips, almost as if he didn't quite believe she had said *yes*, and a rush of words came all at once as if she might convince him.

"I thought I was too brash, that I was too bold. The ladies of the *ton*, they would whisper about how I was odd, far too brazen to be a true duchess. But—"

She was rambling, and her words made no sense to anyone but her, but it didn't matter. Everything rushed from her in a single stream of suddenly released emotions.

She would have time to think of it later, so very much time, but she thought just then it was because she was overwhelmed with a rainbow of emotions.

But then she said the very thing that could still hurt her.

"I love you," she whispered.

CHAPTER 15

I *love you.*

She may have whispered it, but he heard her clearly nonetheless.

I love you.

The words played over and over in his head, and he wondered if they would replace the litany that had tormented him until then.

You hurt me.

He supposed he could only hurt her if she did love him.

In that moment, he wished himself the cad she had thought him, the Rogue Duke society had always believed.

But instead, he was just a man. A man who might one day love the woman in his arms. He didn't know. He'd never considered love. He'd never witnessed anyone in love. He knew nothing of it, but he did know the feeling her words carried was foreign to him.

While he might suspect he could love her, he knew for certain he could not trap her with the emotion.

He eased her from his arms and stood, pacing several steps away from the bench.

"Ryder." Her voice had gone weak and wondering, tinged with a worry she did not know was warranted.

He was a few feet away when he realized he'd left that horrid cane abandoned against the bench where she still sat, and his right leg wobbled beneath him.

"Viv, I must tell you something."

He hated himself for not being able to look her in the eye. A visceral pain started in his chest and began to spread. It numbed him until it was all he could do to speak.

"Remember when I told you why I was heading to London when I crashed the phaeton?" He did look up now. "I was going for you. Do you remember?"

She nodded and gave that soft tremulous smile. "Of course. Ryder, what is it? What is this about?"

He wished he did have the cane now, something he could hold in his hands to distract him from what he was about to do.

Namely, break her heart for the second time.

He squared his shoulders. She deserved the truth, not to be trapped in some lie.

"I was going after you because…" His throat closed on the words.

She stood and came to him, catching his hands in hers.

"It's all right now, Ryder. I understand. It all makes sense. Why you would want me to stay. You wanted to—"

He couldn't bear to hear it. He couldn't stand to know just how effective his scheming had been.

"Viv, it wasn't love."

The words shot out of him more forcefully than he had meant them to, and she dropped his hands. It was that moment that he'd remember. The moment she let go.

"What?" She took a step back, her eyes wide, her lips slightly parted.

"I've had this feeling." He'd never described the restlessness before, and now he struggled to name it. "It's a sort of unease, like I was missing something or something wasn't right."

She took another step back, and he reached for her, his hands finding nothing but air.

"I didn't know what to do, and I thought if only I could get to you, you would make the feeling go away."

She shook her head. "What do you mean?" Her voice had gone cold and steely, and he knew her defenses were back up.

That more than anything he felt, almost as if he'd been plunged into icy water and he'd been forced to watch it close over his head.

"I don't know," he said, his hands still reaching into nothingness. "I don't know. I just knew I had to stop it. I had to stop the feeling from consuming me, and I thought the only person strong enough to stop it was you."

This, he realized too late, was the absolutely wrong thing to say.

Her eyes flashed, and the hurt he had seen there was replaced with anger.

"Strong enough?" she repeated. "You mean you think me headstrong? Someone manly and controlling? Someone bossy enough to expel a...what did you call it? An unease?" She scoffed. "I should think one of your whores would be sufficient enough to settle any of your woes, Your Grace."

The words struck him. Not for their meaning, but that she would still think of him like that. But he deserved it. He deserved it for always doing this to her, always tormenting her, always playing some kind of vicious game with her emotions.

She didn't deserve this. She didn't deserve him.

The thought spiraled through him, and he thought he might be sick.

Never had he ever considered himself unworthy of another, but just then he did.

Because if there was one person who deserved more than anything he had to offer, it was Viv.

And he had to let her go.

He folded his hands in front of him and gave away everything he wanted, only to save the one he cared about most. "I shall keep your words in mind for the future."

It was as though he had slapped her, and he hated himself with a vileness he'd never before experienced.

He was the worst kind of creature, and it was all he could do to maintain a vacant expression as she backed away, her eyes glassy with tears.

"See that you do." She turned on her heel and with careful measured strides disappeared along the garden path in the direction of the house.

He waited until she was out of sight to stumble back to the bench where she had declared her love for him. His right leg gave out before he got to it, and he fell more than sat down. He didn't cry. He didn't lament and didn't rue. He was numb, utterly and completely. There was no restlessness. Far greater and more vital emotions were there to overrun any unease he might have felt.

He wasn't sure how long he sat there, but the sun had dipped low in the western sky before Mrs. Olds approached him, her arms full of a wool blanket.

"She's gone, Your Grace," was all that she said as she laid the blanket next to him on the bench and slipped away.

* * *

THE HOUSE WAS QUIETER NOW than the last time she'd run home.

Eliza and Louisa were gone, ensconced in homes of their own with husbands who loved them. Just as Viv had wanted.

The thought hadn't been so painful before she'd gone to Margate. Before it had given her happiness, even if it had been tinged with her own regrets.

Now her heart hurt too much for it to be anything else.

Jo had greeted her with a frown and a mutter about needing to write a letter. The fact that her other sisters had arrived within the hour of Jo's muttering was not at all a surprise to her.

Louisa had strode in as though she were not about to give birth any day now and demanded to know what Margate had done. Eliza had been much more circumspect and had merely asked if Ryder were alive and doing well.

She'd written to them, of course, while she had been away, but they wanted to hear the whole of the tale again from her own lips.

It had been an exhausting day, but it had been a balm to her heart to see her sisters again.

She'd gone to bed that night and allowed exhaustion to take her. She'd slept the kind of hard sleep that only a body on the edge could muster.

She stumbled through her first few days home. Samuels helped her to unpack and sort through the invitations that had already arrived. By the following week, it almost felt normal again.

"We'll want the ball to be one of the first of the season. It's still rather early, but that works in our favor. We'll have time to get new gowns made for you and plan the guest list. We'll want to be exclusive in our invitations."

Jo sighed and sank back against the cushions of the sofa in the drawing room. "I don't see the reason for such fuss. It's not as though this is to be my first season."

Viv set down the invitations they'd received in that day's

post. "That's precisely why we should cause such a fuss, as you put it. You'll have been out for three seasons now, Jo, and you haven't secured a husband."

Her little sister slid her a none-too-thrilled glance. "I am well aware of the fact, dear sister. It's not as though I have failed to notice my lack of a husband."

Viv frowned. "You know it's only that I want the best for you."

Jo dropped her feet to the floor from where she'd hung them over the arm of the sofa. No matter how Viv had told her to sit up and act the lady, Jo never seemed to listen.

"Have you ever thought, dear sister, that what you think is best for me is not really best at all?"

Viv was growing tired of people telling her what to think. "You must trust me on this, Jo. I do know what's best."

Jo turned to the chair set just outside the seating arrangement. "Do you hear her? Will you allow her to direct me about like this?"

Her brother, Andrew, did not look up from where he'd plopped himself an hour previous, the letter he was reading perched between his hands.

Viv sat back and folded her arms across her stomach. "He agrees with me."

"He made no sound. You cannot claim he agrees with you."

They both looked to Andrew who was still fastidiously reading.

"Do you think he's finally done it?" Jo muttered.

"Do you mean has he finally accomplished the art of completely ignoring us?"

"Yes, that." They were both leaning close now over the low table that separated them as they peered at their brother.

Viv realized with a jolt that she'd done exactly what she'd set out to accomplish. She'd married off all but one of her sisters. Soon Andrew would have the house to himself, and he could find his own duchess.

The thought saddened her at the same time it bolstered her.

That was the way things should be. It was about time for Andrew to find his bride. He deserved nothing less. He'd taken exquisite care of his sisters after their father's death. It was his turn now to have someone to care for him.

The thought stabbed her, and she swallowed to stop herself from choking. When Andrew married, she would be forced to find residence in one of the Margate homes. She would be forced to confer with Ryder to ensure they didn't accidentally occupy the same place. How terrible it would be for him to suffer the presence of his wife.

"Are you thinking of finding a wife for Andrew?"

Viv sat up straight in a flash. "Whatever do you mean?"

Jo raised an eyebrow as she crossed her arms just under her bosom. "Well, if it isn't so. You *are* thinking of finding a wife for Andrew." She slid a glance in their brother's direction. "And here I believed only we sisters would be subject to your ministrations."

Viv set down the invitations on the table between them. "Do not think anyone in this family is immune to my care, sister."

"Care?" Jo gave an unladylike snort. "More like demands."

"Call it what you will, but I shall see you happy."

Jo leaned forward, her eyes suddenly earnest. "But are you happy, Viv?"

She'd been about to say *yes* when the word caught in her throat. In her mind, the previous two months flashed past like a horrid carousel, reminding her of what she'd had, of what she'd believed, of what had turned out to be all a lie.

"I shall be," she said instead, and the words seemed to surprise her sister as the concern cleared from Jo's face.

Viv picked up the letters that had also come in the post and shuffled through them.

"What will make you happy?" Jo asked, her tone wondering now.

Viv might be with child.

She couldn't be certain, not for another few days, but she thought if she wished fervently enough, it might come true. She'd given it ample opportunity to occur. Now she had only to allow nature to take its course.

But even if she found she were not pregnant, there was more to her life now, she knew. She would no longer wait on the periphery, pining after a husband she had once believed herself in love with.

She would no longer listen to the rumors that filtered through the *ton* about her either. She was so very tired of it all. The past two months had taught her that while her personality may be left wanting, her body was not. She was perfectly capable of pleasuring a man, and she wasn't about to live out the rest of her life celibate.

The thought had her stomach turning, bile rising in her throat.

She swallowed it down. If Ryder could take lovers, so could she. After all, wasn't she one of the lonely wives she knew he liked?

Only he didn't like her. He'd made that clear. She was nothing more than a distraction to him. Well, she hoped he'd gotten what he wanted. She pressed a hand to her stomach. Because hopefully, she'd gotten what she wanted as well.

"Seeing you married," she said truthfully now.

Jo scoffed and got to her feet and made her way over to the piano, shuffling through the music discarded on its bench.

Andrew had finally looked up as Jo had passed him.

"What is this about a ball?"

"We must host one of the first balls of the season to properly present Jo," Viv answered.

"Present Jo?" He frowned. "Isn't this her fifth time out?"

Jo set down the piano music with a huff. "I beg your pardon. I am not that old, dear brother."

Andrew shook his head. "It was not meant as a slight, sister. I am only mentioning the confusion I have fallen under, having so many sisters underfoot."

Viv felt a stab of guilt. Not for the first time had she come running back to Ravenwood House when, under most circumstances, she should have truly been settled into her own household by now.

"I should think it better now that Eliza and Louisa have married," Viv offered.

Andrew looked about as though confused. "Eliza and Louisa have married? I hadn't noticed." He grinned as he picked up the letter he'd been reading, his attention fully diverted to the script.

"Andrew?" Viv called, attempting to pull back his focus.

Andrew was not one to receive weighty letters. Nothing more than the standard missive meant to conduct business. This letter, however, had clearly gone on for more than two pages.

It took Jo poking him in the shoulder for him to look up again.

"That letter is awfully intriguing." She pointed at the paper in hands.

"Mmm," Andrew said. "It's from Ben." His eyes drifted back down to the letter.

Had she not been watching so carefully, Viv would have missed how Jo stilled at the mention of Andrew's closest childhood friend.

"How is Ben? I trust he's finding America to his liking. Where is he again?"

Andrew made another noise. "Boston, but that's just the reason for this letter."

"What is?" Viv prompted when Andrew did not continue.

Finally, he set down the letter against his bent knee.

"Ben's brother died last month."

"The duke?" Viv said. "I didn't hear anything of it."

"You wouldn't have in Margate, but it was quite the gossip for several weeks. The rumor is that his lover pushed him down the stairs, and he broke his neck."

Viv glanced at Jo. "Really, Andrew."

Jo glanced at the two of them. "I've already heard the rumors, Viv. You were gone a very long time."

Viv sat back on the sofa. "I'm terribly sorry to hear it."

"Well, Ben must come back to settle the estate he's inherited."

Jo dropped the music she was leafing through and bent, scrambling to put it back to rights.

Viv eyed her even as she spoke to Andrew. "It's hard to think of the boy who chased me with frogs as being a duke now. Even though the circumstances could be improved, it will be nice to see Ben again. How many years has it been since he was wed? I think that's the last time we saw him, wasn't it? Right before he left for Boston?"

"I can't remember that, honestly. It was so long ago now."

"Five." The single word shot through the drawing room and brought Andrew to the edge of his seat to look back at his little sister where she stood at the piano slightly behind him. She shuffled piano music into a neat pile. "Ben has been gone five years."

Viv raised an eyebrow as she caught Andrew's attention.

"Does he say when he's due to arrive?" Viv asked.

Andrew picked up the letter. "That's just it actually. He was writing to say he's been delayed. Minerva succumbed to consumption."

Jo knocked the metronome from the piano. In a resounding crash, it hit the instrument's string box on the way down, sending a vibrating echo through the small room.

Viv did not move, a knowing eye on her sister as Andrew stood from his chair.

"I...I..." Jo stammered. "I'm terribly sorry. I just remembered I have an appointment." She scurried from the room.

Andrew turned, his brow wrinkled in confusion. "Whatever was that about?"

Viv stood and brushed her hands down her skirt. "I think it will not be long before you have the house to yourself, dear brother," she said by way of an answer.

CHAPTER 16

"*I*sn't it a little early to be imbibing?"

Ryder wasn't sure whether or not he was surprised when Daniel sat down next to him on the garden bench with two dark glass bottles and a long, thin parcel. It had been over a fortnight since Viv had left, and he'd done little more than walk out to the bench, sit, and let the restlessness consume him.

Only it didn't.

He'd spent so much time running from it, he'd never thought to wonder what might happen if he just stopped.

He was surprised to find nothing did, in fact, happen.

The restlessness was there; he could sense it just off the horizon. But it wasn't the endless clawing he had felt for more than a year. It was almost as if he'd very nearly figured something out.

Only...what was it?

If it was Viv, he was damned unlucky, because he'd gone and let her go. No, worse than that—he'd driven her away.

He sometimes liked to think of her in London and

pretend she was happy. He'd done what was best, so why didn't he feel better about it?

"I know you pretend to be a rogue and all that suggests, but I know you are secretly a kind and caring person." With the parcel in his lap, Daniel set the bottles on the ground so he could tuck his hands into his coat pockets as the day was bright but chilly.

"Dear God, have you started without me?" Ryder eyed the two large bottles at Daniel's feet.

"I also know you know the name of each and every one of your servants."

Ryder raised an eyebrow and looked his friend in the face for the first time. "What is this about?"

"I'm courting Sarah Walker."

Ryder leaned back and clutched a dramatic hand to his chest.

"My upstairs maid? Well, why on this earth are you doing that? You're going to put me in a position which will require me to find a new upstairs maid, aren't you?" Ryder shook his head. "Mrs. Olds will not be pleased."

Daniel laughed. "I don't find I care very much for Mrs. Olds's thoughts on the subject."

"So my servants are spreading rumors that I've turned into a brooding monster, is that it?"

Daniel frowned. "Your servants care about you and have confided your recent state of affairs to a friend who they felt might be able to help you."

Ryder's chest twisted uneasily as gratitude welled up inside of him. He'd forgotten what it was like to have friends. He tapped the long, thin parcel Daniel still held in his lap.

"And this?"

Without ceremony, Daniel lifted the lid from the parcel revealing a bed of midnight blue velvet on top of which was nestled the finest cane Ryder had ever seen.

"My father carved the shaft. He's picked up a bit of a hobby with wood since leaving the estate. But I inserted a core of steel, so it's light yet strong." He lifted the cane from the box deftly with two fingers as if it weighed nothing at all. He spun it in the air to give Ryder the top.

Ryder could only stare for several seconds. He had seen many fine things in his travels. Exquisite, unique items crafted lovingly by skilled artisans. But he had never seen anything like this.

The top of the cane was a ball of polished jet set on a crown of molded silver that extended down the top of the cane by a couple of inches. But there was a break in the silver cuff where a small strip of steel wrapped around like a band.

Ryder took the cane and tilted it so he could see the band better.

"It's from your phaeton."

Ryder looked up sharply, eyeing his friend.

"They brought the wreckage back for salvage, and this piece came from one of the wheels." Daniel tapped the slim band of steel. "I thought perhaps you might wish for something on which to reflect from this time in your life."

Ryder had no words, so he traced the lines of the silver-work as it wound its way to the ball of jet. Finally, he took the cane in both of his hands, setting the bottom to the ground.

"Thank you." The words came out softer than he had intended, but his throat had closed itself against further speech.

They sat like that for several minutes. The sound of the wind whistling through the budding trees, the scamper of some woodland creature, and the call of the sea birds along the coast the only sound. If he drew a deep enough breath, he could almost smell the ocean from here.

Almost.

"Why did you let her go, mate?" Daniel finally said, his voice crisp with concern.

Ryder palmed the cane.

"It was the right thing to do," he decided to say.

"It was the right thing to do?" Daniel laughed. "If it were the right thing, why do you look as though I've forced you to drive a coach and four?"

Ryder looked up from the cane. "I've driven a coach and four. I don't recommend it. Do you realize how tedious those things can be?"

"They are not meant to be raced." Daniel's eyebrows went up in concern.

Ryder could only smirk. "Everything can be raced. It's only a matter of imagination."

"Dear God, I'm starting to see how it *was* for the best."

What little elation he had managed at seeing the cane his friend had made for him vanished at the reminder of Viv's absence.

Daniel placed a hand on his shoulder. "I'm sorry, mate. I truly am. Are you sure there's no hope of making amends?"

Ryder cut him a glance. "Why do you think I must make amends? Perhaps she's the one who's done something wrong."

Daniel shook his head. "Sarah became quite close with your wife's lady's maid while she was here. They've even taken to exchanging letters. I hear there's to be a ball in London tonight for the youngest sister's season. Quite a big to-do from what I hear. You would not look like this if you were not drowning in your own guilt, and your lady wife wouldn't be throwing a ball."

"I'll have you know I look remarkably well today. I've even dressed myself." He brushed the front of his jacket as if to emphasize his point.

So Viv had already put together a ball for Jo. He wasn't

surprised by her efficiency, and he couldn't help the smile the thought brought to his lips.

Daniel's face fell. "Does that mean you haven't always been getting out of bed?"

Ryder shrugged. "What's the point?"

Daniel set aside the bottom of the cane box and crossed his arms. "I should say there's many points. You've got Margate to care for and the hops to—"

"The ruined hops?" Ryder scratched the back of his neck in irritation. "I'll be lucky if I'm ever able to bring them back." He stared off in the distance as if seeing the hops fields before him.

Daniel followed his line of sight before saying, "Tell me the truth, friend. What happened? Surely there can be a way to make it all right."

"She's in love, Daniel." Hearing himself say the words sent a pang through his chest, and Ryder rubbed at the spot as if to make it stop.

Daniel sucked in a breath. "She told you that? That she loves another man?"

"No, you daft idiot. She's in love with me."

Daniel canted his head. "I'm afraid I fail to see how this is an issue."

Ryder pushed to his feet, using the cane to help him stand. His newly healed leg was getting stronger every day, but he felt more confident having the support under his hand. And it was a good deal more manly than that purple monstrosity he'd been sacked with.

"Because I don't love her in return." The words sliced through him, and he staggered, clutching the top of the cane. He whirled to face his friend still on the bench. "I trapped her here with my injury as an excuse. I thought—" He swallowed. "I thought she could distract me from the horrible sense that I've accomplished nothing in my life." He stepped forward, his earnestness driving him. "I had to let her go. I couldn't pretend to feel something I don't, and I couldn't keep her here because she believed my lies."

Daniel blinked. "You seduced her."

He crossed his arms over his chest, but he couldn't say anything more as Daniel seemed to work out the rest.

"You seduced her for your own reasons and then found yourself in love." He shook his head. "No wonder you're in a terrible state."

Ryder blinked. "I beg your pardon."

Daniel smiled. "Of course you love her. If you didn't, you wouldn't be feeling this way right now."

Ryder shook his head. "You don't understand. It's not love that I feel. I was merely—"

Lying to himself?

The restlessness that he sometimes went days without feeling now. The restlessness that he forgot for hours at a time. The restlessness that he knew he was so very close to solving.

Without Viv.

Viv wasn't the answer to his restlessness. She wasn't a distraction at all.

She had been…well, what really?

He sat back down, his mind awash with thoughts that refused to fit together.

"You were merely what?" Daniel prompted.

But Ryder could only shake his head. "I don't know."

He cast his mind back on those first days when he felt the restlessness eating at him. Every day he heard news of a man making a mark on this world, and every day he raced another race, drank another drink, bedded another woman.

But not anymore.

And Viv had nothing to do with it.

He looked down at Daniel's feet where he'd set the dark bottles.

"Did you bring that for looks or for drinking?"

Daniel bent and picked up one of the bottles. "I thought you said it was too early."

Ryder reached for the bottle and, bracing the cane between his knees, used both hands to pry loose the metal bands that held the lid tightly to the neck. He put the bottle to his lips and tilted his head back for a long, deep swallow.

He let the ale run down his throat in great, refreshing gulps until the taste flooded his mouth and hit his senses. He pulled the bottle away with a cough, staring at it.

"Hell's teeth, Daniel. Where did you get this?"

Daniel stared at the second bottle he now held in his hand. "I made it. Why? Has it gone off?"

Ryder placed a hand on his friend's arm. "You made this?"

Daniel nodded. "Yes, of course."

"Where did you get the hops?"

"From the cottage garden. Years ago my father gave me some of the discarded hops to replant, and I—" Daniel stopped speaking at the same time the thoughts finally connected in Ryder's brain.

Daniel swallowed and looked at his friend. "I have the hops in my garden, Ryder."

"You have the hops to save Margate." For the first time in what felt like years, Ryder smiled and meant it.

He stood so quickly he forgot his need of a cane and tumbled forward. Daniel caught him neatly and held him upright.

"I have the hops that can save Margate," Daniel repeated, his own smile plastered across his face. "I must see if there's enough. We'll need to be careful if we are to sow an entire field from it this year."

Ryder shook his head, forgetting his hands were still on

234

Daniel's shoulders. He simply couldn't let go of his friend for the excitement.

"This year will be a small crop to test the soil and make some sample batches to share with potential brewers. We'll need your father to help us."

"Us?" Daniel blinked as if coming awake. "I'm the black-smith. I can't bloody well—"

Ryder shook his head. "You'll be a silent partner if you wish. Your work as a blacksmith is remarkable, and I shouldn't want you to give it up. But if you wish, I'd love to have you as my partner, in truth."

Daniel shook his head. "I can't just leave—"

"I'll have a cottage built on the estate for you and Sarah, and then maybe I won't lose my upstairs maid and be forced to listen to Mrs. Olds lament either."

Ryder's lungs burned for air as he watched his friend. He didn't know how much this meant to him, his friend agreeing to the partnership, until he thought he might be sick with the anxiety.

Daniel tried to object once more, but his smile had grown too big. "Well, I should demand ten percent of the profits if we are to use my hops."

Ryder laughed. "Ten percent? You're my partner, you bloody idiot. It's fifty percent or nothing."

Daniel's face went pale. "Partners?"

Ryder was not so far out of touch to understand what such a thing would do for Daniel Stoker. He would no longer be a village blacksmith. He would be a merchant now and a wealthy one if Ryder had anything to do with it.

"Partners." Ryder finally let go of Daniel's shoulders to extend his hand.

Daniel took it, his eyes still wide.

"Partners," he said again as if trying out the word for the first time.

"Partners." Ryder pulled the man in for a tight hug and a slap on the back. "Now then," he said, snatching up the cane from where it had fallen at his feet. "I'll need to borrow that phaeton you acquired."

Daniel's eyebrows shot up. "Whatever for?"

Ryder had already turned in the direction of the house. "I need to get to London."

"Don't you have a carriage?" Daniel called after him.

"A carriage won't do."

"Why ever not? London's at least a two day's ride."

Ryder turned, a smirk already on his lips. "Because I plan to be there by nightfall."

* * *

She wore her finest emerald silk gown, but it might as well have been a flour sack for all she cared.

She shook her head. This wasn't about her. Tonight was about Jo.

Ravenwood House sparkled with all the preparations she had put into tonight, and Viv knew it would be a smashing success. Jo would be launched into what Viv sincerely hoped was her little sister's last season. And then Viv's work would be complete.

How dreadful.

When she'd set herself on this path to see her sisters wed, she had never understood that at some point she would be finished. At some point, they must all be wed. And then what was she to do?

She really must stop doing this to herself. She drew a deep breath and snatched a champagne flute from a passing footman.

She simply must stop thinking about Ryder.

He had made it perfectly clear just exactly what she was to him. It was her fault for falling in love with him.

Again.

Hadn't she learned?

She took a sip of the champagne and cast her eyes about the room.

Only to have her gaze land directly on the Kingsley widow.

Viv's stomach turned, and a sour taste filled her mouth. She made to turn away and stopped.

What had Ryder called her?

His brazen siren.

She squared her shoulders and turned back, plowing through the crowd until she reached the dowager countess.

"Your Grace," the woman cooed, dipping her head in greeting, a patently false smile showing her white teeth.

"Ryder never pounded you into a piano," Viv stated.

The space around her went utterly silent.

The gaggle of women the countess had been speaking to shared similar looks of astonishment.

The countess stammered out a noise that might have been a defense. "I beg your pardon." Her eyes had gone wide, spittle collecting at the corners of her mouth.

"You claimed that my husband pounded you into the keyboard of a piano with such vigor it required the restringing of the middle C. I assure you he did not."

The dowager countess swept her eyes back and forth. "Are you calling me a liar, Your Grace?"

Viv shrugged. "Yes."

The dowager countess gasped. "What nerve."

Viv gestured as if it were nothing. "Your mistake was in thinking I wouldn't ask my *husband.*" She said the word with enough force to cause the woman to remember her place.

The dowager countess snapped her mouth shut, casting her eyes to the floor.

The gaggle of women surrounding them drew a collective breath.

Viv fluttered her fingers at the countess. "I do hope you enjoy the ball. It looks like it's to be a crush."

She sauntered away, downing the rest of her champagne in a single gulp. If society thought her too bold or too brazen, so be it.

It was her bravery that had secured her the man she loved even if she meant nothing to him, that had to count for something, and she was damned if she was going to let a bunch of gossiping harpies tell her who she was supposed to be.

The evening *was* a crush by anyone's standards, and Viv eyed each of the more eligible bachelors she had ensured would be in attendance, feeling the power of triumph coursing through her veins.

There were a couple of earls and a few viscounts. Jo could have her pick.

If she ever deigned to accept a dance from any of them.

She watched her sister hold court at the side of the dance floor. Not once did Jo extend the wrist that held her dance card. Viv stepped forward to go speak with her, but a hand closed over her arm.

"Louisa is going."

Viv looked over to find Eliza standing beside her, her lips curved in a soft knowing smile.

"I wasn't going to—"

"You forced the Jilted Duke to dance with me, Viv. I can't imagine Jo would be keen on seeing you approach."

Viv handed her now empty champagne flute to another footman.

"And wasn't I right about that?" Viv tried to hide her

smile, but it was hard when her sister's love for her husband was so clear on her face.

The pain returned with an added flourish, and she swallowed and looked away.

Eliza touched her arm again. "I know you said you've told us everything that happened at Margate, but I can't help but think maybe it wasn't everything. It must have been hard to see him, Viv."

She shook her head. "It wasn't difficult at all. He was indisposed most of the time. I was simply there to ensure his needs were met. Don't you think Jo looks lovely in that gown? I had it—"

"Is she continuing to deny anything happened with Margate?" This from Louisa as she appeared through the crowd.

"Shouldn't you be resting?" Viv reached forward to take Louisa's shoulders and steer her toward a chair, but Eliza intercepted.

"Do you see what I mean?" Eliza raised an eyebrow, and Viv dropped her hands.

"I do. Louisa, how are you?"

"Fat." Louisa giggled at her pronouncement. "Any day now I assure you this little one will make its debut."

Viv's smile was genuine even as her heart ached. Her sisters were so beautiful with their heads bent together speaking of babies and husbands and swollen ankles.

"I hope mine do not swell as much as yours this time," Eliza said.

"Well, I should—" Louisa stopped on the word.

Viv leaned forward and gripped Eliza's elbow. "You're expecting again?" she whispered, the pain of the last few weeks freezing in anticipation of what Eliza might say.

But Eliza only smiled.

And then she nodded.

Viv didn't give a fig about decorum and pulled her sister into a tight hug as Louisa flailed her arms uselessly in front of her, her stomach too round to get her arms around anything.

Eliza took pity on her and gave her a squeeze from the side.

"Another little one. Just think of holidays now with the children underfoot. How splendid!" Louisa cooed.

Eliza laughed. "Splendid? I should think it shall be quite tiring."

Louisa laughed along with her sister, but Viv couldn't force herself to do so.

"Viv." Louisa stopped laughing, her eyes riveted to Viv's face.

Had the tears come to her eyes? She didn't think they had. She thought she was holding it quite nicely together. If she couldn't laugh, at least she could pretend—

"Oh my," Eliza breathed, and Viv realized they weren't looking at her.

They were looking slightly behind her.

Jo appeared from what seemed the air itself, thrusting her body between two gossiping debutantes, and then pushing herself between her sisters until she stood in front of...

In front of Viv.

Viv looked around. "What is going on?"

"I swear to God if he hurts you," Jo muttered.

"He who? Jo, straighten your shoulders. Look what you've done to your coiffure. You must look—"

She saw what her sisters had seen moments earlier.

Ryder.

Standing just inside the ballroom.

He wasn't dressed for a ball, though. He wore black breeches tucked into tall boots, his greatcoat dusty and swirling about him as he strode into the crowd. Gentlemen made way while ladies craned their necks to see him better.

He'd come after her.

The thought was like exploding light inside of her, illuminating all the places that had been so dark and cold. Ryder was here. He'd finally come after her.

A touch on her arm and she saw Eliza's smiling face.

"Someone wise once told me they only come after you if they care for you."

The words were so familiar, ones Viv had said herself, and a smile threatened to split her face.

But she didn't know why he was here.

Eliza turned and gathered her sisters, pushing them into the crowd in some sort of sense of privacy. How Viv could find privacy in this crush she didn't know, but she loved her sister for attempting it.

And then Ryder was there, the smell of wind and road and earth on him.

"I love you," he said without greeting. "Your brother and brothers-in-law look as though they may toss me from the building, and I want you to know that should I be unable to converse with you further."

Viv looked behind her. Ryder was correct. Andrew, Dax, and Sebastian were pushing their way through the crowd toward them. At the last possible moment, her sisters stepped in front of them, buying Viv some time, as Jo mouth the word *Run* at them.

She didn't hesitate. She grabbed Ryder's hand and plunged into the crowd opposite, heading for the doors behind the refreshment tables. Two footmen stood guard there as the doors led into the family rooms of the house, and she didn't want strays wandering through Ravenwood House.

The footman on the right stepped up to open the door,

and she pulled Ryder through, not letting go of his hand until the door snapped shut behind them.

They were plunged into the dimness of the corridor, and they both breathed heavily.

"You got a new cane." It was the first thing she noticed when her eyes adjusted to the dimness.

"Daniel made it for me."

He held up the cane for her to examine, and she touched the silverwork at the top of it with a delicate finger before dropping her hand entirely.

"I'm sorry. Did you say you love me?" It was absurd to have this conversation in the dark like this.

"Yes." He put the cane back on the floor with a sharp ring. "Yes, I did say that, and I do. Love you, that is."

She pressed a hand to her forehead. Perhaps she'd had too much champagne, but this was not what she'd imagined when she pictured Ryder coming after her.

She snatched his hand again and dragged him down the corridor. The green drawing room was lit only from the moon outside, but she was able to find the candles atop the piano, and soon the room was filled with a soft glow.

She turned, taking in Ryder's costume now.

"How long were you on the road?"

He was covered in dust, the black of his greatcoat gone murky with clay and soot.

"I left this morning."

Trepidation raced through her. "This morning? Left where?"

"Margate."

She took an involuntary step forward. "You left Margate this morning?"

"I did. I borrowed Daniel's phaeton." His smile was utterly arrogant.

Fury drove her. It was the only thing for it. She raised a hand, pointed her finger in accusation, and charged at him.

"Ryder, I swear to God if—"

"I promise never to do such a thing again. It was only that I had to see you, and I couldn't wait any longer," he said and silenced her with a kiss.

And it was wonderful.

She sank against him, the hurt she'd carried for the past few weeks, the loneliness and heartbreak she'd carried for years, slid from her like a discarded gown. She came up on her toes and wrapped her arms around his neck, pulling him closer and hanging on for all she was worth.

But she still had so many questions.

"But why now?" she gasped, pulling her lips from his.

This, however, did not stop him as he trailed kisses along her jaw. "Daniel helped me to see the truth." He lifted his head. "I've loved you for some time now, I suspect. I just didn't realize it."

He dipped his head again, his teeth catching at the sensitive spot behind her ear. Her stomach clenched in response, her fingers digging into his shoulders.

"What do you mean you've loved me for some time?"

He pulled back and this time he cupped her face in his hands. "Viv, my love, why are you always asking so many questions? I'm clearly not keeping you occupied well enough, am I?"

She tore herself from his arms, stumbling backward until she came up against the piano.

"Oh no. I have questions, and I will get my answers."

His head tilted slightly, his eyes wandering behind her. "Is that a piano?"

She looked back as if seeing the piano for the first time.

"Yes, but what—"

Her question was interrupted by the sound of the key turning in the lock of the door. She swung her gaze around.

"Weren't you telling me a rumor about a piano? I seem to recall something about a certain key as it relates to my legendary reputation as a lover." He'd discarded his great-coat. It lay on the floor behind him, and his fingers were busy unbuttoning his waistcoat.

She swallowed.

"Middle C. It had to be restrung."

His coat hit the floor next. "How odd. I think it would take a great deal of—" He shed his waistcoat. "Vigor to accomplish something such as that."

"You said I was distraction." The words were much louder than she meant them to be, but the sight of his clothes accumulating on the floor was proving itself a terrible deterrent to her questions.

He was directly in front of her now, and she forced herself to meet his gaze. Even as his fingers unwound the folds of his cravat, and she could see the first curls of chest hair poking from the collar of his shirt, that small dip at the base of his throat where she liked to lick—

"I did think you were a distraction, but I was wrong. You weren't a distraction at all. I had just never seen love before. I love you, Viv, and I can never tell you how sorry I am to have missed it." He placed his hands at her upper arms where the edge of her long gloves ended and the sleeves of her gown had yet to start. His touch was cool and sure, and she trembled. "Although you are proving to be quite a distraction in this gown." He bent and scraped his teeth ever so gently at the base of her neck.

She shivered and reached, grabbing blindly at something to hold her up. Her fingers found muscle and heat through the thin cotton of his shirt.

"How do you know this?" Her voice was becoming strained, and she feared soon she'd be unable to speak.

He lifted his head, and his gaze was direct, his eyes clear.

"Because I realized you are not responsible for the burden of my happiness, my love. Instead, I want to celebrate my happiness *with* you."

She searched his face. "What is your happiness then?"

"Having a purpose. Having a reason for being here other than racing phaetons and outdrinking dandies and cads."

Fear gripped her, but it was tinged with anticipation. He talked once of explorers and travel. Would he leave her now that he'd declared his love for her?

"You've found your purpose then." She licked her suddenly dry lips and watched as his eyes lit at the gesture.

"I have." He slipped his arms around her until she was snug against his chest. "It's you."

She shook her head. "No, I can't possibly—"

"Be enough?" His laugh was soft. "You are more than I can ever imagine, Viv. More than I ever expected. As your husband, you are my purpose." He pressed a kiss to her temple. "As my love, you are my purpose." He pressed a kiss to her forehead. "And as my duchess, you are my purpose." He kissed her softly on the lips.

She sifted through his words as warmth spread through her. "You're staying."

He leaned back and studied her face. "In London? God, I hope not. Too many people. Did you see how many were in your ballroom alone?"

Her lips trembled with a laugh, but she pushed her hands flat against his chest.

"No. I mean…yes. I mean…" She sucked in a breath. "I mean, you're staying…with me."

"Of course I am, love. I'm not meant to be anywhere else. I'll never forgive myself for taking so long to realize it."

He kissed her deeply now, his hand cupping the back of her head as he tilted her back against the piano. She clung to him, her body pressed against his until she disappeared and only they existed.

Complete.

Whole.

Loved.

"Ryder," she breathed after some time. "I still don't understand what it is you plan to do."

His smile was bright and wide. "We're going to grow hops."

She laughed, a burst of wonder and sound. "You got the hops then?"

He shook his head. "My partner has them. We must return to Margate for the planting, but we'll work the schedule around Johanna's needs. She seems to be a smashing success if the turnout tonight is any indication."

He drew her closer against him and shifted until he pressed her down on the bench of the piano, coming to kneel between her spread knees.

"Your partner?"

He nuzzled her neck. "Daniel, of course."

"Daniel Stoker. The blacksmith? Why would he have the hops?"

He grabbed her face in both of his hands. "Now is not the time for questions, love."

Instead of kissing her, his head disappeared as she felt her skirts rise up.

Fire sparked deep within her in nothing but a moment, tension coiling low in her belly.

"Ryder."

His lips first found the sensitive skin of her inner thigh, sucking and nibbling until she nearly slipped off the bench.

He wasted no time in moving deeper and soon, oh God, soon his lips closed around her sensitive nub.

"Oh God," she cried, her fingers clenched around the edge of the piano bench. "Ryder, we mustn't."

He either didn't hear her or he didn't care. She thought it the latter, but just then, she didn't care so much either.

His lips and tongue did wicked things to her until she could bear it no longer.

"Ryder, please," she moaned.

He reappeared in a flash from under her skirts, his hands fiddling at the front of his breeches.

And then he was inside of her, full and hard and hot. He slammed into her, and her body convulsed around him. But he kept going, again and again and again. The tension built until she thought she couldn't stand it anymore.

Then he leaned forward and whispered in her ear. "I love you."

She came apart with the words of love spilling from her lips.

"*And* that is how you can tell the soil is properly prepared for the planting of the hops?"

The elder Mr. Stoker scratched his forehead under the brim of his felt hat. The day was hot for so early in the spring, and Viv hoped that boded well for the success of their first planting.

"Well, now seeing as how this soil has been used for gardening the last several years, I have hopes the soil should be primed for such cultivation."

Ryder came up behind her. "Are you asking the poor man more questions?"

Viv shrugged. "I should only like to know how it is that he can tell the soil is ready. He is rather gifted, wouldn't you say?"

The older man blushed and pulled a handkerchief from his pocket to dab at his cheeks. "I should say it's a talent crafted after many years of hard work." He gave her a smile and tipped his hat before moving off to follow the lads distributing the hops along the rows Daniel had marked earlier.

She leaned back against her husband, only to straighten immediately.

"Your Grace, what is the meaning of this dishabille?"

He looked down at his shirtfront.

"I found the jacket to be far too constricting for such labor."

"And the waistcoat?"

He nodded. "Same."

"And your cravat?"

He squinted at the horizon where the sun baked the earth beneath it.

"Too damn hot for such frivolity."

She pursed her lips to stop the laugh that threatened to spill forth. She turned back to the men at work in the field. "Shall you miss the gardens?"

They'd commandeered the rear gardens for the test crop of hops. It was large enough to provide ample room for the samples they had gathered, both from Daniel's own house garden and the generous donations of local estates. It appeared a good many landowners in the area were curious as to what to do with the hop problem and were eager to see what the Duke of Margate might make of it.

He frowned, a crease appearing between his brows.

"I never really enjoyed the gardens as such, but I shall look forward to the day we might restore them and all the tenants are growing their own hops for harvest."

"That is something to look forward to."

They spent several seconds in silence as the men moved up and down the rows, planting. Ryder had prioritized the rebuilding of the hops workers' barracks, calling on every able-bodied person to help in their reconstruction in time for the planting. Viv had even taken a turn at some painting only to discover she should not be allowed to attend to such work.

The smell of fresh-turned earth filled the air, mixed with the slight tang of the breeze from the ocean.

She leaned back, nestling into her husband's shoulder as his arm came automatically about her.

"I shall miss this when we must return to London next week."

"Mmm," he said somewhere above her as he rested his chin atop her head. "Is Johanna any closer to choosing a suitor?"

Viv shook her head. "I'm afraid we must wait and see." She turned in his arms and snaked her hands around his waist to feel the contours of the muscles of his back under her fingers. "It will be so lovely to see wee Simon, though, won't it?"

"Does he do more than cry and sleep now?"

She batted his shoulder playfully. "He's only weeks old. Give him time." She shrugged. "He also poops a great deal, or so Louisa tells me."

Louisa had given birth to Simon not a week after Johanna's ball. He was a perfect bundle of joy who quickly became a prized possession of Eliza's dog, Henry. It seemed the collie had taken it upon himself to protect all young members of the family.

Viv sighed in contentment as her eyes caught sight of something in the distant.

"Do you know I believe you can see this field from the duke's bedchamber?"

Ryder turned his head in the direction of her gaze.

"Do you know I think you're right, Your Grace?"

"Do you suppose we should verify the matter?"

His smirk was thoroughly mischievous when he turned back to her. "I think that a wise proposition, Your Grace."

He scooped her up in his arms before she could take a single step in the direction of the house.

"Your Grace!" she cried, but her protests were drowned by her own laughter.

"You shouldn't be traipsing through the fields in your condition." He silenced her with a quick kiss.

She'd missed her courses the previous month and while she'd not felt ill other than being a little tired, they had summoned Dr. Malcolm just to be certain. It was clear family holidays would be quite a to-do, and Viv feared for poor Henry's stamina.

"Who am I to argue with a duke?"

"You are the very person to argue with a duke," her husband replied and strode toward the house as the sound of her laughter was carried away on the wind.

ABOUT THE AUTHOR

Jessie decided to be a writer because the job of Indiana Jones was already filled.

Taking her history degree dangerously, Jessie tells the stories of courageous heroines, the men who dared to love them, and the world that tried to defeat them.

Jessie makes her home in the great state of New Hampshire where she lives with her husband and two very opinionated Basset hounds. For more, visit her website at jessieclever.com.

Printed in Great Britain
by Amazon